**Here's what critics are saying about
Gemma Halliday's books:**

"A saucy combination of romance and suspense that is simply
irresistible."
—*Chicago Tribune*

"Stylish... nonstop action...guaranteed to keep chick lit and
mystery fans happy!"
—*Publishers' Weekly*, starred review

"Smart, funny and snappy... the perfect beach read!"
—*Fresh Fiction*

"The High Heels Series is amongst one of the best mystery series
currently in publication. If you have not read these books, then
you are really missing out on a fantastic experience, chock full of
nail-biting adventure, plenty of hi-jinks, and hot, sizzling
romance. Can it get any better than that?"
—*Romance Reviews Today*

"(A) breezy, fast-paced style, interesting characters and story
meant for the keeper shelf. 4 ½!"
—*RT Book Reviews*

BOOKS BY GEMMA HALLIDAY

High Heels Mysteries:
Spying in High Heels
Killer in High Heels
Undercover in High Heels
Christmas in High Heels
(short story)
Alibi in High Heels
Mayhem in High Heels
Honeymoon in High Heels
(novella)
Sweetheart in High Heels
(short story)
Fearless in High Heels
Danger in High Heels
Homicide in High Heels
Deadly in High Heels
Suspect in High Heels

**Hollywood Headlines
Mysteries:**
Hollywood Scandals
Hollywood Secrets
Hollywood Confessions
Twelve's Drummer Dying
(short story)

Jamie Bond Mysteries
Unbreakable Bond
Secret Bond
Lethal Bond
Dangerous Bond
Bond Bombshell
(short story)

Tahoe Tessie Mysteries
Luck Be A Lady
Hey Big Spender
Baby It's Cold Outside
(short story)

Young Adult Books
Deadly Cool
Social Suicide

Other Works
Play Nice
Viva Las Vegas
A High Heels Haunting
(novella)
Watching You (short story)
Confessions of a Bombshell
Bandit (short story)

BOOKS BY T. SUE VERSTEEG

Danger Cove Mysteries:
Killer Closet Case

Tahoe Tessie Mysteries
Luck Be A Lady
Hey Big Spender
Baby It's Cold Outside
(short story)

Other works:
My Ex-Boyfriend's
Wedding
Twisted Fate
Secrets of the Sapphires
Another Time, Another
Place

HEY BIG SPENDER

a Tahoe Tessie mystery

Gemma Halliday
&
T. Sue VerSteeg

I've been blessed with great friends throughout life, but this book is dedicated to my two BFFs since grade school, Patty and Donna. I love you girls more than you could ever know. Oh yeah, and GO HAWKEYES! ;)
~ T. Sue

A huge thank you to my dedicated editorial team who tirelessly work to take the suckage out of my writing. Susan, Jackson, Michelle, and Dori—appletinis all around!
And a special thanks to Casey and Lake Tahoe Brand for the awesomely inspired woodwork likeness of Tessie!
~ Gemma

CHAPTER ONE

———

"Strippers are not prostitutes." The smooth timbre of Rafe Lorenzo's voice made the sentence sound so much more beautiful than the subject matter.

From my perch on the third-floor balcony of the Royal Palace Casino and Resort, I looked across the bustling casino floor. Below me spanned a wide stretch of burgundy carpet filled with the bright lights of slot machines, happily dinging out their songs in neat little rows as retirees indulged in their afternoon sport of choice: video poker, keno, or bingo. Beyond them were groups of the card tables where men in suits sat wearing poker faces and sunglasses indoors, smoking cigars (which was still legal on this side of the Nevada-California border), and hopefully losing a fortune as they downed our complimentary drinks. Surrounding the scene were marble walls trimmed in ornate gold finishings where large family crests—most of which were completely faked—hung in an effort to give the Palace its regal medieval flair. The occasional tourist or ski bum mingled in with the crowd, though it was early for the post-slopes rush we'd have later today.

"Tessie, are you listening to me?"

I spun around at Rafe's voice and gazed up into the greenest eyes known to humankind. I'd been a sucker for his green eyes as a starry-eyed teenager doodling our names in hearts in my Trapper Keeper. Tall, dark, and dangerously handsome, the man could talk an elderly woman out of her panties. Not that he'd ever done it, at least to my knowledge. But once you tossed in wealthy, professional snowboarder, *and* bigwig board member for my casino, Rafe hit the trifecta of hotness. He blinked his dark, thick, and insanely-long-for-a-man eyelashes at me, and I could see a mysterious twinkle take hold behind the eyes that had doomed me to teenage crushdom once upon a time. "I believe we were discussing strippers?" he said, a teasing edge to his voice this time.

My heart skipped a beat, but I managed to keep my cool. Just barely.

"Strippers, prostitutes. Po-tate-o, po-tot-o," I enunciated. "Same thing." I crossed my arms over my chest in an effort to appear more forceful than my skipping heart felt.

His mouth pulled into a grin, puckering his dimples to maximum depth.

Damn, I couldn't help but smile back.

Rafe heaved a reluctant sigh before pleading his case. "Strippers take their clothes off and dance for money. Prostitutes take it a step further and accept money to perform..."

I stepped toward him and pressed my finger to his mouth, a sensual hum ringing through my entire body at the contact.

A single brow rose almost to his hairline, letting me know that the contact hadn't gone unnoticed by him as well. I quickly yanked my hand away. "You don't need to spell out the details. I know what I'm talking about."

"Oh, so, you *know* strippers and prostitutes?" His head cocked to the side, his arms crossing over his broad chest to mirror my posture.

I had known *one* stripper in my tenure at the Palace since my father had passed away. I'd also caught her doing the walk of shame from a high roller's room one morning, glittery stiletto heels in hand, hair smooshed against one side of her head, and makeup smeared like an '80's music video gone horribly wrong.

I shook my head. "It doesn't matter. What does matter is that you're just going to have to convince Mr. Sicianni that he can do without either strippers *or* prostitutes while he's at my casino."

The smile fell from Rafe's face, taking those amazing dimples with it. "I get it, Tessie. But you know how badly we need to keep Mr. Sicianni happy."

Unfortunately, he was right. I did know how badly we needed him.

When my father had passed away last year, the casino had been left in a sort of limbo without his commanding presence. Richard King had been the king of the Palace in more than just name, building it from the ground up into a premier resort destination in California's winter playground of South Lake Tahoe. His death, an embezzlement scheme, and the ensuing scandals had taken their toll on both the Royal Palace's reputation and its bank accounts. Its board of directors had been on the verge of shutting the casino down and selling it off piece by piece to the highest bidder, when, by a weird twist of fate, I'd been voted in as chairman and operating director.

Temporarily.

The board had originally given me a three-month probationary period to prove I wouldn't burn the place to the ground or run through what was left of their accounts in record time. Admittedly, when the probationary period had started, I'd had about as much doubt as the board of directors. While I'd grown up spending summers and holidays at the casino with my father, it turned out there was a lot more involved in the day-to-day operations of a casino hotel than sunning myself by the pool and hitting the buffets. Not to mention planning the special events that kept the regulars coming back for new and exciting experiences. While I'd inherited my father's blue eyes and strawberry-blonde hair—which usually leaned just a tad more to the strawberry than blonde—I hadn't initially shared his love of the gaming industry, instead opting to study art in college. That had landed me a job as a curator for an art gallery, but it hadn't exactly qualified me to head the casino.

However, I was proud to say that at the end of three-month probation, I hadn't royally screwed anything up. Unfortunately, I hadn't actually turned the profit margins around either. The board had extended my tenure as chairman for the rest of the year, but they'd assured me that I had to show "significant" revenue growth in the next four quarters to keep them from voting at the annual shareholders' meeting to close the casino doors for good.

But if anyone had a passion for keeping the Palace alive, it was me. Well, me and Rafe.

Like me, Rafe had practically grown up at the Palace, my father having sponsored his snowboarding career when Rafe was still in his teens. Even when Rafe had opportunities to be sponsored by much larger names, he'd stayed by my father's side right until the end.

It had been Rafe's idea to invite Mr. Sicianni, the producer of the Food TV's megahit television show *Battle Buffet* to the Royal Palace to film the final episodes live in front of a studio audience. His celebrity chef and star of the show, Bastien Dubois, had helped bring in food critics and some much-needed positive press to the casino. And the foodie fans clamoring for tickets to the tapings and accommodations had us fully booked— a phenomenon that had even the board of directors smiling. Smiles I definitely needed, as the end of my twelve months was only a short week away.

I let out a resigned sigh. "Yes, I'm aware of just how badly we need to keep Mr. Sicianni happy."

Rafe slid a hand across my shoulder and down my arm. Warmth danced through every single spot he touched, filtering southward to regions that made my cheeks warm too.

"And you know what makes Mr. Sicianni happy?" he asked.

I heaved another sigh. "Strippers."

Rafe's grin reappeared. "Let me buy you an early dinner, and we can talk about this."

Teen-me had a moment's giddiness thinking that the cute boy had just asked her out. Regrettably, adult-me knew better. While there had been recent moments where I thought maybe my teen crush hadn't been *entirely* in the past or *completely* one sided, those moments had taken a backseat ever since Rafe had started seeing the latest in his long string of blonde, bubbly, snow bunnies. His current version, Tiffany, happened to be the niece of our rival casino owner, Buddy Weston. My mother'd had a poodle named Tiffany while I was growing up. The dog was undoubtedly the smarter of the two.

I patted his hand, tugging my fingers away. "Sorry, I've already got plans," I told him truthfully.

A small frown settled between his delicious green eyes. "They wouldn't be with a certain FBI agent, would they?"

Any warmth I'd felt earlier froze up faster than a puddle in January. Rafe was referring to Devon Ryder, the special agent who'd been assigned to investigate my father's death and alleged organized crime connections to the Royal Palace. While I had my doubts that the organized crime allegations were anything more than speculation, I had to admit that on a professional level, Ryder had been instrumental in bringing my father's killer to justice. On a personal level, Ryder had shown more than a little interest in me, even going so far as to ask me out for New Year's Eve. Of course, then he'd blown me off, leaving me to watch the ball drop and polish off a bottle of champagne alone, so he was probably the absolute last person I'd have plans with now.

"No!" I said, maybe a little too emphatically. "I'm meeting Tate tonight. Sorry." I glanced at Rafe's flashy, high-dollar watch, flinching at the time. "I'm actually late as it is." I slid from his grip. "Rain check?"

"Sure." His dimpled smile returned with a vengeance, making me a little weak in the knees and causing me to question my decision. But I merely waved good-bye and admired the view as he walked away.

Tate Lopez's squeal from farther down the hall pulled my gaze from Rafe's buns of steel. "Tess!" My best friend's hand beckoned in an erratic flutter as he approached. "Are we still on?"

I waved back, making my way toward him. "Of course!"

I wove my way through the crowd, meeting him halfway in front of the elevators. He looked fabulous, as always, in his oversized, untucked purple paisley dress shirt and skinny jeans that hugged his midsection in a *manly* little muffin top. His dark complexion, hinting at his Mexican heritage, was a stark comparison to his bright bleached-blond hair. It made a statement, and Tate was all about those—the louder the better.

Threading my arm in his, I was glad to be in the company of my bestie, his familiar beachy cologne easing my mind with thoughts of slow rolling waves and hot cabana boys.

"Was that Snowboarder Hottie I saw leaving?" Tate asked.

I nodded, letting him lead me toward the Minstrel Lounge, where our Frank Sinatra impersonator played six out of seven days a week and the steaks were to die for.

"Oooo, deets, girlfriend," Tate insisted.

I shrugged. "No deets to give. At least not about him."

Tate raised an eyebrow. "Do I detect gossip?"

I grinned. "Mr. Sicianni had three girls from the Pretty Kitty lounge up in his room last night for a private dance party."

Tate snorted. "Wait—that strip joint next the dry cleaners?"

I nodded.

"Oh, I bet that went over reeeeeeal well," he drawled.

"Oh yeah," I said, matching his sarcasm. "The older couple on their second honeymoon in the suite next door to Mr. Sicianni's called the front desk to complain about the noise three separate times and threatened to call the police on the 'den of iniquity' that we were harboring here at the Royal Palace."

Tate threw his head back and laughed out loud. "Oh, honey. I've always wanted to visit a 'den of iniquity,'" he said, his manicured fingers making air quotes.

"Yeah, well, you may be the only one." I sighed. "All I can hope is that our celeb-u-chef brings in more *revenue* than his producer does *topless revue*."

Tate cackled again, causing a few coiffed, gray-haired heads from the slot machines to turn in our direction as we made our way to dinner.

* * *

Two steaks and numerous Sinatra standards later, I found myself at the front desk helping Tate check in the latest slew of tourists fresh off the slopes, before hitting the appletinis to wash my day away. I had to admit that the excitement of those just starting out their Tahoe vacations was infectious. As each group of tourists entered the lobby, their eyes pinged from the medieval crests to the shiny suits of armor guarding the elevators to the neon signs touting the King's Court All You Can Eat Buffet. I could feel them being sucked into the fantasy world my father had created and couldn't help the smile it brought to my face.

A smile that froze the second I heard a familiar voice approach the desk.

"Ohmigod, if it isn't Tornado Tessie, live and in the flesh!"

The voice alone set my teeth on edge, yanking me from my happy place and dumping me into the least endearing moments of my childhood. I knew it was LeAnna Aiden before I even turned around.

I could still clearly see her prepubescent blonde curls as she sat at the edge of the pool, taunting, "Look! It's Tornado Tessie, the hottest mess in the West!"

Okay, so I'd been a *little* overly energetic as a kid. And probably a little too eager to make friends during my lonely summers staying with Dad. And yes, I'll admit my hair had been a little frizzy and unruly at that age, making me look like, well, the perfect human embodiment of a spastic tornado. But the nickname that LeAnna Aiden, the daughter of one of the regular high rollers at the Royal Palace, gave me had stuck, and I'd been the butt of her jokes all summer as her father had gambled away a small fortune at my dad's tables.

I inhaled deeply, letting the breath out slowly, in a vain attempt to regain my composure before turning around. I forced my inner Zen to the surface and pulled out the toothiest fake grin I could muster.

"LeAnna Aiden?" I said, turning my attention toward the bane of my nine-year-old self's existence. I scanned the woman in front of me up and down a few times, hating to admit that she still looked fabulous. And, she just happened to be wearing the red print Michael Kors jersey dress I'd been admiring in our boutique earlier.

Damn.

Her smile faltered as I faced her, but only for a moment. "Girl, you know I'm just kidding about the Tornado Tessie thing, right? We're grown. And as of last year, it's LeAnna Aiden-*Taylor* now." She shoved her left hand so far in my face the ashtray-sized diamond practically grazed my nose.

"Taylor?" I asked, the name ringing some sort of bell in the back of my mind that I couldn't quite put my finger on.

LeAnna's grin widened to Cheshire cat proportions. "*Gerald* Taylor. Of the Napa Valley Taylors?"

I raised an eyebrow in her direction. That was the name I knew well. Gerald Taylor was a regular at Royal Palace. He owned a very successful winery in Napa, spent big at our high-roller tables, where he had a habit of passing out after one too many glasses of Cabernet, and was also well over seventy years old.

"Congratulations?" I forced, though I was afraid it came out more question than statement.

LeAnna just fluttered her fake eyelashes, seemingly oblivious to my hesitation. "I know, right? How did I get so lucky!?"

Karma? I bit back the sarcastic reply, proud that the people skills I'd acquired since taking over the casino were keeping my smile in place.

"Anyhoo," LeAnna went on, "we're in town for the big *Battle Buffet* taping. Gerald, of course, got us VIP spots. Isn't he a dear?"

I opened my mouth to respond, but she didn't give me a chance, clearly not really interested in my opinion on Gerard's "dear" status.

"But enough about me." She propped her fists on impossibly tiny hips as she let her eyes do an up and down of their own over my person. "What are you up to these days?"

I found myself tugging at my blouse and smoothing my pencil skirt. Even though both were from one of our high-end shops, I suddenly felt very underdressed.

"I'm actually the owner of this casino," I heard myself announcing. At least for the next week.

Her eyelashes did the flutter routine again. "No way!" she gushed. "Who ever thought that Tornado—" She paused, clearing her throat, a slow smile creeping into place before she reworded her barbed statement. "Who would have thought *you* would be owner of a cute *little* place like this?"

"Excuse me?" I heard Tate bristle, suddenly appearing at my side. Apparently he'd heard the call of the she-devil voice too. The bright spot in my first memory of LeAnna's taunts was that was also the day I'd met Tate. His mother worked in housekeeping at the Royal Palace, and he'd "accidentally" nudged LeAnna into the pool head first, knowing she was only torturing me while on hiatus from taunting him. We'd bonded over our tiny victory, becoming fast friends and spending every second of our summer vacations together from that point on.

I put a calming hand on his sleeve and shot him a look that I hoped told him not to go for the jugular, as tempting as I knew it was.

LeAnna shrugged. "Oh, honey, I just meant that compared to the places in Vegas that my Gerald has taken me...well, this is a darling little hotel you've got here." She waved her arm around her, and I felt Tate tensing beside me again. His face was so red, I was beginning to worry he might bust something internally.

"Anyway," she continued, "how did you get saddled with this place? I thought you were into arts and crafts or something?"

"Fine art," I shot back through what was becoming an increasingly tight smile. "I curated at a gallery."

"Ooo, fancy!" LeAnna punctuated the comment with the sarcastic wink.

I felt my eyes narrowing. "Until my father passed away and left me the casino."

LeAnna's haughty face dropped for a moment, genuine emotion peeking through. "Oh. Wow, sorry. That sucks."

"Thanks."

LeAnna shifted on her spiky heels, clearly more comfortable with thinly veiled sarcasm than sympathy. "Well, good to see you again. I should go find Gerald..." She trailed off, pointing vaguely in the direction of the card tables.

"Try the poker room," I said, once again proud of my customer service skills and that I didn't add there was a good chance he'd be passed-out drunk there.

She shot me one last saccharine smile before she turned and I was forced to watch what *had been* my favorite Michael Kors dress walk away.

"If she wasn't such a class *A* bitch, I'd feel sorry for the girl," Tate clucked, finally relaxing beside me. "What is Mr. Taylor, like, eighty?"

"Well, don't feel too sorry for her. I know how much that dress costs."

"Amazing what a good sugar daddy can do for your wardrobe, right?" Tate winked at me.

I opened my mouth to respond with an equally snarky comment—the kind every childhood nemesis deserved—when a chirp from Tate's phone interrupted me.

He fished it out, and the smile tumbled from his face as he read the text message.

"It's Britton. Code Black."

* * *

I trailed behind a distraught Tate all the way to the elevator, where he turned and waved me on urgently. "Hurry up! How can you not take Code Black seriously?" he scolded.

I keyed my code for the penthouse into the elevator and waited the few Muzak-filled seconds for the carriage to take us to the top of the Royal Palace's East Wing. We entered the penthouse to find a very nervous Britton pacing the living room, twisting the same bleached blonde curl around her finger over and over.

In addition to being my current roommate sharing the large penthouse suite overlooking the crystal-blue waters of Lake Tahoe itself, Britton was also my father's young widow. Which, yes, made her my stepmother. I'll admit that fact had bothered me to no end when my father had first announced he was marrying a twentysomething former cocktail waitress whose cup size seemed to rival her IQ. In my mind, Britton had *gold digger* written all over her. However, since my father's passing, I'd come to realize that I'd been a bit hasty in my judgment of Britton on several items. First of all, she might be blonde, but she was a lot smarter than everyone gave her credit for. And secondly, Britton had actually loved my father and, if I had to guess, was still mourning the loss.

"What took you so long? Hashtag urgent!" Britton squealed as soon as we walked in.

Well, mourning in her own unique way.

"Didn't you get the Code *Black*?!" she added, scaring my cat, Captain Jack, back into my bedroom. He was nothing more than a fluffy black-and-white blur. "I expect *her* to ignore my Code Black," she balked, pointing a perfectly French-manicured finger at me.

I barely resisted the urge to roll my eyes.

Then she honed in on Tate again. "That's why I sent *you* the message." She waved frantically toward the dozen or so designer dresses draped on the back of the sofa. Her voice returned to the high-pitched squeal as she cried, "I'm meeting an old friend for a girls' night, and I have to look perfect. It's been, like, forever since I've seen her. I don't know what I'm up against."

"What do you mean 'up against'?" I asked, fingering a gorgeous black dress in shimmering silk. If I got a vote in this fashion crisis, I'd go for that one.

Britton's panic level rose along with her pitch as she explained. "The woman is loaded and knows fashion like no one else I've ever met." She turned to Tate and pointed toward the pile of designer garments. "I need to make sure I'm wearing the latest-and-greatest style dress I own. Like the ab-fab best."

"What's wrong with the number you've got on?" I asked, eyeing her charcoal-gray sleeveless dress. Well, aside from the fact that it was so formfitting that it left absolutely no room for anything else, including most of her cleavage, which I had a sneaky suspicion my father had paid for. Seriously, if the dress had pockets, you'd be able to count her change.

All I got back was a blank stare. I wasn't sure if that was because of her Botox treatments or just a statement in and of itself. Finally, she turned toward Tate and whimpered.

Tate sprang to attention, nodding briskly before turning back to the dresses. He gently searched the pile, scanning tags, hemlines, and necklines before turning to her and assessing the one she wore. "Tessie's right. I'm pretty sure you're wearing the latest."

"Pretty sure?" she yelped. "You must be *totally* sure. God, I need a drink."

Now that was something I agreed with. I rubbed my temples, dreaming of those appletinis as I watched Tate scour the web on his phone while Britton paced behind the sofa.

My phone jingled from my pocket, and I was extremely happy to attend to *anything* other than what was unfolding before me.

That is until I took the call.

"Tessie King," I answered.

"We have a situation at the high-roller blackjack table," came the deep, gravelly voice of my director of operations and security manager, Alfonso Malone, or Alfie, as I'd always known him.

"Define situation."

"We got a whale passed out."

I closed my eyes and thought a dirty word. Oh, the glamorous life of a casino owner.

* * *

I stared down at my "whale," or high-rolling client, who, true to my earlier predictions, just happened to be LeAnna's beloved hubby. He was passed out cold, his butt slowly sliding out of the leather chair and his Armani-clad torso sprawled along the edge of an empty high rollers' blackjack table. A trail of drool pooled under his cheek. For a split second, I was conflicted about who I felt sorrier for: him or LeAnna.

I quickly came to my senses. Him, of course.

Nudging his shoulder gently, I bent down to speak directly into his ear. The noise of the slot machines, his advanced age, and the Cabernet-induced coma drowned out my first few attempts to rouse him.

"Mr. Taylor," I repeated, growing louder with each try.

His eyes fluttered open, a grin stretching across his weathered face into the slobber puddle before he pushed himself into a sitting position. "Well, Ms. King, are you trying to kiss me?" he chided.

I used a cocktail napkin to dry his face. "You caught me," I fibbed.

I'd had to wake him up so many times during his stays at the Palace that I was running out of new excuses to get him back to his suite to sleep off the booze.

Almost running out. "I saw LeAnna stifling a yawn a few minutes ago," I lied, only feeling the teensiest bit guilty. "I think she needs you to escort her back to your room."

"Really?" he asked, his tone disbelieving.

I nodded somberly.

"You're a terrible liar, kid." He lifted a shaky hand, pointing one finger toward the Golden Chalice bar that sat just beyond the card tables.

LeAnna's designer-clad form stood next to a slightly younger version of her husband. I heard their giggles carrying across the casino floor as she seductively brushed her breasts against his arm.

I rolled my eyes before turning back to Gerald's knowing glance. "Sorry."

He shrugged. "Thanks for trying." He signaled for a passing cocktail waitress. "Gin and tonic, please. Light on the tonic." He dropped a fifty on her tray.

"Right away, Mr. Taylor," she gushed.

After releasing the girl with a slow wink—which she graciously tolerated due to the cash now crushed in her clenched fist—he turned back to me.

"Are you sure about that gin and tonic?" I asked, trying my best to think of some way to politely dissuade him from inducing another drool-worthy moment.

He gave me a watery-eyed smile. "You're kind to want to look after an old man like me."

"Oh, you're not old, Mr. Taylor," I quickly shot back. "Ruggedly mature," I added, coming up with a positive spin.

He chuckled and patted my hand. "Believe me, my dear, some days I think I'm much *too* mature." He shot a glance back at his wife again, the smile dropping from his face, replaced by the sadness that had his jowls hanging in a very un-rugged way. "My wife informed me early this evening that she thinks she's pregnant." He grabbed his nearly empty glass and tipped it to his thin lips to polish off the last few drops.

"Uh, wow. Um, congrats?" I tried to picture LeAnna as a mother, but the only image that came to mind was a reptile eating her young.

"You can save those congrats." He paused. "Unfortunately, I'm going to have to break it to my dear wife that my doctor disagrees with her. At my last visit with him, he told me that I'm sterile."

I choked on a laugh, which I poorly attempted to turn into a cough. For once I actually felt sorry for LeAnna. Though as I looked down at Mr. Taylor's sad face, I had much more sympathy for him than the cheating gold digger he'd been blind enough to marry. "I, uh, I'm sorry." As soon as the words left my mouth, I knew they were inadequate for the situation. But unfortunately, how to comfort a man faced with proof his wife had been cheating on him wasn't in the Hospitality 101 manual.

"I suppose I should have said something when she told me," he went on. "But it was all a bit of a shock. Could you imagine?" he scoffed.

I nodded…then switched to shaking my head. I wasn't quite sure if I was supposed to be agreeing or not. Luckily, the cocktail waitress reappeared with Mr. Taylor's gin and tonic, which, at this point, I was willing to concede him.

Mr. Taylor took a healthy gulp and then continued his monologue. "Chronic pancreatitis. The doctor said it's probably a result of too much…" He trailed off, looking at the glass in his hand. "Well, that I should think about cutting back on the wine. But in my case, it's already resulted in an inability to father any more children. When he told me, I didn't know how to break the news to my wife, but I suppose that conversation will be a bit more awkward now, won't it?" He attempted a smile as he took a generous gulp form the glass.

I nodded sympathetically, my eyes scanning the casino floor now for a nice escape from the beyond-awkward conversation. A card counter situation? An underage kid on the gambling floor? Even a maid in need of a hand cleaning up after a sick spring-breaker's beer binge would have been welcomed.

"You know, I secretly always wanted another child," he said, his eyes gazing off into the distance. "My son was such a joy to watch when he was young. Children really do breathe life into you, you know? I had such big dreams for my boy." He cleared his throat, bringing himself back to the present. "But I suppose he's destined to be an only child now."

"How old?" I asked.

Mr. Taylor chuckled. "Oh, he's been grown for a while now, though sometimes you wouldn't know it by the way he acts. Fact is, he's even older than..." He trailed off, pointing his now half-empty gin glass toward LeAnna at the bar. He watched her giggle and rub up against the unsuspecting stranger again before they headed in the direction of the craps table together.

I honestly tried to dig deep and pull up some kind of pity for LeAnna. Hand to God. But I'm sure it was buried right next to her apology for calling me Tornado Tessie, which would undoubtedly require a jackhammer and backhoe after all this time.

Mr. Taylor crunched an ice sliver then muttered, "She really is a sweet girl."

LeAnna's voice carried above the casino noise, "I'm your lucky charm tonight, baby!"

Oh yeah. A real sweetie.

Mr. Taylor released a long sigh. "Unfortunately, she's really sweet to most men." Then he stood and assured me, "Don't worry. I've only got one more little drink in me tonight before I retire to our suite. I promise to at least keep *myself* in line." He waved a dismissive hand toward his wife.

I smiled at him before he turned to leave, knowing I'd be called to another part of the high rollers' gaming area to wake him again before his stay at the Royal Palace was over. I'd seen Mr. Taylor's *one little drink* turn into several, which usually turned into a scene like I'd just witnessed—him passed out, drooling on some table or other. However, for the time being, crisis was averted, so...

I pulled my phone from my pocket and dialed Tate's number. "Tell me your Code Black is contained. It's so appletini time."

CHAPTER TWO

———

The next morning I was awakened bright and early with another call from Alfie, whose gruff voice jarred me out of a lovely dream about hot snowboarders.

"Situation on the *Battle Buffet* set. Now," he barked. Then he hung up.

I glared at the bright-green numbers on my alarm clock beside my bed, blinking back at me with an angry 6:02 a.m. Ugh. I thought a few choice words then roused Captain Jack from his perch at the end of my bed to do a quick shower, makeup, and hair routine. I tossed on a soft-pink blouse, a pencil skirt in heather gray, and a pair of black high-heeled boots to cap off the outfit before making my way to the pending disaster on the set.

In just two days the *Battle Buffet* show was set to begin taping the final rounds of competition, where the celebrity chef would whittle his final six contestants down to one lucky winner over the course of three rounds of competition. The show would be taping one round per day in front of an audience, who had paid handsomely for their tickets to the event. Everything culminated in a huge, live grand finale on Sunday. In addition to the regular tickets sold to the show, Rafe had come up with the idea to add on a special invitation-only VIP package, which included seats in a plush, exclusive section of the auditorium right in front of all the action, and a cocktail party and gourmet dinner prepared by the celebrity chef on the evening before the finale. While I'd initially had my doubts, when the VIP packages had sold out almost immediately after the invitations had been issued, I'd given him a well-deserved pat on the back.

I firmly held on to the idea of just how much revenue this event was bringing in to the casino as I pasted a smile on my face and entered the kitchen stage to contain whatever *situation* was brewing.

Immediately I could hear someone slamming kitchen utensils. Sigh. Calming a celebrity temper tantrum wasn't exactly my idea of starting the day off right. A never-ending cup of coffee at the Java Joust and a few glazed donuts might have at least softened the blow.

I cleared my throat as I watched a slim man in a black chef's jacket shout what I could only assume were French curses at a pair of bubbling pots while pouting like a spoiled toddler. "Uh, Mr. Dubois?"

The curses came to a screeching halt as he threw a pan into a sink in the center of the set, the sound of clanging metal echoing off the high ceilings of the Palace's auditorium long after it'd come to a rest. He turned his narrowed gaze toward me, his nostrils flared. In a heavy French accent, he shouted, "*Chef* Dubois. It is always *chef*!"

His dark hair was camera-ready perfect, as if it received daily salon treatments, sporting just one small streak of white down the side in what I assumed was an attempt to be edgy, rather than nature's hand. His brows were neatly trimmed, and a slight dusting of stage makeup covered his forehead. Beneath his black chef's coat he wore deceptively casual jeans and sneakers. From the bright white of the shoes, I had the feeling they'd never been worn outside a soundstage. He was only slightly taller than I was, which made him perfectly suited for the magic of television angles and a Napoleon complex. He reminded me of a cross between Bobby Flay and Pepé Le Pew.

I took a deep breath. "Excuse me. My mistake, *Chef* Dubois," I enunciated.

Regaining his composure just a tiny bit, he added, "Anyone who has even seen a *commercial* for one of my *award-winning* cooking shows knows that." He turned away, straightening his starched coat and muttering, "Imbecile," his thick accent making the single word sound even more insulting.

I smacked on my *the customer's always right* smile. "I'm told you have a problem?" I prompted through clenched teeth.

I glanced around at the beautiful kitchens the crew had built in our auditorium that was usually used for flashy stage shows and the occasional midlevel band when we could book one. While I'd only seen *Battle Buffet* a few times on television myself, I had to admit that this seemed to be an almost perfect match for the show's usual soundstage. Top-of-the-line appliances, sparkling new mixers, pots, pans, and even a few gadgets that I had no idea how to use littered every surface. Was that a liquid nitrogen tank?

While Chef Dubois had his own large kitchen at one end, there were six smaller prep areas for the competing chefs—each one nicer than my penthouse kitchen. All of the plumbing had been installed so the sinks and appliances worked and drained properly, and each station was stocked with the latest in upscale cookware and utensils. I had absolutely no idea what Dubois's problem was.

The man pivoted slowly, facing me, his nose scrunched. "You seriously do not see what is wrong with this set?" He stretched out his arms.

I looked around again, this time noticing that the six contestants were there, but each one was hiding next to a prep station or crouched behind the nearest counter. Pleading, wide-eyed gazes locked with mine as I scanned from one to the next.

I looked back at him, shrugging my shoulders. "I'm sorry, sir. Whatever it is, I'm sure we can get it fixed before taping starts."

He shook his head, his lips puckering into an ugly snarl. "*Mon chéri*," he spat sarcastically, "my viewers demand *cohérence*. I was promised an *identique* set. I demand an *identique* set, or I will pack up and abandon this charade."

Alfonso Malone's voice boomed from behind me. "Bastien Dubois, what an honor it is to have you in our casino. What can we do for you?"

I turned to see our director of operations filling the entryway. Dressed in his trademark black suit, shirt, and tie, his choice of wardrobe blended seamlessly with his dark hair and deeply Italian complexion. A faint scar running across his cheek and a slightly crooked angle to his nose were the only remnants of the hard life he'd left behind to become my dad's right-hand man. Now he was all expensive suits, strict adherence to gaming regulations, and a strong hand when it came to running his security crew. He'd bailed me out of my fair share of tight spots in the short time I'd been in charge, and I felt better knowing he was there.

And I must not have been the only one, as Dubois pulled out a smile like he'd just hit triple sevens. "Monsieur Malone," he drawled as he walked over to shake Alfie's hand.

"What seems to be the problem, Chef?" Alfie peered over the shorter man's head, giving me a hard look that clearly let me know he was begrudgingly there to bail me out yet again. "Whatever it is, consider it fixed."

"Do *you* see it?" Dubois asked, his voice calm but an octave higher with hope as he waved toward the sink.

Sure, give Alfie a hint. This was so not fair.

Alfie nodded knowingly. "I was hoping you'd miss that. We have a new faucet coming. That was as close of a match as we could get for you locally. I just checked the shipping details, and it'll be here this afternoon."

"Oh-ho-ho," Bastien laughed, releasing a large sigh. "I can practice with this, yes. You had me very worried, *mon ami.* I was wondering how to work with a faucet a *un centimètre*—" He held his fingers a small fraction apart. "—shorter than the one I use."

A centimeter? For real? The coffee was no longer just something I wanted. I needed it or there would be consequences that would not make this situation any better.

Alfie clamped a hand on my shoulder and whispered, "Smile."

It was then that I realized I was glaring. I popped on my professional, toothy smile and bubbled, "Well, you obviously have this handled, Mr. Malone. Is there anything else I can help with, *Chef* Dubois?" I asked, emphasis on the title.

He locked a narrowed gaze with mine and flicked his hands in a little shooing motion. No words, no thanks—he just dismissed me. It was my turn to bristle with anger as I stomped out of the soundstage, across the lobby, and right into the Java Joust.

"Venti vanilla latte with an extra espresso shot," I pleaded at the barista.

The lanky teen behind the counter gave me an understanding glance as she quickly backed away to start my coffee. The whir of the espresso machine calmed me some, but it was the intoxicating aroma of the brewed beans that brought me back to non-murdering notions. She handed me the drink, and I dropped a tip in her jar. Smiling, I slowly raised the cup to my lips and took the first glorious sip.

"He's harmless," Alfie said directly in my ear from behind me.

I snorted part of my coffee in surprise. After regaining my composure from a coughing fit, I muttered, "He's still a jerk." I scanned my general area for anyone else who might be lurking, before taking another drink.

"If you could have attended to the situation sooner, maybe it might not have gotten so out of hand," Alfie chided. "Since when does 'now' mean in twenty minutes?"

"Don't push your luck," I mumbled, taking another sip.

Alfie raised an eyebrow at me, but he was wise enough to drop it until I got some caffeine into my system. Instead he motioned toward a table with a view of the courtyard.

I walked to it, staring out the window at the melting snow spotted with patches of bright-green grass. Spring was my favorite of all seasons, more so in the Lake Tahoe area, where there was actually a big change in the scenery, than in my previous home of San Francisco, where the changing seasons only vacillated between blue skies and foggy ones. I loved to see the grass and flowers fighting through the dissipating snowbanks, bringing splotches of color to the bland grayscale of the winter palate. From a business standpoint, we were hitting the tail end of the hustle and bustle of ski season, too, which meant a nice pause from the breakneck pace. The months between the end of ski season and the beginning of summer usually slowed and brought a more relaxed crowd, here to enjoy the gorgeous views of the mountain range, lounge poolside, and take boat tours on the lake.

Of course, that also meant a drop in the number of visitors to our hotel—a fact that I hoped the board would not pin on their new chairperson. Assuming I was still owner after their shareholders' meeting.

Alfie pulled out my chair, and I sat.

"About Dubois…" he started.

I gave him a hard stare. "Please don't defend that pompous celebu-chef's behavior."

He snorted a laugh as he sat across from me. "Never. But he is a necessary evil. His pompous self is bringing in a lot of revenue. Besides, you'll probably be dealing more with James Sicianni, the producer of the show. You'll see that his wit and charm will more than offset Dubois. He's got quite a way with the ladies, from what I've heard." Alfie waggled a bushy brow and almost smiled, his eyes glinting just a bit.

"The more naked the better, from what *I've* heard."

A real smile tugged at the corner of his mouth as he leaned back in his chair and laced his fingers behind his head. "You heard about the strippers, huh?"

"Me and every other patron on the fifth floor."

Alfie chuckled. "I'll make sure Sicianni keeps his visitors on the down-low from now on."

"Good," I said, taking a heavenly sip that did wonders for my mood. "I'd appreciate that."

Alfie paused, and I could tell there was something else he'd sat me down to talk about other than Mr. Sicianni's appetite.

"What?" I asked, staring at him over the rim of my cup.

Alfie narrowed his eyes, as if sizing me up, before he asked, "Have you gone to see him yet?"

My cup froze. I was pretty sure I knew who he meant, but I asked anyway to stall for time. "Who?"

"You know who. Your father."

Damn. I had to pick now to start being right. I looked deep into my coffee cup to avoid eye contact.

"You visited his grave yet?" Alfie pressed.

I shrugged, trying my best at nonchalance. "Not lately."

"It's one year on Saturday."

I took a deep sip of coffee that now tasted like bitter sludge. I didn't need Alfie to remind me of the anniversary of my father's death. It was something I'd been pushing to the back of my mind for weeks, watching the days tick down on the calendar and feeling the same emotions of grief, guilt, and regret that I'd felt at his passing all suddenly being rubbed raw again. I'd done a bang-up job of burying them in work during the past year, and the last thing I wanted was Alfie digging them back up again.

"I'll go soon."

"Good," he said with finality that thankfully meant he felt he'd done his duty as my dad's right-hand man. "Take Britton with you."

"Sure," I said, waving him off.

"I mean it," he said, stabbing a finger at me. "You'll regret it if you don't go see him."

I nodded, though I knew deep down what I would always regret was not seeing enough of him when he was still alive.

Thankfully, Alfie stood, letting me off the hook for now. But he paused before he walked away. "I, uh, I wanted you to know I'm going to be putting in for some personal time off soon."

My head shot up. "Why? What's wrong?" I immediately asked. *Alfie* and *personal* were two words that didn't go together in my mind. Alfie lived for the casino. He ate, slept, played, and worked here. If I had to guess, he'd made marriage vows to the poker tables long ago.

He made a big show of crinkling a napkin and tossing it into the nearby garbage can, not meeting my eyes. "Nothin'. I'm just taking some time off, is all."

I opened my mouth to delve further, but he didn't give me the chance, turning his back to me and quickly walking away.

* * *

I spent the rest of the morning knee-deep in accountants, going over the numbers for the previous quarter's returns in anticipation of my board review. To say they weren't pretty was like saying a bulldog needed a facelift—obvious to even my own untrained eye. I sorely hoped that the *Battle Buffet* finale was a hit, or else the Royal Palace might be saying its final adieu right along with Dubois's season.

I was just leaving the conference room, visions of a lunch at the Castle Cafe dancing in my head, when my phone buzzed in my pocket. I briefly contemplated not answering it. But the truth was that whoever was on the other end knew where I lived. The hazards of living where you worked.

"Tessie King," I answered.

"This is Maverick in security."

"Yes?" I asked.

"We have a small disturbance at the slots."

"Define disturbance."

"Mr. Taylor's passed out again."

I glanced at my phone read out. It was just past noon. "Already?"

"'Fraid so."

"I'm on it," I said into the receiver as Maverick directed me to the particular bank of *The Price is Right* themed machines holding the snoozing vintner.

I glanced down aisle after aisle of clanging devices until I found him slumped against one at the far end. One of my regulars, Mrs. Schnatz, was standing in the middle of the row, arms crossed tightly over her chest and erratically tapping the toe of her Velcro-strapped tennis shoe.

"Finally!" the older woman said, jutting her meaty arm out toward Mr. Taylor. I tried not to look as the under part of her arm took way longer to stop moving that the rest of it. "That's my machine. He can nap in his room."

I set a comforting hand on her shoulder. "Give me just a minute, and it's all yours."

It was a little early in the day for a bender, but it didn't exactly surprise me either, considering the situation he'd outlined for me the previous night with LeAnna.

But as I approached him, something didn't look right. His complexion was blue, almost purple, and his drink was spilled on the floor. He would never allow that, no matter how many he'd already downed. Adrenaline-infused panic flooded my body. Instead of nudging him like usual, I put my fingers to his neck. His skin was cold and clammy, and his pulse was nonexistent.

"Call 9-1-1," I yelled to a now alarmed-looking Mrs. Schnatz. She complied, pulling out a cell. "Tell them we need an ambulance at the Royal Palace Casino."

She nodded, turning away as she put her phone to her ear.

I bit my lip, forcing myself to face the truth. It was too late for an ambulance. I tried to pat his face, and his head shifted toward me, revealing a small pair of scissors protruding from the side of his neck.

And blood.

A thin line of it trailed down the side of the slot machine, pooling between it and the neighboring machine.

I heard a scream that very well could have been mine.

CHAPTER THREE

———

Once uniformed officers had secured the crime scene (which was going to be just dandy for business) and medics had taken Mr. Taylor's body away, I tried my best to falsely assure the remaining casino patrons that everything was under control. Then I made my way to where the detective in charge of the investigation had set up camp to speak with witnesses in my dad's office.

Wait, *my* office.

After I'd taken over the casino, one of the first things I'd done was girlie up the office a little bit. I'd gone with some lighter paint, replaced the random liquor decanters with framed photos and flower vases, filled the bookshelves with novels a little more to my taste, and moved the Vermeer painting from the penthouse to the wall behind the desk where it sat as a reminder that someday I might have time to take up painting again. I'd also upgraded the outdated, clunky PC with a slim little laptop I could take with me anywhere. But even with all of those changes, every time I sat at the massive, dark cherrywood desk, I always felt like I was twelve years old and would get in trouble if I got caught there.

I opened the door and found the police in full interrogation mode, and LeAnna bawling and slobbering into the scarf I'd left on the lounge chair in the corner where she currently sat. I forced myself to feel sorrier for LeAnna than my poor pashmina. A man in a suit sat next to LeAnna, asking her questions as he scrolled through an electronic tablet in his hand. I could only assume he was the detective in charge of the case. Alfie paced the room behind him, monitoring the scene carefully.

A man I'd never met stood by the bookcase. His tailored dress shirt hugged his muscular frame, the unbuttoned collar showing a hint of smooth, tanned skin, and an undone bowtie hung from his neckline. He turned toward me, his impeccably styled salt-and-pepper hair sparkling in the light. He looked a lot like George Clooney, but I was pretty sure *he* wouldn't be in my office with the cops.

A girl could dream though.

Forcing a half smile to his face, he extended his hand. "You must be Tessie King. I'm Gerald Taylor."

I shook his hand, but I couldn't help looking around the room as though someone was going to break away from a murder investigation to clarify things for me.

"Oh," he interjected, "you must know..." His words trailed off as he swallowed hard then took a deep breath. "You must have known my father. I'm Gerald Taylor Junior. Please, call me Jerry. And, uh, excuse my disheveled monkey suit. I was at a charity function at Edgewood when I got the text from LeAnna. I'm renting a house in the Keys, but I didn't want to backtrack to change."

I had to admit that the family resemblance was certainly there.

He must've seen me scrutinizing his features as he added, "I'm told I look a lot like him, but I personally never saw it."

"I'm so sorry for your loss," I told him.

His forced smile fell, shoulders sagging. "It's just tragic. I can't imagine why anyone would want to kill my father."

Clearly I had no answer for that one, so I did my best to give him a sympathetic smile and nod.

LeAnna's wails cut through our conversation from across the room. "What do you mean they were my scissors? Why would *I* kill my husband? What possible motive would *I* have?"

I looked over my shoulder as LeAnna blew her nose into my scarf. I was fairly certain she didn't want me to rattle off my list of possibilities, so I turned back toward Gerald's son. "So, you're her..."

"Her stepson?" he answered in more of a question, his top lip ticking up with a tiny bit of distaste. "I guess it is what it is. And, as it turns out, it sounds like I'm about to have a brother who would be young enough to be my..." His words trailed off as his face fell into a dark scowl. "Well, you've met LeAnna," he finally ended, spitting out the last word with what I could only describe as disgust.

I nodded, both in sympathy and genuine agreement.

"Jerry," LeAnna whined. "Please come tell these awful men that I'd never ever hurt your father."

"If you'll excuse me..." Jerry nodded toward me then reluctantly wound his way through the room to LeAnna's side.

I watched as he placed a comforting hand on her shoulder, which she immediately latched on to, rubbing her cheek against his fingers. Yeah, so not polite of me, but I couldn't help it. Her step*son* was at least a decade older than she was, possibly two. Damn gorgeous, but still. It was a lot to process. A text from Britton pulled me from staring.

Penthouse STAT!!!

I quietly excused myself and made my way to the elevators. When I got to the penthouse, Britton pounced, grabbing me by the shoulders as soon as I stepped through the door.

"What's going on? Who killed Mr. Taylor? How did he die? Is there a killer on the loose in the casino!?"

"Pause. Take a breath," I instructed and gently navigated her toward the sofa.

"Ohmigod, ohmigod. I can't believe this is happening. What are we going to do?"

"*We* are not going to do anything. The police are going to find out who killed Mr. Taylor, bring them to justice, and everything will be fine," I told her, going for my most soothing voice, even though I wasn't sure I entirely believed that statement.

"Do they have any ideas who could've done this?"

I shrugged, thinking of the interrogation I'd overheard in my office. "If I had to guess, I'd say they're focusing on his wife at the moment."

If it was possible, Britton's panic level rose. "What? No, there is no way they can possibly think LeAnna had anything to do with this. I know she would never!"

"Wait—" I held up a hand in front of me. "You know LeAnna?"

"Honey, everyone knows the Taylors." She sighed, putting on her *mother knows best* look. The woman was only a couple of years older than I was, but she had a habit lately of slipping into this mode when it served her. "Your dad, God rest his soul," Britton mumbled, pausing to cross herself for the first time in, well, ever, that I'd seen, "liked to spend personal time with his high rollers, like Mr. Taylor. He and Gerald go like way back, like even before LeAnna came on the scene. Anyway, after he married LeAnna, she and I totally hung out every time they were in town. It's super scary how much we have in common."

Britton had married someone old enough to be her father, and LeAnna had married someone old enough to be her *grand*father. I could see the bond.

"Anyway, I know LeAnna, and I know she couldn't do this. She wouldn't hurt a fly." She jumped up and began to pace the floor of the living room in a bright neon-green blur of spandex topped off by leg warmers. Either she'd been down to the Medieval Torture Chamber (a.k.a. our hotel's fitness center) working out, or the look was unfortunately coming back as a casual option.

God forbid.

I momentarily contemplated letting her in on the torment LeAnna had afforded me during my childhood summers at the casino as an alternate version of her new BFF, but pride squashed those words back in along with all of the repressed memories. Besides, a few childhood taunts weren't the same thing as a cold-blooded murder. Was LeAnna capable of that?

"What makes you think she's innocent?" I grabbed a glossy red apple from the fruit bowl on the table, taking a bite as I waited for an answer.

"Well," she drew out, looking at her brand-new sneakers. "I wasn't supposed to say anything about her little secret. Promise not to tell?"

"That she thinks she's pregnant?" I asked, somewhat coherently through my mouthful of apple.

Britton's wide-eyed gaze popped to mine. "Did she tell you?"

Yeah, because we're close like that.

I swallowed my bite but not the derisive snort. "Gerald told me last night while LeAnna was flirting with a guy at the bar. I'm so glad she's thinking like a mother already." I couldn't help the sarcasm. I took another big bite to keep from expanding on the subject.

She waved a dismissive hand between us. "She was just hanging around the bar while she waited for me."

I raised an eyebrow her way. "So LeAnna was the old friend you had to look fabulous for last night?"

Britton nodded. "I was late 'cause I was trying to figure out which dress to wear. But I'm sure LeAnna wasn't drinking. And I'm sure she wasn't flirting either."

I was pretty sure she was, and I was pretty sure her husband thought she was too. But I kept that opinion to myself, instead asking, "Okay, but how does being pregnant make her innocent?"

Britton scoffed. "Why would anyone kill the father of their baby?"

I shook my head and dumped the apple core into the trash under the kitchen sink. "I think that all depends on her feelings about the father."

"You're wrong. LeAnna is too sweet," Britton objected.

I snorted loudly, crossing my arms over my chest.

Britton threw me the cynical side-eye stare. "I've spent a lot of time with her over the past few years. While she may have a bit of a wild streak, I know she wouldn't kill anyone."

"Wild streak?"

"Sorta." Britton's hand went to twist that poor lock of hair again. "You know how girls are."

"I know how some girls are. I don't have the *pleasure* of knowing how *this* girl is." *Other than her obnoxious childhood self.*

"Okay, fine," Britton said slowly. "It may be possible that LeAnna was flirting just a teeny tiny bit with the guy you saw last night."

I couldn't help a grin. "Go on…"

"Well, she's just really friendly, you know? She's just naturally flirtatious. She never means anything by it. I'm sure. I mean, take last night, for example. She was totally texting with some guy all night, but at the end of the night she shut him down and went up to her suite. Alone. Harmless flirting."

"Hold on. Rewind. She was texting someone all night?"

Britton bit her bottom lip. "That looks kinda bad for her, huh?"

"Kinda."

"Maybe I shouldn't tell the police that part." Britton sucked in a breath, her face scrunching up as much as her excellent plastic surgeon's work would allow. "Ohmigod, do you think the police are going to question me?"

"Who was she texting with?" I asked, glossing over her last question. The truth was, I had no idea what the police were going to do.

She shrugged, blinking at me through her thick, fake lashes. "Wouldn't say. I knew it was a guy though. No one giggles like that at a text unless there's a sexy guy on the other end."

"So, maybe she *was* cheating on Gerald," I said, more to myself than Britton.

"No way. Like I said, harmless flirting."

"Are you sure? Were you with her *all* night last night?"

Britton sighed, plopping back onto the sofa. "No," she admitted. "Like I said, she said she was going up to her room."

I narrowed my eyes at Britton, noticing that she was carefully avoiding my gaze, looking everywhere but at me. "But…?"

"But it was early." Britton blew out another sigh. "Usually when she stays here, our girls' nights last until the sun comes up. But last night she wanted to call it quits around eleven. She said she was feeling a little queasy. You know, morning sickness." Britton's forehead tried to do a frown again. "But I guess it kinda wasn't morning, was it?"

"Did you actually watch her go up to her room?"

Britton shrugged. "I saw her get into the elevators."

"But she could have easily gotten out and gone somewhere else. Like to meet the guy she was texting."

"I guess." Britton squeaked out the admission. "That doesn't look very good for her either, does it?"

I shook my head. "If LeAnna was seeing someone else, that's a pretty big motive to want her husband out of the picture."

Britton jutted her chin forward with defiance. "I still don't think she did it."

I opened my mouth to protest that I, for one, was becoming more and more convinced. Only my phone buzzing from my pocket interrupted me.

I grabbed it and looked down at the screen. Security office. I quickly swiped my phone to accept the call.

"Tessie King," I answered.

"Ms. King, this is Maverick in security. We have a detective from the South Lake Tahoe Police Department here. He's asking for our surveillance files from last night."

I pursed my lips together. Right. Of course the police would want to see our surveillance. Mr. Taylor died on the gaming floor, which had cameras mounted nearly every five feet. There was no way someone could have killed him without being caught on camera. I sent a hesitant glance Britton's direction. For her sake, I hoped it wasn't LeAnna's face the police found on those tapes.

"Right. I'll be right down."

"What? What's going on now?" Britton asked.

I gave her a reassuring smile. "The police want to talk to security. Don't worry. I'm sure everything will be fine." For us. For LeAnna, I wasn't so sure.

On the elevator ride down to the second-floor security office, I tried to look past my mental childhood scars, but I still couldn't see Britton's side of LeAnna. An evil twin was the only logical conclusion.

As the door slid open, I nodded to Larry and Moe, the guards who made sure patrons didn't wander onto the security floor. It was a running gag in security that everyone had a nickname. Most people knew about theirs and laughed them off. Except Alfie, that is. I doubted very seriously that Alfie did humor in any form.

"Ms. King," Larry said. "The police are in Mr. Malone's office."

I nodded my thanks and made my way through the security floor, which was a maze of cubicles cordoned off by glass partitions that afforded privacy, but not *too* much privacy, to their occupants. Each office was furnished in a dark, modern style punctuated by huge screens mounted at eye level, where random shots of the casino floor played on endless loops. Security staff nodded and rushed past me, arms loaded with files and paperwork, as I worked my way down the glass hallway toward Alfie's office in the center of the floor.

By the time I arrived, it looked like Alfie already had the footage cued up. The image on the oversized monitor on his wall was of the same bank of *The Price is Right* slot machines where I discovered Mr. Taylor. Only in this scene, there was no crime scene tape surrounding them or lab techs collecting fingerprints and hair samples. Alfie stood at the monitors, along with two uniformed officers and the same detective who'd been with the bawling LeAnna. Maverick was seated at Alfie's desk behind a computer, queuing up the footage.

"This is from last night, sir," Maverick said.

Alfie nodded. "Time?"

"Two fifteen a.m."

"Run it through," Alfie ordered.

I took a spot near the door to silently watch the footage myself, hoping no one noticed my presence, as Maverick sent the scene on fast-forward. We watched several people crisscross in front of that particular machine before I recognized Mr. Taylor in his rumpled blazer from the previous evening stumbling into the frame.

"There!" the detective shouted, pointing at the monitor.

Maverick slowed the tape, and I watched Mr. Taylor sit down at the *Price is Right* machine, where he promptly passed out. No big surprise there. We waited a few seconds before Alfie motioned for Maverick to speed the tape up again. He did, only pausing when a guy in big puffy ski pants, a plaid flannel shirt, and a baseball cap came into the frame.

I held my breath, watching the ski bum glance over his shoulder, take something out of his pocket, and bend over Mr. Taylor's frame.

"Zoom in on his face," Alfie said, his voice tense.

Maverick complied, pushing in closer on the ski bum. Unfortunately, the cap covered up any hint at hair color, and as the man turned toward the camera, a large bushy beard and oversized black sunglasses obscured most of his face.

"It's a disguise!" I blurted out.

All five men turned around to look at me.

Oops. So much for silence. "Er, I mean, clearly whoever that is has covered up his appearance. Right?"

"Or *hers*," the detective said pointedly.

I bit my lip. He was right. While the outfit had initially given the impression of a male, the bulkiness of the clothes concealed the shape of the person underneath them. The killer could easily have been male or female.

"We're going to need copies of this as well as any other footage you have of this person in plaid," the detective told Alfie.

He nodded. "Of course, Detective Johnson. Anything we can do to help. Follow me, and I can get that for you now."

I moved out of the way to allow the four men to exit the room. Alfie gave me a stern look as he walked out—thankfully leaving any lectures on proper conduct in the presence of police detectives for later.

As soon as they left, the air in the room lightened. "You think we have more footage of that guy?" I asked Maverick.

He shrugged behind the desk. Maverick was slim, shy, and the complete opposite in every way to the *Top Gun* version of his nickname sake. But he'd proven helpful to me on more than one occasion in the past and was sweeter than anyone working security had a right to be.

"If he took the time to put on a disguise, he knew we were watching," Maverick reasoned. "I'm sure he was careful about where else he went in the casino as well."

I nodded. He was right. If there was more footage of the mystery man, it was likely only going in and out of the Royal Palace's front doors.

However, there was someone else who might not have been so careful about her movements that night...

"Hey, you think you can pull up some other footage from last night for me?" I asked.

"Sure," he said, turning to his keyboard. "What do you want to see?"

I gave him LeAnna's name and room number. "Start with early last night." With a little luck, maybe I'd catch her sneaking off to meet the cute guy on the other end of her text messages. With a lot of luck, maybe I'd catch her changing into a ski bum disguise.

He punched some data into the computer, and the footage popped up on the screen. A little box outlined LeAnna's face, her name hovering above, as she left her room for the girls' night with Britton.

"Any way you can send this to another monitor?" I asked. "Like, maybe one in a more private office?" While I wasn't technically doing anything wrong watching LeAnna, I wasn't sure that I wanted to throw any more suspicion on her to Alfie or anyone else. Well, any more than she was currently throwing on herself.

Maverick nodded, motioning to an empty office two cubicles down. "That work?"

"Perfect." I beamed at him, causing his cheeks to turned twenty different shades of pink.

"I'll, uh, send the footage over to the monitor."

"Is there any way I can follow her movements through the casino? Like through the different cameras that might've picked her up last night?"

"Sure. I can auto-set to follow her through our facial recognition software chronologically according to the time stamps on the footage that any of our cameras might have picked up that evening."

Gotta love modern technology. "You are the best! Thank you, Maverick."

He blushed again, his cheeks going an impossible shade of red now. "You're welcome. If you need me to service you..." He paused, stammering over his words as he realized what he said. "I, uh, mean if you need my services, you know where to find me." Then he scrambled back to his office across the hall, eyes firmly on his feet as he scampered past me.

I smiled, quickly scampering off myself to the empty office before Alfie could return to his. As promised, LeAnna's face leaving her hotel room was now front and center on the monitor atop the desk. Using the mouse, I slowly scrolled through watching her get into the elevators and exit them down on the casino floor with just the slightest blip between frames as the different cameras handed her off to one another. From there she made her way to the bar, where the stranger I'd seen from last night came up to her and offered to buy her a drink. I had to give her points that at least it looked like she ordered a Diet Coke instead of something alcoholic. I was almost considering the man at the bar as her possible texter, when I saw her look down at her phone and giggle.

Britton was right. Women did not giggle like that at texts from other women.

After several moments of watching LeAnna text back, flirting with the guy at the bar, and accompanying him to the craps table where she served as his "lucky charm," I saw Britton finally arrive. I had to admit she did look fabulous in the gray off-the-shoulder number, which she'd accessorized with lots of bling. The two women did a squealy-huggy thing. Then what ensued was lots more giggling, gambling, drinks, and flirting.

Hours of it.

After what felt like eons of fast-forwarding through footage, I felt myself going cross-eyed and hit pause to take a break. I rubbed my eyes and leaned back in the chair, which groaned and creaked in protest. I moved my neck from side to side, working out the kinks, and glanced across the hall at Alfie's gigantic monitor.

And froze.

Gone was the footage of Mr. Taylor's killer, but it had been replaced with what looked like Alfie's usual rotating live feed of various parts of the casino floor. On this particular part, a familiar face caught my eye. A face that owed me a damned good reason for ditching me on New Year's Eve.

Agent Devin Ryder, FBI.

CHAPTER FOUR

———

I popped up from my chair and was next door in Maverick's office in two seconds flat. Motioning back toward the room I'd been occupying, I asked, "Hey, would you mind following along with that footage and letting me know if LeAnna met up with anyone last night? Particularly anyone male?"

"Whatever you need. I'm here to service you." He paused, going beet red again, and cursed under his breath. "*Serve* you."

"Thanks. Text me if you see anything," I called over my shoulder as I wove my way through security and into the elevator. I rode it down to the casino floor and frantically scanned random faces until I found Agent Ryder's blond hair bobbing through the crowd.

My stomach alternated between giddy butterflies and twists of anger. It had been almost three months since he'd left me high and dry on the biggest date night of the year. I thought I'd gotten past it—with a little help from Ben & Jerry and their good friend, Jose Cuervo—but the butterflies in my gut that'd multiplied into a flock begged to differ. As I bore down on my prey, I reminded myself to play it cool. I would go for the persona of an aloof, busy casino owner who really didn't have time for a personal life anyway. Because, well, it was sort of true.

I approached my target, who looked to be grilling one of my cashiers. I stopped, inhaled a few deep breaths that didn't really help me relax much, and tugged my skirt into place. I sashayed calmly through the resounding machines, lacing through the crowded lanes until I was standing next to him.

Damn, he smelled good. Even through the haze of cigarette smoke, the familiar pine and sandalwood scent set my knees wobbling. I attempted to regain my composure again and cleared my throat.

"Ms. King." Ryder nodded, turning toward me.

I beamed at Rosalie inside the cashier's cage. "I'll take care of Agent Ryder's needs." I paused, realizing I'd just done a Maverick moment, and quickly corrected myself. "I'll answer any questions he has."

I slid my reserved face into place as I turned my attention to him. It really helped that he'd addressed me so formally. But he was as hot as ever. Even more so, if that was possible. His sandy blond hair was brushed back from his face haphazardly, and a sexy five o'clock shadow graced his chin. His dark-blue pinstriped suit hugged his waist, and the light-blue silk tie set off the blue in his eyes. Part of me wanted to smile and flirt, twisting my hair like I'd seen Britton do on countless occasions. Though, the move probably needed the whole excess-cleavage thing she had going on, for maximum effectiveness anyway. So, thankfully, the other part of me stuck to the *aloof* game plan.

"What brings you back to the Royal Palace?" I asked.

"Is there somewhere quieter we can talk?" He glanced around at the crowd of people surrounding us.

"Of course, Agent Ryder," I said, purposely addressing him as formally as I could. I motioned toward the hall by the front desk that led toward our conference rooms.

As we made our way by the desk, Tate mouthed *oh-em-gee*, licked his finger, and made a scorching sound as he touched his chest.

I smiled and nodded as we passed, sharing a wink with him just out of Agent Ryder's sightline. Then I slapped my *I don't give a damn* face back into position as I turned to Ryder and gestured toward one of the smaller conference rooms. As we entered, two employees were tidying up. They scrambled around to gather their equipment, leaving within seconds. The long table in the center was dressed in a crisp white tablecloth. A huge chandelier dangled overtop, dozens of crystals catching the light and casting rainbow prisms about the otherwise dimly lit room.

Ryder pulled a chair out for me at the head of the table, a hint of a smile curling his lips as he waved his free hand toward the seat. I sat, not wanting to be the one to break the formality.

"Well," he mumbled as he sat just next me. He leaned back, one hand draped over the chair, the other resting on his lap. "I'm sure you're wondering why I'm here."

Forgot to flip your calendar since December?

"I am curious as to the FBI's interest in my casino again, yes." I folded my hands in my lap, trying my best to keep the fidgeting to a minimum.

"I have some questions about Mr. Taylor. How well did you know him?"

"Gerald?" That one caught me off guard. What could the feds possibly want with such a sweet old man? Sure, he was a dead, sweet old man, but homicide was usually a local affair that didn't warrant FBI involvement. "He is..." My words trailed off, still processing his death. "He *was* a regular here. We've seen him a few times a year for quite some time, according to our records." And by records I meant Tate, but he didn't need to know that.

"Does the name Gambia mean anything to you?"

I frowned. "Should it?"

"Members of the Gambia family have stayed at the Royal Palace. Quite frequently, in fact." Whatever he was hinting at, it was well concealed behind his poker face.

"Repeat business isn't unusual. We are one of the top destinations in South Lake Tahoe." I narrowed my eyes at Ryder. "What does this have to do with Mr. Taylor?"

Ryder looked down, and for a moment I thought he wasn't going to answer me. Then he finally said, "It just so happens that Mr. Taylor's last few visits have exactly coincided with those of members of the Gambia family."

"And..."

Ryder cleared his throat and carefully met my eyes again. "The Gambia family *business*."

"Wait, when you say *family*, do you mean..." I trailed off as a lightbulb went on in the dark recesses of my brain. Ryder worked the organized crime unit. "You mean like *mob*?"

He didn't answer me, but his assessing gaze said it all.

I rolled my eyes. "Look, just because somebody with the same last name as some Italian Mafia family stays at the Royal Palace does not mean that we are involved in mob activities!"

"I didn't say *you* were involved."

I narrowed my eyes at him again. "So what are you saying?"

"I'm saying that we have reason to believe that Mr. Taylor had business transactions with the Gambias."

I pictured the kind, weathered old man I'd found drooling all over our high-roller tables on multiple occasions. I shook my head. "There must be some mistake. Mr. Taylor owned a winery. He wasn't a member of the Mafia."

Ryder adjusted himself in his chair and pulled a little notepad and pen from his jacket pocket. "Our information is credible. You'll have to trust me on this."

I scoffed. Trust was something I was a little short on lately when it came to Agent Ryder.

He shifted his gaze, his poker face slipping for just a moment. "Okay, you'll have to trust the FBI on this, I guess." He raised a brow, and I returned the gesture. "So, I can assume you didn't know Mr. Taylor had ties to the Gambias?"

"Your assumptions would be correct," I conceded.

"Since this is still your casino, I need to inform you that we will be involved in the investigation into the murder of Mr. Taylor."

"Wait—" I said, holding up a hand. "You don't think that the mob killed Mr. Taylor?"

"I can't comment on an ongoing investigation." And just like that, the poker face was back.

I narrowed my eyes into catlike slits and crossed my arms over my chest.

"I trust we have your full cooperation?" Agent Ryder stood and extended his hand.

I rose but refused the hand. If he thought we were friends now, he had another thing coming. "We are happy to cooperate with the FBI," I agreed, hearing the sarcasm dripping from my own voice.

He put the notebook and pen back into his jacket pocket as he rose. "Thank you for your time. We'll be in touch."

No sooner had he disappeared into the hall than Tate popped through the doorway. "Damn, girl. That guy is hot!"

I heard Ryder laugh in the hall as Tate fanned himself. Tate shrugged and put his hands to his mouth in an "oopsie" gesture. "Well, I guess he knows what I think, now."

"Sorry, honey, I'm pretty sure he's not your type." My mind involuntarily wandered to the memory of a sensual kiss we'd shared nearly a year ago. I shook it off. Any romantic interest I'd had in Ryder had died the moment I'd read his brush-off-text while waiting for my very late New Year's Eve date in a crowded restaurant wearing the most to-die-for little black dress known to womankind. *Can't make it. Sorry. Call you later.* was all it had said. No explanation, no reason, not even a cute emoticon. I'd used the basic break-up lexicon to translate that he'd found a better New Year's offer. The pity on the waitstaff's faces when they realized I'd been stood up ranked among my most embarrassing moments to date.

And contrary to the text, he hadn't called me later.

I forced my thoughts from my previous pity party and back to why Ryder was crashing my casino yet again.

I'd first met Ryder after my father's death last year, when he'd come sniffing around the casino, investigating mob connections. At that time I'd gone through the classic stages of grief at losing the shiny, good-guy image of my father and his casino. At first I had completely denied that anyone at the Royal Palace would have anything to do with organized crime. I'd been angry that Ryder would even suggest such a thing and quickly moved on to the bargaining stage, looking for alternative suspects who might have had family connections. The first one I'd immediately thought of was Alfie. If anyone fit the stereotypical image of a connected man, it was Alfonso Malone.

While Alfie and I had come to a sort of mutual understanding about our positions at the casino, I couldn't a hundred percent swear that he wasn't connected.

Just like, despite my protests to Agent Ryder, I couldn't a hundred percent swear that members of the Gambia family hadn't been conducting some sort of business on the casino premises.

"You have a memory for names," I said, going with a flattery tactic with Tate as we walked back out into the main lobby. "Do you remember anybody by the name of Gambia staying here recently?"

Tate nodded. "Sure. Lots of times. In fact, Hammerhead Hank Gambia just checked in today."

I exhaled sharply. "*Hammerhead* Hank?"

Tate shrugged. "You know these Italian guys. They're all about those goofy nicknames."

Right. Goofy. I suddenly found myself glancing around the faces in the lobby, expecting to see *Goodfellas* mingling amongst the retirees.

Tate shot me a look, giving me his full attention now. "Why do you ask?"

I bit my lip.

Tate wagged a finger at me. "I know that lip nibble very well. What's going on, Tess?"

"Fine," I breathed, filling Tate in on what Ryder had told me about the Gambia family possibly having Mafia connections. Though I held back the bit about Ryder suspecting Mr. Taylor of having the same sort of connections. If it wasn't true—and I really hoped it wasn't, for Mr. Taylor's sake—the last thing I wanted to do was ruin the man's reputation. And while I loved Tate, I knew he could only handle so much juicy information without fear of his social filter exploding and sprinkling the entire South Lake Tahoe area with gossip.

Tate's mouth dropped open in a *Nooooo!* pose. "So, that's why Hottie McFed came for a visit? He thinks that there are mobsters staying here?"

"Shhh!" I instructed, putting a finger to my lips as a family with three adorable little boys walked by. "Maybe. Possibly."

Tate shook his head. "And to think I sent poor little Juanita up to his room this morning with extra blankets…alone! She could've been whacked!"

I rolled my eyes. "Okay, let's say for argument's sake that Mr. Gambia—"

"You mean Hammerhead!"

I winced. "That *Hank* is in town to conduct some business of some sort. Who do you think he would be been conducting it with?" I didn't add *other than poor Mr. Taylor.*

Tate pursed his lips, but he didn't have to think long. In fact, neither did I as I followed Tate's gaze out the glass front doors of the lobby and across the street to the Deep Blue Casino.

"I can think of one guy who's sleazy enough to move in the same circles as a wiseguy like the Hammerhead," he answered.

I could too. Buddy Weston.

Buddy and I'd had a tumultuous relationship in the past. Buddy was known for loving loose pockets, loose women, and loose interpretations of the law. At current, we tolerated each other. Mostly because we didn't have much choice, with our rival casinos being positioned directly across the street from each other.

"Maybe Rafe would know something? Isn't he dating Weston's niece?"

"Tiffany," I ground out. Maybe a little too forcefully. Not that I was jealous or anything. I mean, the woman was a size 2, 32DD who had never worked a day in her life. What was there to be jealous of?

I shook my head. "Let's not involve Rafe."

Tate nodded, giving me an exaggerated wink. "Riiiiight. Need-to-know basis. Ix-nay on the ob-may."

I couldn't help a grin. "What do you think the chances are that Buddy Weston has room in his schedule for me today?"

"Is that a nice way of wondering whether or not he'd have his goons physically throw you out of his casino?"

I shrugged. "More or less."

"Leave it to me, honey," Tate said, shooting me another wink. He pulled out his phone, fingers flying across the keyboard, face going solemn. Within seconds his phone dinged like expensive wine glasses in a toast, bringing a wicked grin to Tate's face. "Georgie, one of the front-desk guys over there—" He fluttered a hand toward the Deep Blue. "—he says Weston is scheduled for his weekly massage in like thirty minutes."

Pushing past my amazement at how fast Tate had gotten the information, I grabbed his elbows and turned him toward the door. "I think we're due for pedicures. My treat."

Tate squealed, clapping his hands. "Hashtag happy! I love it when you spoil me." He stopped, turning a serious, deadpan look toward me. "How are you not married already?"

"I know, right? I just haven't found a guy who likes pedicures as much as you." I smiled at my friend, patting his arm as I prodded him toward the hall. "And, you know, likes women."

CHAPTER FIVE

The Deep Blue casino was a dark concrete building rimmed in flashing blue neon. It was one of the South Lake Tahoe casinos that were located just over the border on the Nevada side of the state line. The esteemed group included the Royal Palace, the Hard Rock casino next door to us, and Harrah's, just to the other side of the Deep Blue. And Buddy was always trying to outshine the other three...literally. The glare off the neon and the recently installed oversized disco ball above the entrance had me shielding my eyes as we entered the building. An enormous aquarium sat in the atrium-style lobby, reaching four stories tall and nearly filling the cavernous space. It housed all sorts of brightly colored tropical fish and several sleek, gray sharks whose predatory smiles often reminded me Buddy himself.

Tate chatted exuberantly about getting some color on his toes this time as we walked past the front desk then froze in his tracks, his hand going to his collar. "Ohmigod, that's him!"

"Who?" I asked, whipping my head around the crowded lobby.

"James Sicianni, the creator of *Battle Buffet*." Tate pointed toward the concierge desk with one hand and started fanning himself. "He's like Simon Cowell and Channing Tatum all rolled into one. Money, power, and a set of abs you could wash your unmentionables on."

I wasn't sure how he knew about the abs thing, but as I turned in the direction of Tate's starstruck gaze, I had to agree with the rest of his assessment. A tall man with dark hair, perfectly gelled into place, stood near the concierge desk. He wore a dark suit with a classic white shirt unbuttoned at the collar, and had one hand casually tucked in the pocket of his well-tailored pants. The smile he flashed the woman working behind the desk was bright white and filled with charm. She practically drooled in response.

"Come on—you have to introduce me," Tate said, grabbing me by the arm. Before I could protest that I hadn't actually formally met the producer myself, I was being dragged across the lobby.

"James Sicianni?" Tate asked, approaching the man.

He turned our way, much to the annoyance of the female concierge still fluttering her eyelashes at him. "Yes?" he asked politely.

Tate nudged me, not-so-subtly clearing his throat.

"Uh, hi. I'm Tessie King, owner of the Royal Palace."

Sicianni's eyes lit up with recognition. "Of course," he said, quickly extending one hand toward me. "James Sicianni, executive producer of *Battle Buffet*. It's a pleasure to finally meet you."

As I slid my fingers into his palm, he pulled his other hand out of his pocket and skimmed it over mine, firmly clasping. His eyelids went heavy, looking at me through his lashes, a sultry smile curling his lips. "I was told you were beautiful, but the rumors didn't do you justice." He flipped my hand over, planting a small kiss at my wrist. Slowly, deliberately, he let my fingers slide free.

Despite his immaculate look, I felt dirty, like I needed to wash that hand now. He had a tall, dark, and handsome thing going on, but he was a little over the top for my taste.

And then there was his whole love-of-strippers thing.

I looked over at Tate. He stared at Mr. Sicianni, wide eyed, as if he was going to start fanning himself again. He flung a buoyant hand out toward Mr. Sicianni, doing a deep baritone that I knew he reserved for his manly-man mode. "Tate Lopez. It's an honor to meet you, sir. I'm a huge fan of your show." The men shook hands. Tate girly-giggled toward the end, pulling his hand to his mouth once it was freed.

Mr. Sicianni nodded to Tate. "Thank you. It's always nice to meet devoted fans." He shifted to look at me again. "I hear an apology is in order, Ms. King."

"For what?"

"Chef Dubois is a bit…" His words faded, his eyes searching the room as if the right word were etched on the wall. Finally, he nodded, glancing back to me. "Eccentric."

Egotistical jerk was more fitting, but okay. "You don't owe me anything." I wafted a hand in his direction, shaking my head as I backed toward the hallway that led to the spa.

He motioned toward the glass bar at the center of the casino floor to our left. "May I buy you a drink?"

Tate sucked in a squeal beside me.

"We have an appointment." I glanced at my phone for the time then back to Tate. "In ten minutes."

Tate's face fell.

"Another time, then," Mr. Sicianni said in way that made me think that was an order more than an offer. Something told me he didn't take no for an answer very often.

"Of course," I murmured, just a teensy bit freaked out. And kinda feeling like I needed a shower.

* * *

We followed the etched, sandy-looking path off to the right that led to the Deep Blue Beach Spa. We were met at the door by a tiny young girl holding a clipboard. She was wearing a T-shirt with a graphic of a clamshell bra and khaki shorts covered by a plastic grass skirt. She shook her hips halfheartedly and mumbled robotically, "Welcome to the beach. Have we reserved a heavenly slice of our oasis for you?"

"No," I offered, looking past her at the empty overstuffed chairs at the pedicure stations and the hallway past them that led to the massage rooms. Weston had to be in one of them. "Do you have an opening for two pedicures?"

Tate squeaked a bit and shifted his weight from foot to foot in anticipation.

She looked at her clipboard and back at us, her expression never changing from the blank, benign mask. "I'll have to check the computer."

I gazed back into the room, where several employees were sitting on the rolling stools, talking among themselves, painting their own nails. I exchanged a bewildered look with

Tate as the girl walked over to the kiosk by the entrance and logged into the computer.

"Good news," she muttered while splaying her hands to her sides, still not smiling, still in a monotone voice. "You've just booked two tickets to paradise. Pack your bags and follow me, please." Shoulders slumped and hips forcing the skirt to move as she walked, she led us to the pedicure area.

Two of the nail techs bounced to attention, bright smiles lighting their faces. They were dressed just like the young receptionist, though they filled their uniforms out much better. They shook their hips with a bit more exuberance, motioning toward the chairs in a wavy, hula-like dance.

One girl bubbled, "Hi, I'm Amanda, and I'll be taking very good care of you today. Please remove your shoes and have a seat. Would you like a drink before we begin?"

Tate clapped a few times, beaming. "Two appletinis, please." The girl nodded and turned to leave. "Wait," he called, halting her hip-shaking exit. He turned to me. "Did you want anything, doll face?"

I held up a finger and nodded. After she left, I tapped the other girl on the shoulder as she filled the soaking tubs at the base of our chairs. "Can I use the ladies' room first?" I was pretty sure I'd seen the restroom sign at the end of the hall, past the massage rooms. She smiled and pointed in that direction.

Bingo.

I made my way slowly down the corridor in a very James Bond kind of way. Hugging the wall and checking back toward the nail room every few seconds, I leaned toward each door, listening for Buddy Weston's booming voice. If memory served, it had a distinctly lecherous quality that I knew I'd recognize. At the end of the hall, I found my mark.

"What the hell do you mean he's won four straight hands?" I heard his voice yell.

I put my ear to the door.

There was a pause then, "Well, comp him a room and get him the hell off the gaming floor. Now!"

It sounded like he was on the phone. I sucked in a deep breath for courage, not knowing what stage of undress he might be in, and shoved the door open.

I found Buddy sitting on a chaise lounge in nothing but a fluffy white robe and bright-blue slippers emblazoned with the Deep Blue logo. The robe was open to the waist, affording me a view of his chest, where mounds of dark, curly hair fluffed out of the gap. His legs, which were nearly as hairy as his chest, were crossed at the ankles, with the robe tucked between his thighs just enough to cover the goods.

Thank God for small favors.

A slow smile curled his thin lips as he watched me enter. "I'm gonna have to call you back, Bruce. A new bit of business just fell into my lap."

I choked back a gag at the thought of being anywhere near his lap.

Buddy snapped his phone shut and tossed it onto the pile of clothes on the chair next to him.

"Tessie King," he said, drawing out the words.

"Buddy Weston," I replied.

"To what do I owe this pleasure? Oh, wait! Lemme guess. You're my massage girl?" He smiled then stood and began to remove the robe.

"No!" I barked, my hands waving frantically in front of me, as much to block the view as the thought of that much oily hair stuck to my fingers. The very last thing on the planet I wanted to see was this man's junk. "Please keep that on. I just need to talk to you."

"And just what makes you think I feel like talking? Maybe I feel like calling security and having you escorted out instead." He graciously pulled the robe back over his shoulder.

"Because I'm pretty sure you want to keep the FBI out of your casino as much as I do." With his robe securely back in place, I crossed my arms over my chest in a stalemate gesture.

He raised a bushy brow. "You've got my attention."

"I had an interesting visit from Agent Ryder earlier today."

"I'll bet," he teased, his eyes doing an up-and-down thing that made me involuntarily shudder.

"Agent Ryder and I have a strictly professional relationship." *Now.*

"Sure." Weston pretended to agree.

"Anyway, he told me he suspects members of an organized crime family are doing business in Tahoe."

"You mean doing business at the *Royal Palace*," he corrected. "Otherwise, why would the feds be crawling all over *your* joint?" He flashed me a big grin.

I bit back the sour words on my tongue, wanting to tell him where to go and exactly how to get there. Instead, I asked, "Does the name Hammerhead mean anything to you?"

"Hammerhead Hank?"

"So you know him." That sinking feeling hit the pit of my stomach again as I realized that a known member of an organized crime family was staying right under my nose.

Weston's face lit up with a slow, icky smile. He took a step toward me, his robe gaping lower. He placed a meaty hand on my shoulder. "I sure do, princess, and I'm happy to share with you. Every now and again, it's nice to get into bed with the competition." He gave me another creepy once-over, this time with a gratuitous bushy brow-waggle at the end.

I wilted from his grip and inched away, forcing a jaw-clenched, toothy smile on my face. "Let's not get carried away, Weston."

"Then what's my motivation here?" He snapped his jaw shut, giving me a wide-eyed look of indifference.

"How about I don't report the teenager you have working at the desk? She's under twenty-one, I'm willing to bet."

"Come on, now, King. I think we could strike up a deal that could be..." He wiggled his hips in a way that he must have thought was sexy but was actually more along the lines of something Chevy Chase would pull off for laughs, and then continued, "...mutually gratifying."

Ick, ick, ick. "Just tell me what you know about the Gambias."

He paused, narrowed his eyes at me then thankfully pulled his robe tight, covering any hairy little bits that might have escaped.

"Fine," he shot back, returning to his perch on the chaise. "I'll tell you what I know about the Gambias. I know that Hammerhead Hank ain't the only member of the family comin' to town."

I sucked in a breath. The thought of *one* mobster staying at my casino was enough, but the thought of *more...* "What are they doing here?"

Weston's face broke into that big, creepy grin again. "Well, sweets, they're here because you invited them. *Battle Buffet* is crawling with wiseguys."

CHAPTER SIX

———

I clamped my mouth shut to make sure my jaw hadn't dropped to my chest. *Battle Buffet* full of mobsters? I really hoped Weston was pulling my leg.

After inhaling a slow breath and letting it out even slower, I calmly asked, "Are you sure?"

"Honey," he cooed seductively, causing my gag reflex to kick in. "If there's one thing I know, it's how to keep my casino clean. You think I didn't look into stealing the show away from you? Course I did. Only when I found out who was backing it, I figured I'd let you have that headache. You're a lot friendlier with the FBI than I am, you know what I mean?"

I narrowed my gaze on his. "I'm not buying it, Weston. I know that money is money in your book—dirty or not."

Weston shrugged. "Okay, fine. You got me. I *did* try to steal it away."

"So you did meet with Hank Gambia?"

He nodded. "Only Hammerhead informed me, in no uncertain terms, that they were very comfortable filming at the Royal Palace. Which, as it turns out, was lucky for me."

"Why is that?"

"I'm not the one with whales dropping like flies on my gaming floor, now am I?"

I felt that sinking sensation in my stomach again. "You think that Mr. Taylor was killed by the Gambia family?"

"I think the feds do. If they didn't think one of these families comin' in had a hand in the stiff you found, why bother? They generally don't stop by for social calls or tea time." His head dropped back as he released a belly laugh at his own joke.

But I jumped on his wording. "Wait, what do you mean by 'families'?"

Weston paused, his eyes blinking in mock innocence. "What?"

"You said families, *plural*. We were just talking about the Gambia family, singular. Right?"

There went that cheesy grin again that I was really starting to hate. "Can't slip much past you, now can I, doll?"

I narrowed my eyes and cracked my neck from side to side. I took a couple of steps toward him. "Look, Weston," I started. "I've got a stiff at my *Price is Right* slot machine, a crazy French chef shouting curses at my staff, some guy named Hammerhead staying in my casino, my childhood nemesis wearing the Michael Kors that *should* be mine, and an FBI agent, who owes me a New Year's Eve date, running around my casino making accusations about the Mafia." I paused to take a breath, standing just a few inches from him now. "I don't have time for your little games. The way I see it, there's just one thin piece of cotton standing between your hairy little family jewels and my very sturdy Italian leather boots."

Weston's smile dropped, and I saw his Adam's apple bob up and down.

"So," I said, forcing a smile back on to my face, "you want to tell me what my celebrity cooking show has to do with Mafia families? *Plural*?"

Weston swallowed hard. "Hey, no need to resort to that kinda talk. We're all friends here, right, doll?"

"I swear if you call me doll one more time..." I lifted my boot.

"Okay, okay! Geez." Weston adjusted his robe tighter around himself again. "Look, I swear to God—" He flipped a furry-knuckled hand heavenward. "—here's what I know. The Gambia family has some money in that celebrity cooking show. Like, a lot. They're having some sort of big meeting with some other 'businessmen' soon, and they're using the *Battle Buffet* as a cover."

"What do you mean big meeting..." My voice trailed off as my mind tried to catch up. Over a hundred VIP foodies were supposed to be coming in, via the producers' private invitations.

made a mental note to check the names on the guest list. I suddenly had a bad feeling that *foodie* was a cover for *mobbie*.

"I don't know what the meeting is about," Weston went on, "but the Gambias aren't the only ones involved. Hammerhead mentioned some other families comin' into town soon. If you get my drift."

I got it all right. And I didn't like it one bit. "Are you saying there's some sort of meeting between different mob families going on in *my* casino?" Suddenly I felt like I was on a bad episode of *The Sopranos*.

Weston shrugged. "It ain't going on in *my* casino."

"And somehow Mr. Taylor's death is tied to all of this?"

Weston started to shrug again, but any comment he may have had was stopped by the door bursting open.

A petite brunette pushed in, her arms full of neatly folded towels that apparently blocked her view of us. "It needs to be perfectly clear before we begin that there is not going to be a happy ending to your massage, Mr. Weston—" She stopped short as she set the towels down and saw me. "Oh. I'm so sorry. I didn't expect you were with...er, do I need to come back?"

"No, Kayla. Ms. King was just leaving."

No other words were needed for my hasty exit as his robe dropped to the floor, exposing more hairy parts than I ever wanted to see or ever expected to forget. I stood outside for a few seconds, trying to decide if I really did need the ladies' room to purge the sight from my mind and stomach. Swallowing hard, I made my way back to Tate, needing the pedicure even more now. Not to mention the brain-bleaching effects of a few appletinis. It wasn't a permanent solution, but it would do for now.

Tate greeted me with a big smile and a half-empty martini glass as he wiggled is toes in his bubbly water. There were two already empty glasses sitting on the table next to him. I snatched *my* drink from his hand, slamming it back as I kicked off my shoes. I climbed into the big, overstuffed, comfy chair beside him.

Just as my phone buzzed to life.

My head dropped back against the plush headrest as I wavered for a few seconds on whether or not to answer, the steaming, bubbling water in my basin practically begging me to hit the mute button.

Instead, I dutifully pulled the phone from my pocket and saw Britton's face gracing the screen. I swiped it on.

"Hello," I reluctantly answered

"Tess!" There was panic in Britton's voice. "There's an emergency in LeAnna's room. We..." Her words trailed off as she cleared her throat. "I need you."

I froze, my mind immediately going to thoughts of Hammerheaded mobsters. "I'll be right there," I promised, jumping up from my seat.

The nail tech returned with two more drinks as I was slipping on my boots. Well, at least I could have one for the road?

I smiled at her, flashed a remorseful glance back at Tate, and then gulped one of the drinks. "Please put this on my tab. I gotta go."

* * *

My head was spinning partly from the alcohol and partly from my chat with Weston as I made my way back through the shark-infested lobby of the Deep Blue and across the road to the Royal Palace. I found myself scanning faces in an almost paranoid way as I weaved my way through the crowded lobby. I didn't know who I could trust, who I couldn't, and if I even believed Weston's wild story of mob meetings. I mean, wasn't that the kind of stuff that just happened in movies?

I was so engrossed in my thoughts that I almost didn't even see Rafe and his blondie du jour until I practically ran into them. Literally.

"Whoa, Tessie," I heard Rafe's voice call. I looked up just in time to avoid colliding with Tiffany Weston, decked out in a slinky silver minidress that *almost* had her man-made boobs contained.

"Oh, uh, sorry," I mumbled distractedly, my cheeks going warm. As if one Weston encounter a day wasn't enough. I took in Tiffany's short hemline, high heels, and dark smoky eyeliner. She was teetering on that very fine line between red-carpet-worthy and hooker.

"You okay?" Rafe asked, putting a steadying hand on my arm. I hated how warm and safe that hand felt. Especially when Tiffany took a possessive step closer to her man, sliding her hand into the back pocket of his jeans. I looked away, loath to see her cop a tushy squeeze.

"Yeah. Appletinis," I said, hoping they took my clumsiness for being tipsy and not having mobsters on my mind.

"Maybe you should go a little light on the cocktails, huh?" Tiffany chimed in. Her voice was high and perky in a way that made me think of *Sesame Street* characters. And her note of judginess was not lost on me.

"Thanks for the tip," I told her, trying to put on as genuine a smile as I could muster for her.

"You sure you're okay?" Rafe asked. "It looks like your mouth is twitching,"

Okay, so I couldn't muster much. "Yep. Fine."

"We were just going to grab a bit to eat. You want to join us?" he offered.

I took satisfaction in seeing a moment of horror on Tiffany's face (at least the parts her plastic surgeon hadn't gotten to yet) at the idea of sharing her date, before I shook my head. "No. Thanks. Duty calls," I said, pointing to my phone as I quickly slipped into the elevators.

Three minutes later, the elevator dinged, opening to one of our floors filled with high-dollar suites. I squeezed through the sardine can of people, barely making it out before the door closed. Britton paced the marble-tiled foyer just outside the elevator doors. She wore a bright-blue, sequined Kate Spade dress and matching stiletto heels. Which, considering that she was outside LeAnna's suite, I supposed was appropriate.

As soon as she spotted me, she threw herself into my arms, releasing an exasperated sigh directly into my ear. "Thanks for coming, Tess."

"What's going on?" I asked, glancing down the hall toward LeAnna's suite.

"The cops are crawling all over the place! They just burst in and started tearing the place apart, and they wouldn't tell me anything. Not much clout comes from being the *widow* of the previous owner." She nervously switched between smacking her gum and twisting her hair around her finger.

I threaded the digits of her free hand through mine. "I'll see what I can find out." I pulled her along behind me, her heels muffled against the plush carpeting.

LeAnna's suite doors were wide open. Several uniformed officers sporting blue latex-gloved hands milled about inside, collecting fibers, digging through drawers, invading every last inch of her personal space. LeAnna sat straight-backed on her leather sofa, dressed in a skintight zebra-print minidress, hands folded in her lap, uncharacteristically quiet. Her gaze was fixed on the sliding doors directly across from her. I actually felt kind of bad for her. She was handling the situation much better than I'd expected.

An officer came from the bedroom, toting her makeup carrier sealed inside a clear plastic evidence bag.

LeAnna gave a high-pitched squeal that was nearly deafening. "You honestly can't expect me to do without my makeup!" she shrieked, scrambling across the living area, grabbing the officer by the collar, and yanking his face down toward hers. "I'm drawing the line."

Another officer unclenched her fingers, freeing his coworker, and shoved her back toward the sofa. He pushed a finger to her shoulder and warned, "I was trying to be nice earlier, Mrs. Taylor. But, if you do anything, say anything, even stand up from that sofa, let alone manhandle another of my guys I will cuff you and drag you down to the station for obstruction and assault."

Big fat tears slid down her face as she scanned the room honing in on Britton and me at the door. "Did you see that? He shoved me. That's totally police brutality!"

Britton rushed to her friend's side, tugging LeAnna down on the sofa next to her, clutching her hand. "Tessie's here to help."

I pursed my lips together to keep from blurting something insensitive out loud and forced myself into professional mode. I looked around the room, found someone who looked like a plainclothes detective, and made my way to his side.

"Are you in charge?" I inquired.

He turned slowly, his bushy brows scrunching into a single blob in the middle of his forehead. "And you are?"

My hand shot out. "Tessie King."

"Oh," he muttered, recognition dawning in his eyes as he aggressively shook my hand. "I'm the detective in charge of this scene, yes. It's a pleasure to meet you, Ms. King."

I pulled my hand from his sweaty palm, wiping it discretely on my skirt as I pretended to straighten it. "I'd like to see your search warrant, if you don't mind, Detective."

He pulled the paper from his jacket and handed it to me. "I'm sure you'll see that everything is in order."

I opened the document and scanned it. Not that I had a lot of practice at reading search warrants, but I could see that it was signed, listed LeAnna's name and suite number, and apparently allowed them to access anything in the suite. It was pretty much carte blanche to anything they wanted to paw through. "Can you tell me why this was issued?"

He narrowed his eyes at me. "I'm not sure I'm at liberty to discuss that, Ms. King."

I put my hands on my hips. I'd had just enough stonewalling from ego-inflated men in my life today. "Well, how about I discuss it with your boss, Detective Johnson?" I said, remembering the name I'd heard for the detective in charge of the case when he'd been reviewing footage in Alfie's office earlier. "I'm sure he'd love to know what a bang-up job you're doing searching such a *secure* scene." I pointedly nodded toward the wide-open doors to the suite that Britton and I had walked right through without questions.

"Uh...th-that won't be necessary," he stammered. "I'm happy to cooperate fully with you and your security staff," he amended while motioning to one of the uniformed officers to shut the doors on the outside hallway.

"Delighted to hear it." I shot him a big, toothy grin. "So, what prompted this search warrant to be issued?"

The detective cleared his throat, trying to preserve some semblance of authority. "A partial print was found on the cuticle scissors removed from Mr. Taylor's carotid artery. It matched *Leona Helmsley* over there." He flipped a hand toward LeAnna.

I stifled a laugh. This was so not the place. "No one else's prints on the scissors?"

"Nope." He glanced down at me. "That's why we're here."

I nodded then wound my way around officers, who were busy taking pictures of tiny little evidence placards splayed across the floor, to Britton and LeAnna.

Britton's face brightened. "Did you set them straight? Can you make them leave?"

LeAnna leaned forward. "I must insist that they leave. If they need anything further, I'll have them speak with my attorney. Get rid of them. Now!" She waggled a perfectly manicured finger toward the door, but her narrowed gaze remained locked with mine.

"They have a signed search warrant, so I'm sorry." I probably could have said it in a less cheery way. At least I kept the cheeky grin from my face. "There's nothing I, or your attorney," I added, "can do about it."

LeAnna's shoulders sagged.

"What are they looking for anyway?" Britton asked.

I shrugged. "I don't know. But Detective Cocky over there told me they issued the warrant to search through your things because the murder weapon came back with only one set of prints on it." I paused and sent a pointed look toward LeAnna.

"What!" She bolted to a standing position, but Britton quickly yanked her back down. LeAnna leaned toward me, grabbing the front of my blouse, forcing me to sit right in front of her on the coffee table atop a lumpy stack of magazines and God only knew what else.

"They were my cuticle scissors. Of course they had my prints on them," she spat through clenched teeth. "But like I've said a million times, I did not kill my husband." Her voice rose to a squalling shriek toward the end of her statement. Her upper lip quivered with anger, causing her nose to bounce like a rabid bunny. Not her best look. *Would it be impolite to snap a pic?*

"That's all good and well, but they aren't leaving." I plucked her hand from my blouse, shoving it back into her lap. "Besides you and Gerald, who else had access to your room?"

Her anger faded for a moment as she trained her eyes on mine. "Why do you ask?"

"Well," I said slowly, spelling it out for her, "if you didn't kill Gerald, and he didn't kill himself, someone else must have gotten their hands on your cuticle scissors." I moved an oddly placed TV remote out from under my posterior, shifting in an attempt to level myself.

"Maybe you loaned your cuticle scissors to someone else?" Britton offered.

LeAnna shook her head. "Who loans those?"

"When was the last time you saw them?" I pressed.

LeAnna opened her mouth to respond but seemed to pause midthought. "Well, I don't know! I got a shellac before we left Napa." She held out her hands. Her nails were, indeed, freshly manicured and shellacked. If I had to guess, it would be another week before she even needed her cuticle scissors. "I usually keep them in my makeup case, but it's not like I inventoried *everything* in there."

By the size of the case I'd seen, I could tell that prospect would take a while.

"Do you think that Gerald would have given his room to key to someone else?" Britton asked.

LeAnna sniffed, wiping at tears that just weren't there. "No, my Gerald never allowed anyone we didn't know into our room."

"Any friends you might have given your key to?" Britton asked.

Shaking her head so hard it loosened the sparkly clip from her bangs, LeAnna pleaded to Britton, "You know I'd never do that. You also know I'd never kill anyone, right?" She gathered her friend's hands in her own, big doe eyes begging along with her words.

Britton nodded, shifting her gaze to mine. "She wouldn't. On both counts. Even if you don't believe her, you can believe me."

I trusted Britton implicitly, knowing her faith was deeply rooted in her friend, misguided as it was. I, however, did *not* trust LeAnna any farther than I could throw her.

I glanced between the two women a few times but finally stopped on LeAnna. "So, if you didn't use *your own scissors* to kill your husband, who did?"

Leaning in close again, LeAnna spat, "You tell me." Her voice lowered before she continued. "It had to be one of *your* employees, *Tornado Tessie.* Which one of them broke in here and framed me?"

"Wait—what?" I sputtered, her accusation taking me completely by surprise. "My staff would never do anything like this." At least, I hoped they wouldn't. It would be easy enough to check card access and video footage from the hallway to make sure. But I stood my ground (actually, sat my ground), my expression never wavering.

A sound of a throat being cleared loudly behind me pulled me from visions of smacking some sense into the woman. I turned to find Alfie towering over me.

He bobbed his head toward the door. "Can I talk to you in the hall?"

"Sure." I stood, brushing papers and debris from my butt before following him out of the suite.

Alfie pivoted from side to side, staring down the empty hallway in both directions before turning his attention back to me. "My guys just got done with the footage from this morning. We recovered all shots of our fake ski bum."

"Any of them provide an ID?" I held my breath, hanging on his answer, half of me almost hoping to hear LeAnna's name and not that of a certain Hammerhead.

He shrugged his shoulders. "Sorry, nothing definite. He came in through the side entrance from the parking garage, sat at the slot machines for a while, where it looks like he was watching for Mr. Taylor." Alfie paused. "You saw what happened when he found him. After that he just walked right out the front doors and got into a cab."

"Any chance you could track down the taxi driver?"

"We're working on it, but with the amount of traffic we had coming in and out of the casino last night, is unlikely anyone's going to remember any particular skier. Especially if our guy was taking steps to not be recognized. Wherever he had the driver drop him off, chances are it wasn't his final destination anyway."

I huffed out an exasperated sigh. "So, basically were back at square one."

"Pretty much. I'll let you know if my guys find anything else."

"Thanks, Alfie. Can you also have them track anyone who may have come and gone from this room over the last few days?"

His lip twitched, and his jaw tightened. "Feds already have that in the works."

"Thanks," I said, truly meaning it. I turned to go back into LeAnna's suite. She and Britton were waiting right inside the door, an officer blocking their exit. LeAnna crossed her arms tightly across her chest and ground her teeth. "Can we leave now?"

"I'm sure they'll be done soon," I assured.

"Whatever. I just want to go get settled in my new room."

"*New* room?" I asked, casting a glance in Britton's direction.

Britton smiled sheepishly and dropped her gaze to her bedazzled feet. "I sort of invited LeAnna to stay with us in the penthouse. Just until this killer is caught. It just seems safer. You don't mind, right?"

It was my turn to grind my teeth. Great, now I'd be sleeping with the enemy.

CHAPTER SEVEN

———

The sun streamed through my window shades, casting striped sunbeams across my bed. Captain Jack was curled in a tight black-and-white ball next to me, purring up a storm as the warmth permeated us both. As I scratched his ears, he stretched out long and lean. He opened an eye and did a cute little purr/meow. Mornings just didn't get much better.

Unless Bradley Cooper was free.

A blood-curdling scream sounded from the living room, quickly taking me out of a happy cocoon and bringing back the nightmares from the previous evening. The LeAnna invasion was real. I groaned. I'd made a point last night of checking for any other available suites we could off-load LeAnna into, but thanks to *Battle Buffet*, we were fully booked until the weekend. I tried to think happy thoughts about the revenue that would generate and not about how hard it would be to keep from killing LeAnna between now and Monday.

I grabbed my robe, and Jack crept under the bed. He was probably the smarter of the two of us. I smoothed my hair as I turned out of the hall into the living room. LeAnna was wearing Britton's black yoga pants and matching sports top and was holding her palms out in front of her, disgust etched on her face.

"Is everything okay?" I regretted the words even before she snarled at me.

"Can you not see all of the cat hair? This is disgusting." She swatted at maybe three hairs on her thigh.

I crossed the room to Britton's antique writing desk and tossed a lint roller on the mattress of the hide-a-bed. "That's what these are for."

Jack trotted into the living room, making a figure eight around my ankles.

"You just need to drop that thing off at the pound."

"He's not going anywhere, but I'll drop you off there if you need a lift." I gave her my biggest fake smile.

"This is just gross," she said, rolling her thigh like a maniac. "If it were up to me, all animals would live outside. In cages."

Jack hissed at LeAnna, and she lunged toward him.

I scooped the poor kitty into my arms just in time. "I swear, LeAnna, if you touch one hair on this cat's head…"

"Don't worry," she cut me off. "All of his hair is on me right now."

Britton chose that moment to prance around the corner in another neon spandex outfit and matching shoes, this time in florescent yellow. "What's the problem, girls?"

LeAnna and I shared a scowl before I mumbled, "Just setting a few ground rules."

My phone chirped from my room, calling me away from the stare-down. I grabbed a bagel from the basket on the kitchen counter and headed back to my room to check my phone. Jack followed on my heels.

It was a text from Alfie. *Battle Buffet set ASAP.*

Oh, goodie. Probably another French fit, toddler-style.

* * *

After rushing through my morning routine, I arrived on the show set, dressed in a new dark-blue pencil skirt and matching 3/4-sleeve short jacket. I was fully caffeinated and ready for any insults the cranky celebrity chef could throw my way. I was not, however, prepared for Rafe. He was dressed in khakis and an emerald-green sweater that matched his eyes, momentarily throwing me off my game and tossing me into teen-crush mode.

Even when he smiled at me with dimples popping at only medium depth, I couldn't help the girly sigh that escaped. I tried to cover it with a forced cough. "What are you doing here?"

He flipped a hand over his shoulder toward Chef Dubois. "Alfie asked for my help installing the new faucet. The plumber couldn't make it in until this afternoon. Dubois was about to bust something." He looked over his shoulder. "As a matter of fact, he may have actually busted a few set props."

I shook my head in frustration. "I know he's bringing in some big revenue, but is it even worth it?"

Rafe leaned an elbow against one of the contestant's counters. "Yes, it's worth it. And I had to call in a favor to even make it happen."

I raised an eyebrow his way. "I didn't know that."

He shrugged. "It wasn't a big deal. Your father and James Sicianni go way back. He was happy to consider our venue when I mentioned your father's name." He flashed his dimples again.

Sicianni, who was funded by the Gambia family, and *my dad* went *way* back? That sinking feeling from the day before returned to my stomach, mixing with my bagel in a nauseating brew. I stared up at Rafe. Surely I could trust him. I grabbed his arm and tugged him over to the VIP section, out of earshot of anyone on the set.

"Whoa, Tessie, what's going on?" he asked, concern replacing his delicious dimples.

I wanted to be tactful, but the words just poured out. "Is *Battle Buffet* mobbed up?"

Rafe's eyes narrowed. "What do you mean mobbed up?"

"I mean, who are these VIPs that Sicianni invited?"

He leaned back in his chair, dropping his hands into his lap. "I heard you went to Weston, asking about the show."

"Tiffany," I mumbled, more like it was a bad word than a question.

"Yes, Tiffany." He paused. "If I didn't know better, I'd say you didn't like her."

"Ha!" I blurted out before I could stop myself. I quickly pulled my professional face back out. "Sorry. It's none of my business who you date."

His eyes suddenly twinkled with a mischievous glimmer through his thick, dark lashes. "Who says I'm dating her?"

I quirked an eyebrow his way. "So, you're just taking her out to dinner, dancing, and nightclubs?" I asked, ticking off the places that my sources (a.k.a. Tate) had seen the two together in the last few days.

He shrugged. "We may have been to those places together. Doesn't mean we're *together*." He winked at me.

Was he flirting? I cleared my throat, feeling my cheeks go warm. "Are you avoiding the question?"

"What question? Am I dating Tiffany Weston?"

As much as I was suddenly interested in that answer... "No. Did I invite the cast of *The Godfather* to my casino?"

He shook his head. "Mr. Sicianni has invited a group of—"

"Foodies. I know," I said, waving the cover story off.

"And food critics and restaurateurs. VIPs in the *culinary* industry."

"But why would the FBI be here?"

Rafe's easy smile faltered for a moment. "FBI? You mean Agent Ryder?"

Was that jealousy I detected? Wow, flirting and jealousy all in one convo. Teen-me was kinda not hating this.

"They're looking into Mr. Taylor's death. They think maybe, possibly, the Mafia, Mr. Taylor, *Battle Buffet*, and the Gambias are all connected somehow."

"Gambias?"

"And other families. They're all coming for a big all-hands mob meeting."

Rafe's smile fell lopsided, his eyes clearly laughing at me. "Weston told you all of this?"

I swallowed. "Well, yeah."

"And you believed him?"

"Well, sorta..."

Rafe grabbed both of my hands, pulling me toward him. Our noses almost touched. Teen-me's heart skipped a beat and honed in on his lips. Adult-me couldn't help but look too.

"Look, we start taping later today," he said, rubbing the back of my hand with his thumbs. I may have stopped breathing, but I was okay with it. "Let's just take a moment to pause here, okay? I mean, what motive would anyone connected with the show possibly have for wanting Mr. Taylor dead?"

He was right. So far the only person who had motive was sitting in my penthouse, lint-rolling herself into a frenzy.

Clanging pots and a string of thunderous French words grabbed our attention. Teen-me was still captivated, but adult-me sprang into action and made my way to Chef Dubois's kitchen stage.

I cleared my throat, calling his attention away from the female contestant he had cornered. "Chef Dubois, is there a problem?" I bit back the word *again*. "That extra centimeter really does make a difference," I said with a modicum of sarcasm, waving toward his faucet.

He turned to me. "Ah, Meese King. My apologies for my *conduite* the last time we met. I had no idea you were the, how you say? Transient owner?"

"I'm the owner, yes." Not a homeless owner, just a regular one. "How is the new faucet? Up to your standards, I presume?"

"Oh, Meese King, one must never presume. That was our *problème* last time. Today *est bonne*." He motioned toward his sink. "Is very good. My contestants? *Pas si bon*, not so good." He glared at a woman who had escaped back to her own kitchenette. She was busily chopping greens, muttering under her breath.

"Is there a problem with a contestant?" I asked. I had to admit, that seemed like more of an issue for the show's producer than the hotel staff. We'd had nothing to do with the selection of the contestants.

"*Oui!*" he yelled. "She is ten minutes late this morning. Ten!"

I looked back at the woman. She was slim, young, and had a tattoo of a whisk on her forearm. She also looked like she was chopping the life out of those greens. If I had to guess, I'd say she was picturing one French chef as she mutilated them into a pulp.

"Uh, I'm very sorry that she was late," I said.

"And do you know why she was tardy?"

I shook my head.

"Because your breakfast service was late to her room!"

I mentally rolled my eyes but was proud to say I kept the smile pasted on my face.

"These amateurs need all the rehearsal time they can get. I cannot function where precision and adherence to schedules does not exist!"

"I am very sorry. I will do all I can to ensure that does not happen to any of your talent for the rest of the stay," I promised.

His eyes narrowed at me, and his nostrils flared. "*I* am the talent on this show. Everyone would be smart to remember that." He grabbed a meat cleaver, wielded it high over his head, the metal singing as it whipped through the air before slamming into the chopping block in front of him.

I backed away to a safe distance. "Well, if there's anything you need, just let us know."

He yanked the cleaver out and waved it in my direction. "You will let Alfie know I'm grateful for the faucet, no?"

I nodded, hoping I had kept the look of terror from my face. "Of course." Spinning on my heels, I all but jogged from the stage, dodging the setup crew with the bleachers as they brought them down the hall, and headed toward the front desk. Rafe was nowhere in sight. Ryder, however, was near the elevators, chatting with two uniformed policemen. I just barely kept my stomach from doing a little flip at the sight of his perfectly tailored suit hugging his frame. How the guy managed to have sexy five o'clock shadow even before noon was beyond me. I gave my traitorous hormones a *down, girl* and made my way toward him.

I stood a few feet away from him, waiting for them to wrap up their conversation.

Ryder kept looking over at me, a slight smile tilting his lips. Finally, he patted the guy closest to him on the shoulder. "I'll meet you guys there."

He wound past a few people and made his way to me. This time, a real smile graced his adorable features. He was dressed in his signature dark suit and white dress shirt, his tie the only splash of color in his ensemble. This time it was in a striped pattern. It was slightly uneven, and my fingers itched to fix it.

"Agent Ryder," I greeted him, going for the formal feel again. "I trust your crime scene crew is done going through LeAnna's suite?" I was proud of myself that I'd kept most of my snarky comments to myself last night, but I couldn't make any promises about the future if she continued to stay in my penthouse.

"They're not my crew," he answered, the smile never leaving his face as his eyes gave me an up and down that raised goose bumps. Traitorous skin. "They're local PD."

"Whoever they are, I'd like my guest to be able to return to her suite."

My chilly tone did nothing to wipe the grin off his face.

"How about I buy you a cup of coffee, and we can discuss it?"

As much as I didn't trust my body not to react around him, I was all for any discussion that led to getting LeAnna out of my hair. Plus, my morning so far was screaming for caffeine. I motioned toward the front of the building to the Java Joust. "I can get us a couple of cups for free. I have connections." Dang, even my own mouth was betraying me now. Bad mouth. No flirting.

"Well, as long as it's not a bribe," he teased before following me.

After ordering my usual and a cup of black coffee for him, we made our way to a table away from the crowd. He even pulled out my chair for me again. A girl could get dangerously used to this stuff.

He sat across from me and dropped his hands on the table. "So, how have you been?"

I felt my brow furrow at his casual tone and the personal question. "Fine."

"Really?"

"Yes."

He cocked his head to the side, assessing me. "You don't look fine."

"Gee, aren't you the flatterer," I mumbled, sipping at my coffee.

"You look upset about something," he pressed.

I gave him a smile that might have come out looking more like a snarl. "What on earth would I have to be upset about?" I ground out.

He cocked his head to the other side. "Wait—is this about New Year's?"

I opened my eyes wide in mock surprise. "Whatever do you mean?"

He sighed deeply. "It is about New Year's, isn't it?"

"Of course not. I mean, I can't imagine what you think I have to be upset about. It's not like I spent hours getting my hair and nails done, picking out the perfect dress, primping, shaving, exfoliating, and doing a smoky-eye thing that was incredibly sexy looking, by the way, just to sit alone in a crowded restaurant surrounded by lovey-dovey couples and get stood up on the biggest date night of the year!" I practically shouted. So much for the aloof thing.

Ryder's smile was a thing of the distant past now, a deep frown between his sandy eyebrows having replaced it. "I didn't stand you up. I texted."

I narrowed my eyes. "Really? *That's* the defense you're going with?"

"I'm sorry. Something came up," he said, his eyes darting down to the table.

"Right. Something much more interesting." Or, more likely, someone.

"It's complicated." This time his eyes darted toward the floor. Clearly he wasn't telling me the whole story here. Not that I was sure I wanted to hear it anyway.

"Sure. It always is," I mumbled as I took another sip from my cup.

"I did say I was sorry in my text," he said, finally meeting my eyes again.

"You also said you'd call," I reminded him.

Back to the floor went the eyes, followed by a clearing of his throat and shift in his seat. "Right. Well, like I said, it's complicated." He looked so uncomfortable that I almost felt sorry for him.

Almost. He *had* stood me up.

"You were going to tell me what's going on with the local police," I reminded him, trying to regain some of my professional composure.

Ryder cleared his throat again. "You know I can't discuss an ongoing case."

I rolled my eyes. "Look, just tell me if they've found anything else on LeAnna. I have a right to know if the woman I'm sleeping with is a killer."

One sandy eyebrow arched upward.

I bit my lip. "She's, uh, staying in the penthouse with Britton and me," I mumbled, feeling my cheeks flame.

I don't know if it was my obvious embarrassment or the idea of girl-on-girl action that changed his mind, but he pulled a notebook from his pocket and after flipping through the pages read out loud, "Other than the partial print on the murder weapon, no other evidence has been found to implicate LeAnna specifically."

"So she can go back to her suite?" I asked, unable to keep the hopeful note from my voice.

"Not quite yet. They are still looking into a couple of things," he hedged.

"How much longer?"

"Another day or two."

Fab. There was a 50/50 chance I wouldn't kill her by then. "But they haven't found anything else to implicate her?"

"Well," he drew out. "I'm not sure they really need to. The murder weapon did belong to her. She admitted to that already."

"But what about the Gambias? You said yourself, that's why you're here."

"I said we believe Taylor had business dealings with them. I didn't say they killed him."

"Pretty big coincidence that they'd be here when he dies."

"Coincidences happen. More often that most people like to think." He paused. "Why? Is there something you're not telling me?"

"No," I mumbled, running a thumbnail along the rim of my cup, spinning my phone in the middle of the table with the other hand. The last thing I wanted to do was add fuel to Agent Ryder's fire with Weston's accusations that I'd invited a Mafia family reunion to my casino.

He turned his attention back his notepad. "I'm sure Alfie already told you that the video footage we found was a bust."

I nodded. "But if I know LeAnna, there's no way she would have dressed in that ski bum getup as a disguise. I mean, it's not even designer plaid," I only half joked.

Ryder frowned. "Look, I know we haven't found a lot of evidence against LeAnna yet, but we also haven't found a lot to point to anyone else. The only key cards used to open the Taylors' suite that night were theirs and housekeeping. I'm told the staff members in question are being interviewed, so I'll let you know if anything comes up there."

"It won't," I said defensively.

Ryder nodded. "Honestly? I'm inclined to believe you. Which means either LeAnna or her husband took the murder weapon out of the suite that night."

"Or someone stole one of their key cards! Mr. Taylor had a habit of passing out, you know. Anyone could have taken it."

"We have footage from the hallway outside the Taylors' room from the time they checked in until Mr. Taylor..." He trailed off.

I gulped back the vision of his pale, lifeless body.

"For their entire visit," he amended. "No one else entered their rooms."

"Well, maybe they didn't take the scissors from her room. LeAnna wasn't entirely sure she had them with her when she checked in."

"Which is exactly what she'd say if she had used them to kill her husband."

I opened my mouth to protest again, but I was out of arguments. He was right. LeAnna did sound guilty.

Ryder flipped back to the front of his notebook then tucked it back into his pocket. "I wish I could tell you otherwise, but everything we have so far points right at your bedmate."

"*Room*mate," I emphasized, feeling that heat creep up again.

Ryder grinned at me.

My phone buzzed with a text, saving me from his teasing gaze. It was from Maverick.

I've got something you'll want to see.

I quickly covered the phone with my hand before Ryder could read it.

"I, uh, sorry, I've got to go."

"Sure. I understand."

Was it my imagination, or did I detect a look of disappointment in his eyes?

CHAPTER EIGHT

"There." Maverick pointed toward the huge monitor on his wall. LeAnna's face appeared, a box outlining her features and her name appearing above her head. It all looked like a real-life version of The Sims. She stood in front of the ladies' room door just off the gaming floor, smiling down at her phone. "She left Britton a little while before, and she was able to avoid the cameras for a bit. This is her second visit to the ladies' room this evening after checking her phone."

Clearly she was expecting to meet up with her mystery text man.

I stood behind him, watching as she disappeared into the bathroom. I expected the footage to pick up again as she exited. Not so much. It switched cameras and followed her right in.

"Wait!" I swatted a hand against his shoulder. "There are cameras in the bathrooms?"

"Uh, yeah. It's a casino."

"Like, *all* the bathrooms?" I asked, suddenly doing a mental calculation of how many times I'd used that same ladies' room and who might have been watching me. I crossed my arms over my chest in a protective gesture. I suddenly felt very violated.

Maverick just shrugged. "There are a few blind spots, but we have cameras pretty much everywhere. We're very efficient."

My glare made him pivot back toward the screen, solemn faced. He pushed the play button again, and we watched as a man came into the bathroom after her. All we could see was the back of him.

"This is what I knew you'd want to see."

LeAnna doing the nasty in the bathroom? No thanks. I swallowed back the coffee that threatened to escape at the thought. I kept watching as the man pulled LeAnna into a firm embrace. They pivoted sideways, but his face was turned away from us as his arms wrapped around her. Her hands slid down his back, cupping his very nice butt. As far as bathroom hookups went, I guess she could've done much worse. He, on the other hand, needed to run far and run fast.

I cleared my throat, and Maverick paused the footage, swinging a concerned gaze my way.

"Are we going to watch the whole sexual encounter? I'll go grab some popcorn if we are," I teased.

"There isn't much more to show except who the mystery man is."

"Oh." I waggled my hand toward the screen. "Carry on, then." If we knew who the other man was and the possible father of her maybe-baby, he could be a viable suspect in Mr. Taylor's death. As implausible as it seemed to me, maybe the guy wanted Mr. Taylor out of the way to have LeAnna all to himself. Though, the poor guy had no idea what he was getting himself into.

The footage picked up again with a little more back stroking and the mystery man removing her hands from his butt, much to her obvious disappointment. I might have snorted in a most unladylike fashion.

Twice.

Until he turned toward the camera. As the facial recognition software pulled his face into focus, I kicked myself for not recognizing his sleek hair or his buns of steel. In my defense, any normal woman would be in denial at the thought that he would really be meeting a girl like that in a bathroom of all places.

All doubt was gone as the software put a black box around his face and typed his name above him.

Rafe Lorenzo.

The latte in my stomach turned sour.

"What...what were they doing in there?" I wasn't completely sure why I went from believing she was hooking up with some random guy in the john to this blind wonderment.

"Uh," Maverick muttered. "I think it's pretty clear it's some sort of tryst."

"Tryst? Who says it's a *tryst*? Maybe it was just a momentary lack of common sense, at least on his part."

Maverick hovered his finger over the play button for a few seconds, took a deep breath, and then pushed it. I watched as LeAnna nestled against Rafe's chest. Another woman walked by slowly, staring from them to the rows of toilets, obviously confused, with a man in the room. Rafe wrapped LeAnna in his embrace at his side, walking her out of the bathroom, both of them laughing all the way.

With my ego deflated to the size of a pea, a tiny ember of hope still burned that Rafe wasn't that desperate. I muttered, "Can I hear the audio?"

Maverick snorted this time. "Clearly we don't have audio in the bathrooms."

"Right, because *that* would be indecent."

I felt my face burn warmer at the naive thought of anyone wanting Tornado Tessie when Princess LeAnna was on the menu. As always, she reeled in the cute guys like an expert angler. Why would this be any different?

"Are you okay?" Maverick rose, grabbing my arm. Then he dropped it like a hot potato, immediately looking down at the floor, his cheeks flushing pink at his bold move.

I fought back the tears of embarrassment and pride. "Yeah. Sure." I forced a smile to my face. "Uh, listen, could you do something for me?" I asked, trying to switch gears lest I make a total fool of myself in front of an employee.

"Of course!" He jumped.

"Uh, we have a guest staying at the hotel by the name of Hank Gambia." I paused, watching for any reaction. If the name meant something to him, he was a top-notch actor. His face didn't register any recognition. "Anyway," I went on, clearing my throat, "you think you could just sort of keep an eye on him?"

Maverick's forehead wrinkled in confusion. "Any particular reason?"

I really hoped not. "Not really, just...just in case."

Maverick nodded. "Okay. Sure, I guess." I could tell he had his suspicions, but if there was one thing the casino security knew how to do, it was mind their own business.

"Thanks," I told him, turning to leave on what I hoped was professional note.

And not the one of total embarrassment that I was feeling.

* * *

I keyed my penthouse code into the elevators and rode up, my head spinning. If there was anyone I thought I could have trusted, it was Rafe. But what if I'd been wrong? I knew the teenage snowboarding-hopeful Rafe, but I'd only been around adult-Rafe for less than a year. He had poo-pooed my worries that Mr. Taylor might have had some connection to the Gambia and *Battle Buffet*...but had that been strategic? It *had* been Rafe who had set up the deal with *Battle Buffet* to come to the Royal Palace in the first place. Had that been strategic too? Had he possibly been the one who went *way* back with Sicianni, and not my father? And if so, where did Mr. Taylor fit into all of this?

Too many questions and not enough answers had a gigantic headache brewing between my eyes. I prayed Britton and her devil-spawn friend had gone shopping or perhaps skeet shooting, where LeAnna would suffer a horrible, disfiguring accident. Of course, my luck wasn't that great.

As soon as I walked through the penthouse doors, Devil Spawn rolled her eyes at me from the sofa.

Goodie.

"Britton?" I called out, hoping for a buffer, especially after the video footage I'd just watched. All I could think about was LeAnna wrapped in Rafe's arms.

LeAnna scrolled on her phone, her other hand shooing me. "She went to the attorney's office. Something about paperwork or needing to sign something."

"For her allowance," I blurted out without thinking.

She shifted on the cushion to face me. "You make your poor stepmother ask for an allowance like a teenager? Isn't it bad enough that you practically stole this casino out from under her when your father died?" LeAnna's face was scrunched in a very unattractive scowl, not that I'd seen much of the un-scowling version.

"Did Britton say that?" My pulse quickened at the thought.

LeAnna stood, pivoting slowly toward me. She crossed her arms over her ample bosom, still dressed in the workout clothes Britton had loaned her. "She didn't have to. I figured that out all on my own."

I shook my head. "The *allowance* is from dividends on my father's shares in the casino." Making sure a regular, monthly allowance of dividends was paid on his shares had been one of the first things I'd done as acting chairman. Britton wasn't exactly the best at the nine-to-five thing. "And we're not talking gas money here, okay?" I said, trying to defend Britton. I knew the last thing she'd want was someone like LeAnna thinking she was a charity case.

"Well, gee, aren't you generous?" A condescending smile stretched her deflating lips. Someone was going to need a plumping refill, or I was going to enjoy watching them turn into wrinkled, empty balloons. I really hoped for the latter scenario. Her staying with us might as well have a few perks for me, too.

Her gaze narrowed. "What are you smiling at?"

I did a wide-eye-innocence thing. "Nothing at all," I lied, overaccentuating each word as though I were talking to a labradoodle.

Britton burst through the door dressed in a skintight baby-blue minidress, and scanned the mail in her one hand as she held a full takeout bag looped over the other. Without even looking up, she set everything on the kitchen table. "LeAnna, I brought us Thai food from the King's Court. I hope you're hungry. You need to keep up your strength now that you're eating for two." She looked up, glancing between LeAnna and me. "Oh, Tessie, I totally didn't know you'd be here. But I'm sure there's enough to share," she offered.

"That's okay. I just came up here to regroup before the taping this afternoon. I'll get something later." I patted her shoulder and walked toward the hall, my bedroom, and my freedom.

And, most of all, my cat.

Britton grabbed my arm. "Not so fast. Lisa in housekeeping told Ken, the valet, who mentioned to Sharron at the bar, that you had coffee with that smokin' hot fed guy. Agent Ryder? Isn't that his name?"

LeAnna rubbed her hands together. "Hot fed is my favorite flavor."

I narrowed my eyes at her. Was there really a flavor she *didn't* like?

I turned back to Britton. "Yeah, so?"

"So, what did he tell you about the investigation? Is LeAnna free to go back to her suite?"

I released a sigh that was filled with 100 percent genuine disappointment. "No, not for a few days still."

I did a mental search through what I could and couldn't tell Britton in front of the police's Suspect Number One, who had flopped back onto the sofa, phone shoved back in front of her face. I definitely couldn't tell her about the possibility that a mob family meeting was about to take place at the casino or about Rafe and the restroom incident, not to mention that he could very well be LeAnna's mystery texter.

"Do they have any other suspects?" Britton pressed.

I bit my lip. "Possibly..." I glanced to LeAnna. She was sprawled on the sofa—one foot dangling off the arm and the other skewed under the coffee table. Her phone was propped right under her nose with one hand, the other draped over her head, hanging from the armrest.

She caught me watching her and glared up at me. "What?"

"What can you tell me about Gerald's business connections?"

She scrambled to a proper sitting position, dropping her phone into her lap. "Who wants to know?"

"Believe it or not, I'm trying to help." *Help you get back to your own life and the heck out of mine.*

Britton stepped to my side, linking her arm through mine. "You can tell Tessie anything."

LeAnna shrugged. "He owns a winery in Napa. As everyone knows. He had tons of business connections."

"Okay, let me focus the field for you." I paused, not sure how to broach the subject of her husband having possibly been "whacked" by the mob. "Did he ever do any business with Mr. Sicianni or *Battle Buffet*?" Mr. Taylor had owned a winery. *Battle Buffet* was all about food. It wasn't outside the realm of possibility that they had crossed paths at some point.

She shrugged. "They might have bought some wine from him, I think. But Gerald didn't really talk about work with me. He knew that in my world *work* was a four-letter word." She giggled at her own joke.

I just barely bit back actually voicing the labradoodle comparison. It was kind of condescending to the dog. "Did your husband know Chef Dubois?"

She looked down at her feet. "He's a celebrity. We've met him, of course. One of the restaurants where they tape the show is in Napa. We've eaten there a few times." She waved a dismissive hand and stood in front of me. "Speaking of which, I'm hungry, and the baby is probably famished." She rubbed a hand over her extremely flat, practically concave abdomen. "We can do this some other time."

I grabbed her bony arm as she walked past me. "One more question and then you can eat. What do you know about the Gambia family?"

LeAnna gave me the blank labradoodle look, but Britton's eyes narrowed suspiciously in my direction. For all of Britton's blonde-bombshellness, she wasn't as dumb as she often let people think.

Luckily, before she could follow up on that, LeAnna's phone chirped in her hand. She glanced down at the screen, and her face morphed into a giddy grin. She yanked her arm from my grasp and clutched the phone to her chest. "I have to use the little girl's room before we eat."

The thought of Rafe possibly being on the other end of the mysterious text message left a sour taste in my mouth. I made my way to my room, slammed the door, and flicked the lock.

Jack yowled from the bed.

"Don't start with me," I mumbled.

CHAPTER NINE

The energy level on the *Battle Buffet* set was off the charts with people chatting exuberantly, anxiously anticipating the taping to start. Mouth-watering aromas filled the air, sending my stomach into fits, demanding food despite the lunch of Thai leftovers I'd had before arriving. Shiny aluminum bleachers lined one side of the audience section, which was nearly packed full already, while more generous stadium seats with luxurious cushions were erected for the VIPs. People milled about that space, smoking cigars and chatting among themselves in low tones. I scanned each impeccably dressed man as I walked by, wondering if he was "connected."

Tate waved from across the set, and I made my way toward him. Only before I could reach his side, another familiar pair of eyes in the crowd caught mine. Bright emerald-green ones.

Rafe was milling near the VIP section, surrounded by his usual snow-bunny groupies vying for his autograph. He looked straight at me, waved, and smiled at full dimple capacity. I fought the conflicting butterflies and gag reflex as I switched between memories of his hands caressing mine and the restroom footage I'd watched earlier. I broke away from his gaze without returning the smile and swiped a finger across my phone to look busy.

"What was that?" Tate chided as he caught up with me. "When Rafe Lorenzo smiles, you smile back, honey."

"I'm not in a smiling mood when it comes to the men in my life lately," I mumbled. Then I quickly amended, "Present company excluded, of course."

"Of course," he repeated, as if it were a given. "But what gives? I've never seen you give hottie the cold shoulder. Not even when he's had Tiffany draped all over him."

I briefly wondered how Tiffany would feel about knowing her guy was sexting a married woman. I doubted even she would put up with that and had a moment of pity for the girl.

"Hello, Tess?" Tate said, waving a hand in front of my face.

"Sorry, I was...thinking about something..." I trailed off.

Tate pursed his lips together. "Okay, girlfriend. Don't make me force drinks into you to get at the truth. Spill. What's going on?"

"Fine," I said. Though, truth be told, a drink didn't sound too bad. "It's just that..." I backed away and held out my pinkie in front of Tate. "Before I go any further, this is just between us."

Tate locked his pinkie with mine, his face solemn as he traced a cross over his heart with his free hand. "Of course." He took his pinkie-swears very seriously. It was better than an official gag order, as far as he was concerned.

"I think LeAnna is seeing Rafe on the side," I whispered.

Tate bounced back and flipped his hands up in a surrender motion. "Shut. Up." Then his hands flew to his mouth. "Ohmigod, you don't think LeAnna's baby could be..." His words trailed off as he turned an exaggerated glare in Rafe's direction.

There went that gag reflex again.

"No, no way!" At least I hoped not. I shook my head vehemently as I added, "Gerald hasn't been here in months. And I haven't seen LeAnna at the casino at all until she showed up a few days ago. The timing would be all off." I wasn't sure who I was trying to convince more—Tate or myself.

Tate nodded. "No, you're right." He paused. "But how on earth did you find this juicy little tidbit of tasty Rafe gossip?"

I took a step back and lowered my head to look at him through my lashes. "Focus on the pinky-swear. I know that look. You are mentally filing through your phone contacts to figure out who to text first."

"Who me?" he gasped. Though I could tell the reminder had shut the mental rolodex.

I leaned in. "I had security trace her steps the night of the murder. She and Rafe showed up together on some footage." I didn't share exactly where. Pinky-swear or no, that would have been too juicy for him to keep on the down-low.

His eyebrows disappeared up into his bangs. "It so wouldn't surprise me a bit if she offed her husband, the hateful thing."

I couldn't help agreeing on the hateful part, but I still had doubts that she was a cold-blooded killer. Besides, stabbing seemed too messy for her. She wouldn't risk getting blood on her outfit.

"By the way, speaking of gossip..." Tate trailed off enticingly. "Guess what I heard from Juanita this afternoon?"

I raised an eyebrow. I could use a little juicy staff rumor to lighten my day. "Do tell."

"Well, she heard from Jocelyn the blackjack dealer who is dating this cab driver named Danny..."

"Yes?" I urged him on.

"That a certain crotchety security officer was spotted in the back of a cab on L.T. blvd with a hot blonde."

"Alfie? So?" I asked. I was pretty sure Alfie had escorted all sorts of high rollers and their wives around town on occasion.

Tate's eyes sparkled with gossipy glee. "Spotted them *making out* in the back of the cab."

"No way!"

"Yes way!" Tate giggled.

"Alfie *dates*?" I could not picture anything even remotely romantic about Alfie. The thought of him with roses and candy in his arms was almost comical.

"My intel is rarely wrong." He backed away a bit, his chin hitching high with pride and a smidgeon of gloating.

"Yowza. I wonder who the unlucky girl is," I asked, wondering if the blonde had anything to do with his sudden request for personal time as my eyes scanned the assembled crowd. Which I realized, as the crew herded the last few audience members to their seats, was huge. If this whole thing actually went off without a hitch, it was sure to bring some good press—not to mention revenue—to the Royal Palace.

Or course, there was still the dead vintner and rumored Mafia family meeting that could hitch it.

I leaned in close to Tate. "Do you see Hank Gambia anywhere in this crowd?"

Tate stood on tiptoes, peering over the sea of heads. "No. But there's a ton of people here. Wow, this event is a total smash, right?"

I nodded my agreement. "It will be if no one else ends up *swimming with the fishes*."

Tate giggled at my Mafia reference. "Well, if I had to put my money on someone here to be a *made man*, I'd totally go with Sicianni," he said, pointing across the soundstage to where the producer in question was chatting with our celebrity chef-slash-tantrum-toddler.

My radar perked up. "Why?" I pounced, wondering what Tate had heard.

"With a last name like Sicianni, I think that question answers itself. He's about as Italian as they come. Even if he is high-wattage handsome..." Tate fanned himself.

I rolled my eyes. "Just because a guy is Italian doesn't mean he's a Mafioso."

Tate gave me a blank stare.

"Come on—it's like saying that just because you're gay, you're fabulous."

Again with the stare. This time accompanied by some rapid eyelash blinking. "But I *am* fabulous."

I gave him a playful punch in the arm. "Well, even if—and that's a big *if*—Sicianni is personally mixed up with the Gambias, what motive would he have to kill Mr. Taylor?"

Tate pouted. "Good point."

I stared out at the assembled crowd, tapping my lip thoughtfully. I watched as Rafe finished signing autographs and took his seat. Alfie stood as a dark shadow at the edge of the production floor, no doubt acting as a buffer between the crowd and the celebrities. Dubois had about a dozen people flitting around him, powdering his forehead, straightening every crease in his chef's uniform, and shining his mixing bowls to a high gloss. A flash of red caught my attention near the auditorium doors, and I turned to see LeAnna in my favorite Michael Kors making an entrance. She clearly had no intention of playing the grieving widow, dressed more for a night on the town in four-inch stilettos and dangling crystal earrings. She slowly clip-clopped through the crowd toward the VIP area, where Rafe, as the charming host, greeted her. A little *too* charming. I turned away before my stomach could dry heave at the sight of the two together.

"You know, there is one person other than LeAnna who might have motive to want Mr. Taylor dead," Tate mused, his eyes on the VIP area as well.

"Who?" I asked, grateful for the distraction from the scene I was *so* not watching.

"Didn't you say that LeAnna has a stepson?"

I nodded. "Gerald Junior. Or Jerry, he likes to be called. I met him just after his father had been found."

"Well, if Stepmommy really is preggers, wouldn't that mean he suddenly has to split Daddy's inheritance?"

I nodded again, my mental hamster jumping on his wheel. "Unless Daddy dies first, and Junior inherits before the little tyke is born." I paused. I had a hard time picturing the George Clooney look-alike donning the ski bum disguise to stab his dad at a slot machine, but as I well knew, sometimes the relationship between a father and his child was complicated. "I wonder where Jerry is now," I mused, thinking maybe it was time for a little chat with Mr. Taylor, Junior.

Tate was one step ahead of me, swiping his phone on and typing Jerry's name into a search engine. After a couple of swipes, he did a low whistle. "Wow. From his pics on LifeBling, he looks totes hawtness."

"Life what?"

"LifeBling." Tate turned his phone toward me, showing a profile of Jerry Taylor on a social media site. Clicking on the man's profile picture, Tate growled. "Look at that chiseled chest."

It was a pretty impressive chest, no doubt about that. The photo was of a shirtless Jerry on some sort of giant yacht, a glass of champagne in hand as a tropical island provided the backdrop.

My motive idea wavered a bit. It didn't look like Junior was hurting for money.

"Why are all the hot ones always bad boys?" Tate sighed.

"We don't know for certain that he is," I pointed out, trying to keep our theory from tickling Tate's gossip bone.

"Right." Tate nodded. "You need to interrogate him first to be sure."

"Have a *conversation* with him."

He waved me off. "Same diff." He clicked a couple of buttons, bringing up a page with lots of short posts and updates from Jerry. I leaned over his shoulder and squinted to read them.

"He post anything juicy?" I asked.

"Or incriminating?" Tate added, grinning wide as he read my mind. "Let's read, shall we?" His fingers flew over his phone, scrolling through posts. "Well, looks like he had dinner at the Deep Blue last night—not necessarily incriminating. It just means he has bad taste."

I stifled a laugh. "Anything else?"

"A few pics of him on the mountain today. Wow, he even looks good in a ski jacket."

"Focus."

"Right." Tate scrolled some more. "He glittered yesterday that he's heading back to Napa as soon as his dad's funeral arrangements are made."

"He what?" I frowned.

"Glittered." Tate dropped his chin to his chest and eyeballed me. "You know, on LifeBling."

I shook my head, still not understanding.

"It's kind of like sending out a text message to all of your friends at once, only it posts on your LifeBling feed for them to read." Tate raised a brow, but I still gave him a blank look. "Girl, you really need to get caught up to the twenty-first century. I'm totally setting you up an account and dragging you, kicking and screaming, into the social media age."

"Okay, so what else has he 'glittered' on there?" I redirected Tate back to Jerry's profile and away from the idea of creating one for me. While I didn't hate social media, I just wasn't sure I was the type of person who would post photos of herself in a bathing suit on the Internet.

"Oh!" Tate cried, clicking on something.

"What?" Hope fluttered in my chest.

"Looks like he's having a sunset yacht party in the Keys this evening. He's invited everyone on his friends' list in the area."

The hope bubble burst. "Not exactly a smoking gun."

"Noooo..." Tate drew out. "But it might provide a nice opportunity for an interro—er, *conversation* before he leaves town."

I glanced at the screen again. While I wasn't entirely sure I felt comfortable blending with the yachting crowd, he had a point. If I wanted to casually chat with Jerry about his inheritance, this was probably the best chance I was going to get. And throwing a yacht party didn't exactly strike me as the actions of a grieving son. Maybe it did warrant a *conversation*.

And if I thought real hard, I knew one person who most definitely would blend with the jet set.

I pulled my own phone out of my pocket and sent off a quick text to Britton.

Yacht party in the Tahoe Keys at 6. U in?

It took less than a minute before her answer came screaming back.

YES!!!

CHAPTER TEN

Britton and I sat in the back of the casino's limo, headed down Lake Tahoe Boulevard. Kitschy souvenir shops, log cabin inspired vacation condos, and quaint mom-and-pop restaurants lined the streets, giving way to an occasional peek at Lake Tahoe sparkling in the afternoon sunlight to our right.

I fidgeted with my short hemline and attempted to pull the drooping sleeves of my borrowed Donna Karan dress into place.

"Stop it," Britton fussed, pulling my hands away from my exposed shoulders. "It's made to fall that way. It's called a cold-shoulder cut."

I rubbed my arms. "Well, it's doing the job, then."

She dug through the large bag she'd brought and pulled out two cashmere wraps that matched our outfits. Mine was a beautiful emerald green just a few shades darker than my outfit, and hers was the same baby-blue shade as her dress.

"It's in the fifties today. You should be plenty warm in this."

"Do you have one for my legs too?"

All I got in return was a raised brow.

As I wrapped up in the fuzzy warmth, I told her, "We could've taken my car. I'd already have us there."

Britton shook her head emphatically, her blonde waves bouncing across her shoulders. "We need to blend. Thiiiiis," she drew out as she waved her hands about the posh interior of the stretch limo, "is what any guest of Jerry Taylor's would arrive in." She sank back against the plush leather seat. "God, I've missed this." Her head cocked to the side. "So how are we playing this interrogation anyway? You want me to be good cop or bad cop?"

I rolled my eyes. "Tate got to you, didn't he? We are not interrogating. We're simply going to have a nice, polite conversation with Jerry."

"About why he killed his father."

I shifted in my seat, wondering if this was such a hot idea after all. "Look, there will be no interrogating, no accusations, and—"

"No mentions of the *Gambia* family?" Britton raised a knowing eyebrow at me.

I shut my mouth with a click. "I take it that name does mean something to you?"

"Well, duh!" Britton rolled her eyes. "Tess, why didn't you tell me the mob was at the casino?" She shot me her patented *mother knows best* look, suddenly making me feel as guilty as a kid who'd been hiding her broccoli in her napkin. In my defense, she'd had LeAnna glued to her hip for the last two days.

"Sorry," I said, quickly filling her in on everything I'd heard from Weston and Ryder.

When I was done, she had a thoughtful frown between her perfectly waxed brows. Or, more like a small twitch. She had a really good esthetician. "Do we know why Jerry is even here?" she asked.

"What do you mean?"

"Well, I mean it's not like he was vacationing with his parents, right? Is it just coincidence that he's in Tahoe too? Or is he here for something specific?"

I nodded. "Good question." I hadn't thought to ask him that during out brief introduction in my office.

The driver turned off the main road, winding us through side streets lined with quaint cottages and updated rental condos.

Britton leaned toward me. "Let me touch up your makeup."

I pushed her hands away. "I let you do that before we left."

Flipping her hands up, she scoffed, "Fine. But don't come running to me when you catch a glimpse of your shiny forehead in a mirror."

We turned onto Venice Drive and wound our way to the Tahoe Keys Marina and Yacht Club, tucked into an inlet of the lake. The marina wasn't overly full at this time of year, but even had it been, our attention would have gone straight to the mammoth yacht docked near the end of the marina. It was easily twice the size of anything else on the water. Loud music blared from the boat, and men in sweaters and dress pants milled about on the decks with women, dressed in far less than Britton and I, draped on their arms. The women were probably freezing to death, but they'd die happily in the name of high fashion and fast living.

Our lanky driver, dressed in all black, topped with the typical flat black hat, opened the door and extended a hand to Britton first. She practically bounced from the car, giddiness lighting her face as she trotted gracefully across the pavement toward the dock. The chain on her tiny purse tinkled like little sleigh bells with each of her steps.

It took me a little longer to steady myself in the sparkly silver five-inch heels Britton had loaned me. Like a newborn colt's first wobbly steps, I eventually found my stride and followed along.

Piece of cake.

Until we hit the dock. I navigated the wooden slats carefully, making certain each heel made contact with wood, not wedging in the space between. I was thankful that Britton had stopped to wait for me at the footbridge to the yacht.

She slid a finger under my chin, forcing me to look up from my feet. "At least smile," she chided.

"Sorry," I snapped, matching her pained smile. "You didn't have any cute wedges in your closet?"

She waved a hand around at the upper-crust guests milling about. "Did you want to fit in with the guests or blend in with the staff?"

"Whatever," I breathed. "Let's find Jerry so we can get this over with. I can't feel my toes."

A genuine look of compassion softened her features. "You'll get used to it."

I hoped. While I was no stranger to heels, these put me in a different atmospheric layer. I really liked my toes *and* the ability to feel them.

I carefully stumbled after Britton's ever-graceful form. I almost thought I'd gotten the hang of it when I wobbled on the next to last step...and fell into the boat, landing in the strong, capable arms of one of the male guests.

I smiled up into the handsome stranger's warm, brown eyes. "Thanks for catching me. That could've been ugly." I shrugged. "Ugli*er*."

He winked. "I'm always available for a damsel in distress."

The tiny redhead at his side, dressed in a little black halter dress, goose bumps, and not much more, peered down her elevated, perfectly sculpted nose at us. "Damn, Dennis, get a room."

With another wink, he muttered in my ear, "Later, babe," before dumping me onto the nearest leather seating arrangement. The cushion gave way to my sudden pressure, slipping out from underneath me. My butt dropped into the storage compartment beneath.

My knight-in-shining-armor-turned-typical-male stomped along behind the redhead, toward an intricately carved bar. "It's not like that, Donna!" he protested.

No one could say I didn't know how to make an entrance. All eyes were on me, but not in a good way. I gave my best effort to wiggle back to my feet with even a tiny piece of dignity still intact and my tiny dress still covering all of the important parts.

While struggling to scoot to my feet, I glanced around for any sight of Britton. Beautiful people milled about the wide-open deck area, where L-shaped tan leather sofas stretched along most of the wall and wrought-iron tables topped with etched glass sat upon what I really hoped to be *faux* sheepskin area rugs. Others guests sat in overstuffed leather lounge chairs that rested upon polished hardwood floors. The bar was filled with guests at the far wall. Canned ceiling lights spotlighted them and the stark-white marble top of the bar. A couple navigated the tightly spiraled iron staircase that stretched toward the open upper deck; a small stairwell sat next to it in the corner, which undoubtedly led down below.

Finally, Britton appeared and spied my less than ideal situation. Concern etched on her face, she quickly ran toward me. Luckily, she was a lot faster in those sky-high heels than I was. She offered a perfectly manicured hand to me, tugging me to my feet.

"You okay?" she asked.

"Peachy," I lied.

"Jerry is up top." She motioned toward the staircase.

I groaned aloud, and Britton nodded. Not just more stairs but a tiny, tightly wound spiral of death.

"I'll be watching my feet," I muttered as I followed.

"And I'll let you." She stopped at the bottom step, waving a hand upward. "You go first. That way *I* can catch you."

I glanced over my shoulder at the dozen or so people. Their gazes simultaneously snapped away from me, idle chitchat filling the air again. Head held high, watching the steps in my peripheral vision, I navigated each one like a boss.

Coming out into the brilliant sunshine, a cold breeze permeated my dress and ruffled through my hair, instantly puckering my exposed flesh. I'm sure my toes were cold too, though we'd never know for sure. I pulled the shawl tightly around my shoulders to hide the evidence of exactly how cold I was, which I feared my thin lace bra couldn't quite contain.

I glanced out at the massive sparkling lake for a moment then turned toward the mini-Venice of waterways that made up the Tahoe Keys. The view was a skeletal riblike structure of man-made piers dotted with rental cabins and houses, most with their own docks just steps away from their doors.

The small waves coming through the inlet from the lake felt a little bigger up on the top deck than they had on the lower level. I made sure to keep one hand on something sturdy, lest I repeat my earlier stunt.

"Jerry!" Britton squealed.

George Clooney's twin turned our way, and his handsome face lit up. "Britton, you saw my glitter! I'm so glad."

"I wouldn't miss this for the world," she said, giving me a sly wink before air-kissing Jerry on both cheeks.

"How long has it been since I've seen you?"

"Practically ages!" Britton exaggerated.

"You're right. A year or two at least. I think it was the last time I joined Dad at the Royal Palace." His strong arms enveloped her in a hug, the fingers of one hand trailing down her spine, coming to rest at the small of her back, threatening to dip lower.

Britton spun out of his embrace as I came up beside her, expertly sliding her own hand over his, nudging his fingers upward to a safer spot on her back. "I think so. Dickie and I had you up to the penthouse for drinks."

He snapped his fingers, pointing directly at her nose and lightly tapping it. "That's right." He smiled, but his face quickly turned somber. "I was so surprised to hear about his passing. I'm so very sorry for your loss, Britton."

She fluttered a hand in front of her face, tears welling in her eyes. "Thank you, Jerry. I'm sorry to hear about your father as well."

He nodded, his saddened stare dropping to his feet. "Thanks. I'm still processing it. That's the main reason for this party. I needed a distraction." He paused. "Is this the first time you've been on the yacht?"

She nodded. "It's amazing," she flattered.

"I should give you a tour. You know, I have an authentic Gustav Klimt oil on canvas in my stateroom."

I sucked in a breath. "I'd love to see that!" I couldn't help the art curator in me gushing.

Jerry turned my way as if noticing me for the first time.

"Oh," Britton sputtered. "Have you met Tessie King, Dickie's daughter?"

"I have." He patted my shoulder, forgoing the whole hug-and-groping thing, and smiled. "At the Palace when they found…"

I rested my hand over his, bringing his words to an end. "You've got a lovely boat."

Britton snagged two flutes of champagne off of a tray as a waitress walked by, handing me one.

Jerry turned to face Britton, which basically left me staring at his back.

The story of my life. At least I had champagne to occupy me for a bit.

And eavesdropping.

Tucking a stray curl behind Britton's ear, Jerry gushed, "You are such a stunning woman. Blue is definitely your color. It matches your eyes."

Britton girly-giggled and flipped a hand at him, brushing his chest with her fingertips. "Well," she gushed, "someone works out."

He flexed both arms, his back muscles straining against his fitted gray dress shirt. I leaned around, and, sure enough, he was making his pec muscles bounce.

Classy.

I downed my champagne, swapped glasses on the next tray that passed me, and continued to listen in on their conversation.

"So, you were already in town when you got the news?" Britton edged gently, big false-eye-lashed doe eyes fixed on his face.

His headed bobbed. "Yeah, Dad asked me to come. He said he had some business things to discuss."

Britton fussed with his shirt collar, even though it was perfectly straight. I craned my neck around, noting that his entire attention was firmly honed on Britton's cleavage now. She offered me a wink.

"Huh," she muttered, crossing her arms under her chest to give them a boost as she heaved a purposefully large breath. "What kind of business things?"

Jerry shrugged. "I never really got a chance to talk with him much before..." His words trailed off as his eyes blinked themselves away from her girls.

Britton casually glanced my way. I flipped my hand in a rolling motion for her to keep digging.

She reached into her tiny handbag, pulled out bright-pink lip gloss, and slathered it on. Slipping her lips slowly back and forth to spread it, she ended with a pucker, loud smack, and brilliant smile. "Any guesses at what he wanted?"

Jerry tore his eyes off of Britton's lips with difficulty. "Huh?"

"Your dad. Any idea what kind of business he might have wanted to discuss with you?"

"Uh…" Jerry blinked, bringing himself out of whatever fantasy he'd been having about Britton's lips. "If I had to guess, it was probably about LeAnna."

I raised an eyebrow. Interesting. "What about LeAnna?" I jumped in.

Jerry turned my way, apparently surprised I was still there. "Well, I don't think it's a big secret that she's knocked up. The only question is, by whom?"

I bit my lip. After the conversation I'd had with Mr. Taylor about his sterility, I had a feeling Junior wasn't too far off the mark on that one.

But ever the loyal friend, Britton immediately came to LeAnna's defense. "How could he possibly think LeAnna would cheat on him?"

Jerry snorted. "You've met LeAnna, right? Heck, my *step*mommy even tried to get me in the sack once."

Ew! I immediately scrubbed the mental image from my brain. Sure, LeAnna and Jerry were closer in age than she had been with Mr. Taylor, but would LeAnna really stoop that low?

"Please tell me you didn't?" I pleaded.

Jerry shook his head. "I don't even like parking my car in the same garage as my dad. There's not enough tequila on the planet to get me drunk enough to want to *park there*, if you know what I mean."

"But what reason would LeAnna have to lie about her baby's father?" Britton asked, her forehead hinting at a frown-slash-twitch thing again. Clearly she didn't like hearing these things about her friend. "I mean, a simple paternity test would tell who the father is."

"Sure," Jerry agreed. "After the kid is born. Which is why she was pressuring him to change the prenup *now*."

"Prenup?" I asked.

Jerry's handsome features contoured into a smirk. "LeAnna hasn't told you about the prenup then, I take it?"

I shook my head and looked to Britton. She looked as surprised as I was.

"My dad might have been stupidly in love with LeAnna, but he wasn't stupid," Jerry went on. "He had a prenup drawn up that basically says she gets nothing if she ever leaves him. Unless..." He paused for dramatic effect.

"Yes?" Britton breathed, throwing in a couple of eyelash bats for good measure.

"Unless she has a kid."

"Wait—so are you saying that LeAnna got knocked up on purpose and lied to her husband about the real father just to bust her prenup?" I asked. Even for LeAnna that seemed pretty low.

Jerry shrugged. "I'm saying she's been pressuring my father to have the prenup voided from the moment she peed on that stick. My best guess? That's what he wanted to talk to me about down here."

"Just out of curiosity," I said, "what does your father's will leave to LeAnna?"

Jerry shifted on his feet, suddenly looking a bit uncomfortable. "Well, you know I don't like to talk money at a party."

Britton leaned in, laying a hand on his arm. "Oh, Jerry. You can talk with us. We're old friends," she said, practically purring the last word. I had to hand it to her—the woman knew when to turn on the charm.

He cleared his throat. "Well, of course, as his son the bulk of his estate goes to me."

"Of course," Britton cooed.

"But, LeAnna will get the house in Napa and a, uh, decent amount to cover living expenses. My father was not an unkind man."

"How much is decent?" I asked.

"Er..." Jerry looked from Britton's pouty lips to me. "Five."

"Thousand?"

Jerry scoffed. "Million."

I blinked, suddenly feeling a bit lightheaded, and not just from the champagne.

"Jerry!" A leggy brunette in a hip-hugging spandex dress hailed him from the other side of the deck, waving a long, bangled arm in his direction.

"Sorry, ladies," Jerry said, not actually looking all that sorry to escape us. "I must go mingle." He gave Britton one more air kiss before joining the brunette.

I stared after him, processing all he'd just said.

"Well, that didn't go very well," Britton said, pouting for real instead of for sultry effect this time.

"For LeAnna," I amended. "If what he's saying is true— and she knew that her husband suspected the baby wasn't his— she's in a whole lot better financial place now. *Five million dollars* better, to be exact." The sum still made my head spin a bit. People had killed for a lot less.

"But what about Jerry?" Britton countered defensively. "Remember, he doesn't have to split his inheritance now."

I nodded. "True, but if the baby wasn't his father's, he wouldn't have to worry anyway."

"Unless LeAnna convinced his father to void the prenup."

She had a point. LeAnna had an uncanny way of making men do what she wanted. While I knew Mr. Taylor had suspicions about the baby, I wasn't sure even he would have been able to stand up to LeAnna's charms for long. I remember the way he'd referred to her as a sweet girl even while watching her flirt with a stranger.

"And don't forget," Britton added, "if there is another man in LeAnna's life, he's got a heck of a motive too."

"What could his motive possibly be?" I blurted out, Rafe's face popping into my head.

"Well, for starters, he might not have liked the idea of another man raising his baby."

That lightheaded feeling came back with a vengeance and not just from the champagne or the waves. Despite my protests about the timeline, I wasn't completely sure that Rafe couldn't possibly be the father of LeAnna's baby.

I walked to a bench near the railing, sitting carefully so as not to dislodge another cushion. I stared out at the brilliant pinks, purples, and golds of the sun casting its fading glow over the lake, almost not seeing it. I knew there was no way Rafe would be able to murder a man. Right? I highly doubted any woman could entice him so much that he'd kill for her. Of course, it wouldn't be just for her but his possible baby. And five million dollars. If LeAnna was planning to leave her husband for her baby daddy, it would sweeten the deal if she brought five million in large bills with her. That was a lot for any man to resist. Especially when you factored in that LeAnna had some kind of weird sexy voodoo spell effect on most men. Where she was concerned, almost anything was possible. Even murder?

* * *

Britton and I were quiet during the drive back to the casino. Both of us were lost in thought—her mind no doubt turning over the mounting items pointing to LeAnna's guilt, while mine was trying not to picture a baby with a mishmash of Rafe's green eyes and LeAnna's sharp tongue. As we pulled into the circular drive at the Palace, I decided to lighten the mood.

"Great use of the cleavage back there." I nudged playfully at her arm.

As the chauffeur opened the door, she blinked at me a few times before smiling. "Why do you think I scrimped and saved to get them done? Men get stupid around a nice rack. I'm pretty sure that's how I hooked your father in the beginning." She winked at me before accepting the driver's hand.

"Huh," I muttered, following her through the big entry doors past the valets and across the lobby.

As we waited for the elevator, she cocked her head to the side, twirling a blonde curl in her fingers, lips pursed. "You thought your dad bought these for me, didn't you?" She shoved them together very subtly with her upper arms, making them look even bigger, as though I wasn't quite sure as to what she was referring.

I nodded, taken aback at yet another incorrect assumption I'd made of her. "I'm sorry."

She shrugged as the elevator dinged and opened. "Can't say as I blame you, really. A lot of people thought I was after

Dickie for his money." We wove through the people getting off of the elevator, ending up with the carriage all to ourselves.

"A lot of people were wrong," I murmured.

Britton quickly scooped me into a tight hug. I hugged her back just as fiercely. The woman was growing on me. Either that or I'd lost my mind. Both were valid options. The doors opened on the penthouse level, ending our little girly bonding moment.

I was more than ready to ditch the sky-high heels and soak in a long, hot bath. Though as I walked through the front doors and LeAnna's cackle echoed from the living room, followed by the unexpected sound of Agent Ryder's muffled laughter, I froze. My stomach lurched. Et tu, Ryder? Was no one impervious to that she-devil's charms?

Britton scanned my face, obviously sensing my hesitation. "Should we go get something to eat?" She had that worried-mother thing going on again.

I took a deep breath. "No. I'm fine." And I was. It wasn't like I had dibs on Ryder or anything. He was free to date whatever woman he wanted, even if it was a succubus like LeAnna.

I held my head high as I made my way toward the voices like I owned the place, because I pretty much did. I forced a smile to my face and smushed Tornado Tessie as far back in my psyche as she'd fit. Though my steps might have faltered just a little at the sight of LeAnna decked out in a slinky, sparkling evening gown, sitting so close to Ryder on the sofa that she was practically on his lap. Her hand rested lightly on his arm in a possessive manner.

I pushed my grin to full-tooth mode. "Agent Ryder, to what do we owe the honor of this visit?"

"He's here to see me," LeAnna snapped as she tried to scoot closer to him. She blinked innocently up at Ryder, her syrupy smile never wavering. "Would you like to continue this conversation over dinner? I'm famished," she cooed, sliding his tie through one hand. "We can have a little more privacy that way."

If I didn't know better, I'd say Ryder was blushing.

Ryder patted her hand then awkwardly dislodged himself from her grip and stood. "Uh, thank you. But I think you've answered all of my questions for now. I actually need to discuss a few things with Tessie." He turned and offered me a lopsided grin, sending my heart into an erratic pitter-pat.

LeAnna's eyes narrowed at me.

"Well, I'm famished too," Britton announced, pouncing on LeAnna before she could respond. "Hey, why don't *you and I* go get something to eat?"

It was LeAnna's turn to force a smile as she stood. "Sure, why not," she muttered in a monotone that didn't quite match her sunny demeanor.

As Britton tugged her toward the front door, LeAnna turned to Ryder. "Rain check on dinner, okay?"

Ryder just smiled and waved as they walked out the door. He released a heavy sigh, shaking his head. "She's, uh, subtle."

"As a freight train barreling toward a stranded vehicle," I couldn't help adding.

His head tilted back with a hearty laugh. "I was trying to be nice, but I think your description is more accurate." He sat on the sofa again, motioning to the seat beside him.

I sat, choosing the other half of the cushion so the man could breathe. I did briefly consider assuming LeAnna's position when I caught a whiff of his heady cologne, but instead I folded my hands on my lap like a good girl and tried not to fidget with the too-short hem of my dress.

"So, you needed to discuss something?" I asked, trying my best to keep things casual. Even though they suddenly felt way too intimate with the two of us alone on my sofa.

Ryder nodded, a grin tugging at his lips as if he could sense my discomfort. "I did. I heard you went to talk with Jerry Taylor today."

My attention flipped from my hem to his steady blue gaze. "Really? How'd you hear that?"

"Britton glittered about the party."

"Seriously?" I rolled my eyes. "Am I the only one who isn't on that site?"

He pulled out his phone and swiped it on, showing me the bedazzled app. It sparkled, tossing rainbow-colored glitter across the screen when he pressed on it. "It's actually a very good place to get evidence and information. You'd be surprised at the number of people who don't lock down their accounts. Anyone can see what's being said, where people are, and who is with them. You would be surprised how many arrests I have to thank LifeBling for."

"Huh." I made a mental note to make sure Britton and Tate had their security settings at max on their accounts. Not that they would do anything that warranted an arrest, but I suddenly felt a little too vulnerable knowing that my moves could be tracked through my friends' social media posts.

"So, what did Jerry have to say?" Ryder asked, swiping the app off.

I shrugged, not sure how much to divulge. If the police had looked into LeAnna's life, it was likely they already knew about the prenup. But if they hadn't, I wasn't about to add fuel to their fire. "Mostly small talk. It was a party."

"I figured that much," he said with a glance down at my dress that might have lingered just a bit too long in the hemline area. "I also figured that you weren't there purely for social reasons."

"Who me?" I blinked in mock innocence.

"You know, you're kinda cute when you pull out the dumb blonde act like that." His grin widened.

I rolled my eyes again. "Fine, I might have had a little chat with Jerry at the party."

"Did he mention his stepmother?"

"A little." I paused, choosing my words carefully. "He said that his father wanted to meet with him here in Tahoe to talk about something. Jerry thought it might have something to do with LeAnna's pregnancy." I left off the part about it probably being about that pregnancy likely not being due to Gerald's swimmers.

"I take it Gerald didn't get a chance to chat with Jerry before he died?"

I shook my head.

"That's convenient," Ryder mused. "At least for LeAnna."

As much as I wasn't a fan, I felt myself coming to LeAnna's defense. "There are lots of other people who that might have been convenient for too, you know?"

Ryder raised an eyebrow. "Really? Like who?"

"Well...for starters, how about Jerry himself?" I said, jumping on the theory Britton had floated earlier. "If Gerald was planning to change his will to split his estate between his children, Jerry stood to lose half the fortune."

"Was he planning to change his will?"

I shrugged. "I dunno," I said, playing dumb again.

"Hmm," Ryder said, clearly not convinced.

"Okay, how about this one," I tried again. "What about Hammerhead?"

The other eyebrow went up. "Excuse me?" he asked, his poker face slipping into place.

"Oh no." I wagged a finger at him. "Don't play coy with me, *Agent* Ryder. Look, you're the one who said Mr. Taylor might have connections to the Gambia family in the first place. I know about Hammerhead Hank, and I know about the other family men coming to town, too. And no, they have nothing whatsoever to do with the casino."

"Except that they're all staying here."

I waved that small detail off. "So maybe Mr. Taylor had a falling out with the Gambias, and Hammerhead bumped him off."

Ryder's lips quivered. "'Bumped him off?' Have you been watching *Mob Wives* again?"

I narrowed my eyes. "I'm glad you find it humorous that there may be Mafia hits happening in my casino."

He tried to swallow the smile. "Look, I promise you that the FBI is looking into all angles when it comes to who killed Mr. Taylor."

"Uh-huh." My turn to play at unconvinced.

Captain Jack took that moment to make an appearance, pouncing into Ryder's lap. He immediately began head-bumping Ryder's hand in a not-so-subtle attempted to be petted. I realized I had no idea if Ryder was a cat person or a dog person or a no-animals-of-any-kind person. Within seconds my question was answered as Ryder tucked his fingers under Jack's chin and scratched. Loud purring filled the room as the cat seemed to lose all skeletal shape, forming a limp, furry black-and-white rug across Ryder's lap. I couldn't help but smile.

"I think he likes you," I said through my grin.

Ryder's eyes scanned me from his peripheral vision. "And what about his owner?"

I coughed, the question taking me off guard. "I...uh..."

He laughed, a low, warm, rumbling thing that made my skin tingle.

"She's undecided," I finally settled on.

"So I still have a shot?"

"Maybe," I found myself answering against my better judgment. I tried to keep that humiliating moment on New Years' Eve in my head, but the image was growing fuzzier by the moment. Maybe due the effects of champagne and his cologne. And, I mean, he *had* apologized. Didn't everyone deserve a second chance? At least someone who smelled this good.

"Would it tip the scales in my favor any if I mentioned how amazing you look tonight?" he asked.

I fought back a big, goofy smile and tugged at the hem again. "Uh, thanks, I think. It's Britton's."

"The color was made for you." His gaze locked with mine. His free hand trailed up my arm toward the nape of my neck, and a sensual hum lingered on every place his fingers had touched. He leaned in closer, and I think I stopped breathing, feeling as though his touch was the only thing keeping me from floating right off of the sofa. I watched through heavy-lidded eyes as his face inched closer to mine, his hand guiding me to him. His lips touched mine in a soft kiss...

Just as someone began banging on the penthouse doors.

We flew apart to opposite sides of the sofa like teenagers caught making out in the basement. Jack regained his bone structure and fluffed to twice his size, hissing his displeasure. He leapt from Ryder's lap and spun out on the coffee table before scooting down the hall toward my room in a fuzzy blur.

"Tessie!" Tate yelled from the other side of the door. "Open up! Code Black!"

CHAPTER ELEVEN

———

I flung the door open, not sure if I was grateful for the interruption or annoyed with it. Tate came bouncing in from the other side, squealing like a chased pig in his paisley shirt, pink today, as he clutched a large metal case and oversized shopping bag. "Girl, have I got a plan!" He paused when he spied Ryder. "Oh. Sorry. I didn't know you have company." His eyebrows both rose up into his bangs as he turned a questioning gaze on me.

"That's okay. I was just leaving," Ryder said, standing and striding toward the door. He gave me a quick wink as he slipped past Tate and toward the elevator doors. My lips still tingled from his kiss as I reluctantly watched him go.

The second the doors closed on him, Tate stared fanning himself. "Wow, that man is smokin'."

I touched my lips, not able to contain the huge smile stretching them taut. "Agreed." I shook myself back to reality, taking in Tate's bags. "What's all this?"

Tate clapped his hands, a wicked gleam lighting his eyes. "I'm going to make you into a stripper!"

I blinked, hoping I hadn't heard him right.

"You're going to what now?"

"I just got a juicy tidbit of info from Colene in entertainment. Mr. Italian Stallion Sicianni ordered some 'girls' tonight." He made air quotes with the word *girls* then pulled his phone out and checked the time. "Like, in an hour!"

I shook my head, palms stretched out in front of me, still not understanding what was going on. Whatever he had up his sleeve, I feared I wanted no part in it.

He released a huge sigh. "Work with me here. Rumor has it he gets very chatty with the ladies from the Pretty Kitty."

"Okaaaaay," I drew out, still very leery of his plan.

"You're going in so he can chat with *you*."

My outstretched palms of confusion turned into flailing hands of complete defiant understanding. "No. No, no, no. There's no way I'm going to strip for a guest!"

Tate waved me off. "Oh, honey, you don't have to take it that far. Just mingle with him, look seductive, and chat him up."

"And I would do this why?"

He rolled his eyes. "Duh! To find out what he knows about the Gambias!" He shook his head at me. "Girl, do I have to spell out everything for you?"

Apparently so, because I still thought this scheme had *harebrained* written all over it.

"Mr. Sicianni had met me. Won't he know I'm the casino owner and not a...party girl?"

"Never fear, my cute little BFF. I've brought in the big guns." He opened the metal case and bag, revealing a huge makeup assortment and several wigs. "When I'm done with you, no one will recognize you."

"Can you really do that?" I asked, more out of curiosity than as consent as I snuck a peek at the array of makeup.

"You bet your little booty I can! Besides, he's only met you, like, once, right?"

"I don't know..."

"Well, luckily for you, *I* do. Sit," he ordered, pointing toward one of the kitchen stools at the counter.

"There's no way I can talk you out of this, is there?" I asked in vain.

He shook his head. "No, because you know I'm right. This is a fab idea."

While I wasn't sure *fab* was the word I would use, he had one thing right. I was dying to have a candid chat with Mr. Sicianni about just who was backing his show. I wasn't sure what I'd do if it was true that *Battle Buffet* was being used as a cover for some sort of Mafia meeting, but if there was any way that Mr. Taylor had gotten wind of it, it provided the Gambias a strong motive to take him out of the picture. Unless of course Mr. Taylor had been in town for the meeting himself.

"Where did you get all of this stuff?" I asked, sitting reluctantly as he pulled out a platinum-blonde wig.

"Oh, I have my connections," he said, a sly smiling lighting his lips. "There's this adorable drag queen who does a show on North Shore."

"Great. I'm going to be a drag queen stripper."

"Hush!" Tate commanded. "You just leave it to me. When I'm done, even your own mother wouldn't recognize you."

I was counting on it. Because I had a bad feeling that I'd never live it down if someone did.

* * *

After Tate's makeup magic and platinum-blonde-bombshell wig, I turned out looking a lot like Marilyn Monroe and Lady Gaga's love child. Between the amazingly transformative effects of his shadowy bronzers and thick eyeliner in several different shades, I looked absolutely nothing like me. I'll admit, I had doubts at first when it seemed like the makeup was heading more toward Marilyn Manson, but Tate pulled it off. I just needed a stripper-type outfit to go with it. I'd raided Britton's closet first, even considering a couple of LeAnna's dresses. They each had many outfits befitting of a party girl. However, they were all way too big in the chest area for me.

Go figure.

Donning Britton's trench coat over my underthings, I slipped the sparkle heels back on, and Tate and I made our way down the service elevator into the entertainment division's costume storage area. Digging through the rack of leftover outfits from our cocktail waitresses and various performers, Tate found a white halter dress with an extremely short hem.

"You need to change quickly," Tate warned me, pulling out his phone again and checking the time. "The girls are supposed to be arriving at Sicianni's suite in ten minutes."

I nodded and slipped into the female employees' locker room, panic buzzing through me as I hoped no one recognized me. Luckily we were midshift, and it was nearly empty. Only a cocktail waitress swapping out her sparkly tutu for a pair of jeans and a server from the Minstrel Lounge tying on her black apron were in the vicinity. I quickly found a quiet corner, wondering how Tate had talked me into this as I tried to put the tiny halter dress on over my bra and panties. Which totally showed beneath the white dress, I realized as I turned toward the full-length mirror hanging at the end of the row of lockers. Crap. The thing was wet-suit tight, making comical outlines of everything I was wearing beneath. Making the only decision I could, I slipped my undies and bra off and went au naturel beneath the formfitting dress. While the effect was much smoother, it made my stomach do flip-flops as I stuffed my undergarments into the pocket of the trench and stowed the whole lot in an empty locker. Tate may have made me look like a lady of the evening, but I had much less confidence that I could act like one. Sure, I was no prude. But I usually wore panties when I danced.

Get in, chat with Sicianni, and get out. I mentally made my game plan as I forced one stilettoed foot in front of the other toward the elevators. I arrived on Sicianni's floor just as a second bank of elevators opened to reveal a group of similarly scantily clad women. I hurried to catch up to them.

A girl in a long red wig that hung down past her booty turned and gave me the critical once-over. "Who are you?"

I smoothed my dress, nervously alternating between having my hands on my hips and dropped at my sides. "Marilyn Monroe."

Her brow crinkled in confusion. "You filling in for Kelsey Jo?"

I hadn't even dreamed there'd be a roster. "Uh, yeah," I lied again, hoping Kelsey Jo wasn't just stuck in traffic.

She squinted at me. "A little heavy on the makeup there, girlfriend."

"Uh...I'm trying a new look."

"Huh." She flipped her hand in a tiny wave. "Well, my name's Candy. You know, Candy Striper the Stripper. Get it?" She motioned at her red-and-white-striped apron, which barely covered much of anything, snorting at her own joke.

I forced a smile and turned to the scantily clad girl next to her. "Who are you?"

The tiny brunette fidgeted, shifting her weight from one bedazzled hooker-heeled foot to the other. "Marcy the Weird," she mumbled.

"Marcy the Weird?" I repeated, wondering exactly what kind of *weird* stuff she did but not really wanting to know.

"Marcy DeWeerd," she loudly corrected.

"Oh, sorry."

Candy slapped her hands to her thighs and barked, "No, you're Marcy's *Playground*, remember?"

Marcy's eyes went to the floor again. "Right."

"And you've got to kind of pout and draw your hands down your sides all seductive-like when you say it." Candy huffed. "Newbs."

We made it to Sicianni's suite, and I could hear music and raucous laughing through the closed door. I could just imagine the complaints about the noise we'd be getting at the front desk from the honeymooners next door tonight.

Candy turned on her heels to face us. "It's showtime, ladies. Smiles. And remember, stay in character and follow the dance routine."

Dance routine? Crap. The nervous flip-flop of my stomach turned into gut-wrenching fear.

I took deep breaths, trying not to hyperventilate as Candy knocked on the door. It was opened by a burly-looking Italian guy in a suit whose face lit up like Christmas when he spied us. "Entertainment's here," he called over his shoulder.

I heard Sicianni's voice respond, "Cut the lights, and show the ladies in!"

Cut the lights? Oh Lordy, what had I gotten myself into?

Candy led the way into the suite. I let the other girls file past me, joining in as the last to enter. The room was dark, strategically placed black lights casting an eerie glow over the shadows. I could make out several men lounging on sofas in the suite's sunken living room. The rest of the suite's furniture had been tucked away somewhere, making a large dance floor in the center of the room. Everyone had a drink in their hands except for two bulky guys standing guard by the door.

Beyoncé's voice, crooning "Dance For You," filled the room, spurring all of the girls into a well-choreographed, sexy dance routine. Their hands slid across their own bodies, hair flinging and tossing as they ground their hips and moved to the music. I hung to the back, gyrating to the best of my ability and slowing down an old high school cheerleading routine into what I hoped was a similar dance. Thankfully, I had the good sense not to start it off by screeching, "Ready? Okay!" and left out the high kicks and jazz hands. All was going well until the other girls started easing down shoulders on their dresses, pulling off tear-away skirts and pelting the men with their discarded items. No way was I following suit. My cheeks burned hot as I tried not to look conspicuously overdressed. I was just finishing the fifth round of my cheer routine as the music thankfully came to a stop.

All of the men applauded and amped up the catcalls. The girls ate up the attention, blowing kisses and shifting from one seductive pose to the next as the lights went up.

All except for one girl.

Poor little Marcy's Playground just stood at the end of her line, a look of complete horror plastered on her adorable face. I saw an immediate career change in her future.

One of the shadows stood, walking into the middle of our group. I could finally make out Mr. Sicianni's handsome features. "Great job, girls."

Most of the girls flocked around him, giggling and fighting for his attention.

Sicianni broke away from the pack, sauntering my way, a look of passionate appreciation directed at me. "Nice moves."

I swallowed hard. "Thanks."

He squinted at my face. "You look familiar. Have you danced for me before?"

"No!" I said, maybe a little too quickly. I cleared my throat. "No, I would have remembered *you*," I amended, doing my best seductive-like voice.

"Well," he drawled, stroking my shoulder. "You look like you're wearing altogether too many clothes, my dear." He paused, sending me a slow wink. "We'll have to work on that."

Apprehension fluttered in my stomach. There was no way I was going to be able to pull this off. "Why don't we get to know each other a little better?" I asked, my voice coming out surprisingly more seductive than I thought I could muster.

"Oh, I like that idea," he said. He grabbed my hand in one of his sweaty paws and tugged me back toward the sofa, pulling me down onto the cushions practically on his lap.

I wiggled away, putting at least a hair's distance between us. Fear surged through my veins. I had the chance to pump him for information, but I was afraid of what he thought he was going to get in return.

Tate so owed me drinks after this.

One of the bulky shadows at the door moved toward us and leaned in to Mr. Sicianni. "Anything I can get you and your lady friend?"

I felt my heart freeze in my chest. I'd recognize that deep, rumbling voice anywhere.

Rafe.

While keeping one hand on Mr. Sicianni's shoulder, I reached out and grabbed Rafe's tie.

"I could use a drink," I said. *Boy, could I!*

I clamped my fingers in a death grip around his tie and tugged him closer to me.

"Uh, sure, honey." He looked me up and down, a small grin of approval gracing his handsome face. When he finally looked me straight in the eyes, a flicker of recognition dawned behind his.

I gave him the smallest, almost imperceptible shake of my head, hoping he caught on.

Thankfully, he did, quickly pasting the smile back on his face. "Right. Champagne?"

"That would be heaven," I said. The first true thing to come out of my mouth all evening.

"Scotch?" Rafe asked, pointing at Sicianni but his eyes still on me.

"Neat," Sicianni added, nodding.

"I'll be back in a sec," Rafe promised.

I prayed he meant it as Sicianni scooted closer to me. "So, where were we?" he asked, his voice low and soft, like he was uttering dirty words.

If I'd felt like taking a shower after meeting him in the Deep Blue's lobby, I felt like standing in a monsoon now.

"Getting to know one another," I purred, channeling Captain Jack. "What brings you to Lake Tahoe?"

Sicianni grinned, showing off about a million teeth. "Small talk? Really?"

"Humor me," I said. I slid my hand onto his knee for good measure.

His gaze went from the knee to my face again. "Okay, doll. Business."

"Oh, what kind of business?" I asked, trying my best to mimic a breathy Marilyn voice.

Sicianni grinned. "I'm a producer, baby doll."

"Really?" I cooed. "Wow, how exciting. Done anything I'd know?"

He rolled his shoulders backward as he stuck a posture of pride to rival any rooster. "Ever heard of *Battle Buffet*?"

I squealed in a Tate-ish way. "You do that show? Wow, I'm such a fan."

He smiled wider than I thought humanly possible, and I mentally amended my tooth count. Turns out he actually had about two million.

Before he could respond, Rafe reappeared with drinks in record speed, handing Sicianni his scotch and me a flute of champagne that looked a lot like liquid courage to me.

I took a big gulp as Rafe sat on the other side of me. Very close.

Sicianni's smile drooped at the edges a little.

"I've always been a fan of Marilyn," Rafe said, putting an arm around my shoulder. I noticed the comment was directed more at Sicianni than it was at me.

The producer punched Rafe playfully in the bicep. "You told me this wasn't your scene. But didn't I tell you? You just needed to give it a chance." Grabbing my hips, he stood me in front of him, swatted me on the butt, and shoved me at Rafe. I awkwardly flopped onto his lap. Hard, if his exasperated grunt heaved directly in my ear was any indication.

I leaned in and whispered, "Sorry."

A small grunt was all I got in response.

Sicianni reached a hand out and pulled Candy, now clad in sparkly pasties and a matching sequined G-string, toward him as a replacement. She giggled and simultaneously shot me an evil eye, like I'd let her down on the job.

"So, Mr. Sicianni, tell me what it's like to be the *genius* behind *Battle Buffet*," I said, laying it on thick as I took another large sip of champagne.

I felt Rafe pinch me in warning, but I ignored him.

"Well, I don't know about 'genius,'" he said with mock modesty as Candy made herself busying doing odd things to his earlobe. "Maybe 'driving force' is more like it."

I poured on the excited girly giggles and tried not to bounce too hard on poor Rafe's injured area. "So, you're Mr. Big Stuff, huh?" I bubbled, suddenly sounding like I was Betty Boop's long lost sister. Too much?

"Well," he hedged, clearly not caring who I sounded like as long as I kept making googly eyes at him. "It's not my money, but I do run the show."

"Really?" I gushed. "So, you secure the big-time investors? You know, like Richard Branson?" I snapped my fingers and clapped. "Oh, or Bill Gates? I'd *love* to meet him." I carefully twisted a wig curl around my finger, channeling my inner Britton. "Maybe he could, like, I dunno, give me a new computer or something."

Sicianni tossed his head back in a full, deep belly laugh, dislodging Candy from his neck. "Oh, honey, my investors couldn't care less about computers. They prefer to keep a low profile." He brushed a finger across my cheek.

"I'd love to meet some big shots," I said. I felt Rafe lean forward, snaking a hand around my waist, pulling me next to him. Probably to keep me from falling off his lap, but I was enjoying the feel of his firm pecs nonetheless. Teen-me instantly melted into a puddle.

Sicianni nodded. "That could be arranged. I'm sure some of my associates would love you." He winked at me.

"You got names for these associates?" I pressed.

I felt Rafe's arm tug harder, though this time it was definitely more of a warning than a friendly gesture.

Sicianni's gaze narrowed. "You ask a lot of questions for a dancer, baby doll."

Candy's head popped up, her gaze mirroring Sicianni's. I wasn't sure who I was more afraid of.

I blinked and twirled a strand of wig hair. "Oh, you know, I'm just makin' chitchat."

"Huh." Sicianni leaned back into the cushions. "Well, you're gonna have to keep that kind of chitchat to a minimum around my friends. They don't like a lot nosey girls asking dumb questions."

I nodded. "Okeydokey!" I said, maybe a little too cheerfully.

But it seemed to placate Sicianni, who then turned to Rafe. "That reminds me of another thing my investors don't like."

"Which is?" Rafe asked. His mouth was so close to my ear I could feel the vibration of his breath. I didn't altogether hate it.

"All the cops swarming around this place. You gotta make sure they stay away from my VIPs."

"I'll do my best," Rafe said, nodding. "But you have to understand that we've had a homicide on the premises."

Sicianni blinked, doing a great poker face. "That's got nothin' to do with me."

I suddenly wondered if he wasn't telling the whole truth there.

"Trust me—we have an amazing evening planned for the VIPs tomorrow," Rafe reassured him.

Sicianni nodded. "You better, Rafe. Some of these guys have come a long way to meet up at this dinner you're throwing."

I froze. Did he just say that *our* VIP dinner was a *meeting* place for his *investors*? I felt my throat go dry. *I* was hosting the big interfamily mob meeting?! Oh, Agent Ryder was going to have a field day with this one.

"Anyway, just keep the cops on a leash till we finish taping," Sicianni told Rafe. "Man, I can't wait. I'm ready to get out of this kitschy little joint."

"Hey," I snapped without thinking.

Rafe clamped his hand around my wrist just as Sicianni turned a confused look my way.

I cleared my throat and channeled my inner Britton again. "I just don't want you to leave, is all." I sent him my best impression of bedroom eyes and licked my lips.

Sicianni didn't get to answer me as Candy quickly turned his face toward her and devoured his lips, staking her claim

Eww! I looked away, suddenly feeling like an unwitting voyeur.

Rafe's phone buzzed to life in his pocket, which just so happened to be situated right under me. I let out a high-pitched squeal.

He resituated me and pulled it from his pocket. After glancing at the screen, he turned his attention to Mr. Sicianni. "I really should take this, James." He pointed to his phone as he helped me to my feet.

Sicianni tugged me back to the sofa next to him. "I guess I'll just have to see what the three of us can come up with, then."

I smiled coyly at him but turned a wide-eyed look of desperation toward Rafe.

He muttered into his phone, "I'm going to have to call you back," and then he returned it to his pocket. "If you don't mind, James, I think I'll take her with me." He winked at the other man and tugged me up next to him again, holding me tightly.

Sicianni waved a hand in our direction. "Suit yourself." He then turned his full attention to Candy and her earlobe fixation.

Rafe guided me nonchalantly toward the door with a possessive arm around my shoulders, tucking me next to him. He turned and waved as we left, a big smile in place.

One that dropped the instant we were in the deserted hall.

His fingers dug into my elbows as he spun me to face him. "What the hell were you thinking?" He narrowed his gaze on me, his jaw clenched tightly and not even a hint of a smile anywhere.

I scoffed defiantly. "I was trying to find out who might be funding the show. I've heard a rumor that it isn't anyone above board."

"What are you talking about?" he asked, waving his hands in the air.

"I'm talking about *the mob*!"

"Shh!" Rafe grabbed my elbow again and steered me toward the service elevators with a backward glance over his shoulder.

"So it's true!" I said, not *shhing* at all. "And you knew!"

"I don't know anything," he said, his voice coming out in a hiss to rival my cat's. The way he was dragging me toward the service elevator brought back memories of the fourth grade and a fateful day on the jungle gym. I'd won the race across the bars, but I'd paid the price for knocking Scotty Cook into the mud in the process. The recess monitor had treated me pretty much the same as Rafe was now while I'd been herded to the principal's office.

"All I know," Rafe amended, "is that you were playing with fire back there."

I released an exasperated sigh as I crossed my arms over my body at a sudden chill. "I bet I could've kept him talking and found out just who was coming to this Mafia Jamboree that we're apparently hosting, if Candy wouldn't have been attached to his face."

"No," Rafe snapped. "*You* would have been attached to his face, whether you liked it or not." He wriggled out of his suit coat and draped it over my shoulders. "And then been dragged back to his bedroom to *party*."

As we waited for the elevator to lower to our floor, and since I was in that fourth grade frame of mind anyway, I took the opportunity to gloat. "Told you strippers were the same as prostitutes." My posture straightened with pride as I pulled his coat tighter around me.

Shaking his head, he looked down at me. "He doesn't pay anyone to sleep with him. Which technically means they aren't prostitutes. They're just…"

"Slutty," I finished as the elevator dinged.

CHAPTER TWELVE

———

"Huh," I muttered to myself, standing outside the penthouse doors, wiggling my bare toes against the cool marble floor. Britton was right. I did get used to not feeling them.

I threaded my arms through Rafe's coat, tossed the spike heels on the hall table, and crossed my arms over my chest as I leaned against the wall. No key, no phone, not even my own jacket, but I did have my pride.

Sort of.

When Rafe had put me in the elevator, insisting that he'd get his jacket later because he had to return the call, I'd kept my mouth shut. I didn't say a thing about not being able to get into the penthouse. That's where the pride part had come in.

And, you know, the not thinking the entire situation through too.

Now it was just a matter of working up enough nerve to call housekeeping from the hall phone so they could come unlock the door. I could already hear the runaway rumor train screaming along at full speed with Tate frantically shoveling coal into the firebox, after I was seen in nothing more than a skimpy stripper dress and Rafe's suit coat.

The elevator dinged, and I tugged the jacket closed around me. When the doors opened and Britton appeared, I nearly burst into joy-filled tears. I stood up, hooked my fingers into the shoes, and darted toward her for a comforting hug.

Britton dodged my embrace several times, yelling, "Who are you?"

Wow, Tate was right about my own mother not being able to recognize me. Well, stepmother at least. I dropped my arms to my sides, deflated. "Britton, it's me."

Her head slowly cocked to the side, realization dawning in her eyes. "Tessie? Why are you dressed like that? And is that Rafe's jacket?" She dropped her chin, waggling an eyebrow as she peered through her lashes.

"It's a long story but so not what you're thinking. Needless to say, I'm really glad LeAnna isn't with you."

Britton pulled the key card from her purse and unlocked the door. "We split up after dinner. She said she wanted to go out dancing or something."

"And you didn't go with?" I asked, thinking that was unlike Britton.

"I, uh, had other plans," she mumbled. "But that just gives us more time for whatever *this* is." She shook a hot-pink-tipped finger in my face as she quickly changed the subject.

I slumped onto one of the kitchen stools, releasing the shoes and letting them clomp onto the floor. "Like I said, it's a long story."

"Then start talking, girlfriend," she said, dropping onto the seat next to me.

I gave in and rattled off the highlights, leaving out the details about my cheerleading routine and moving on to the part about the *rumored* Mafia investors being maybe not such a rumor after all. And meeting at our VIP dinner tomorrow.

"Wow, I totally would have gone as backup." She put a hand to my shoulder and squeezed.

"Thanks. But you did enough today at Jerry's yacht and with keeping LeAnna out of all of this."

She glanced at my makeshift outfit again. "Where did you even get this?" She pulled the jacket away, her eyebrows rising at the outfit.

"Entertainment," I mumbled, dropping my gaze to the shoes next to my chair. I released a long breath. "Would you mind calling them and letting them know that your good trench coat is in locker 103?"

"What?" She laughed.

I scurried off to my room, pulling the door closed. I popped it open a crack and begged, "And my undies, too?"

"Seriously?" she offered from down the hall.

"I owe you one!"

Jack sat on the bed, his narrowed cat glare judging me as he kneaded the blankets.

I snapped my fingers and pointed at him, but he still stared. It was more than likely a *get your butt in bed and love me* glare, but I was feeling a little raw and judged. I hung Rafe's jacket in my closet and dug for something a whole lot more comfortable than that strapless torture device that had been digging into my armpits. I nearly purred too as I slipped on cutoff sweatpants and an old concert T-shirt speckled in paint. My hand swept across the rough flecks, my mind contemplating an empty canvas and free time that I wished I had. The itch to paint, to create something from nothing with a brush and colors, had been strong. I hadn't touched anything paint related in months, and the withdrawal was getting worse.

As I stretched across my bed, burrowing in the covers, Jack settled himself on my chest, his nose nearly touching mine.

"So, do you think LeAnna was the call Rafe ditched me for tonight?" I asked Jack, scratching the sweet spot just under his chin. His eyes glossed over as his head went limp, melting into my hand, half asleep. "You know, not that I'm jealous or anything," I told him.

He just purred. I'm pretty sure he believed me.

I tossed an arm over my eyes, praying for sleep. When it eluded me, I stomped to my desk and pulled out my sketch pad and graphite pencils. It wasn't as satisfying as painting, but it worked in a pinch. My fingers flew across the page, outlining, shadowing, and smudging in much-needed therapy. I found myself creating a grayscale version of the scenery outside my window as I tried to erase the events of the evening from my brain.

* * *

At 8:00 a.m., I walked by the front desk, sipping on my first latte of the day. My morning had barely started, but I'd already handled a day's worth of work. Paperwork for the next board meeting (which was approaching all too quickly!) had been signed at the attorney's office, the police had me sign off on releasing LeAnna's room back to her (words could not convey how freaking happy that signature made me!), and feathers had been smoothed after a heated exchange at the craps table between a Japanese tourist and one of our regular skiers. I'd even put in a text to Maverick, who had informed me that Hammerhead Hank had a very boring evening last night listening to our faux Sinatra during a steak dinner in the Minstrel Lounge, doing a little browsing in the gift shop—where he'd picked up a porcelain figurine of a knight in shining armor—losing $1,200 at the blackjack table, and then ending his evening stumbling back to his room after downing several scotches at the bar. No one had been whacked or otherwise manhandled. Thank God for small favors.

I was just making my way to the front desk to fill Tate in on the fruits of his labor last night, when, as if thinking about it brought it back to life, I spotted Marcy, a.k.a. Marcy's Playground, pulling a suitcase across the lobby. Her head was down, and she was practically running for the front doors. Her conservative jeans, T-shirt, and hooded sweatshirt fit her personality much better than the largely nonexistent outfit from the night before. I only prayed this was not a morning-after walk I was witnessing.

"Marcy!" I yelled.

She stopped in her tracks, whipping her head around and looking for the source of her name. I popped my hand in the air, waving in her direction. I yelled her name again and moved toward her.

Her gaze shifted between me and the floor as she pressed a finger to her chest and eked out, "Me?"

Realization hit me that she had no idea who I was, thanks to Tate's magical makeup case. "Yes, you," I said, scrambling to come up with a cover. "My name is Tessie King, owner of the casino. A friend of mine told me you might be looking to change careers."

Her eyes stayed rooted to the ground, and her chest heaved. "Who? How?" was all she could get out as she gasped for air.

"A friend of a friend, but that's not important," I soothed, placing a gentle hand on her shoulder. "What's important is that we have several positions open at our restaurants, and I believe even one at our front desk."

Her breathing returned to normal after a big sigh, but she continued to study her shoes intently. "I don't have any training in either area, but thank you for the information." She turned to leave, but I firmed up my grip, keeping her next to me.

"We will train the right person. You come highly recommended."

"Really?" A tiny smile curled her lips as she looked up at me through her dark lashes.

I nodded, guiding her back toward the front desk. Unfortunately, Tate wasn't in sight, but a perky blonde attendant was. Her head shot up at my approach.

"Alicia," I addressed her. "Could you please give Marcy an employment application?"

Alicia nodded, turning to grab the piece of paper.

"Be sure to list me as a reference," I told Marcy.

"Yes, ma'am," she answered enthusiastically.

Marcy seemed to bloom right in front of me. Her posture straightened, and her face brightened as she accepted the application from Alicia.

I brushed a hand down Marcy's arm. "I'll leave you in Alicia's capable hands. Please call if you have any questions."

Her head bobbed. "Thank you so much. You have no idea…"

Oh, but I did. With a playful wink, I left her and headed down the hall to the *Battle Buffet* set.

Taping was in full swing as I entered the arena. I tugged the sleeves of my heather-gray dress shirt back into place, smoothed my black A-line skirt, and checked my patent leather pumps for scuffs as I worked my way through the enthusiastic crowd. Wondrous smells of roasted garlic and sautéed peppers mixed with sounds of searing, whisking, and condescending broken French. The bleachers were stuffed with fans, some of them holding up handmade signs for their favorite competing chef and others for the judge, Chef Dubois, all hoping to catch the attention of one of the camera operators for their fifteen seconds of fame. Even the padded VIP section was completely full. Overflow milled about at each side of the seating area. The fact that most of the people there were also staying at the Palace—spending money at our boutiques, restaurants, gaming areas, and attractions—made me almost giddy.

However, seeing Mr. Sicianni slink away in the company of a large man, whose nose appeared to have been broken so many times it was at a permanent ninety-degree angle, doused my enthusiasm much like a bucket of ice water on a January day.

Was that one of his *investors*? The big guy certainly had more of a Mafia air about him than billionaire.

Sicianni looked up at me and winked before disappearing into the hall with the man. Fear paralyzed me. Had he recognized me? The memory of his hands on me threatened to make breakfast reappear.

Surely that was just his usual flirtatious way, and he hadn't figured out my stripping debut, right? I took a deep breath, let it out slowly, and assured myself that no one on the set knew my little secret.

Except Rafe.

I felt his eyes on me before I spotted him. I looked over at the VIP area to find his gaze locked on me. His face held an expression I couldn't read. It wasn't exactly welcoming, but it wasn't anger either. I wondered again who had called him the previous night. He and Sicianni had certainly seemed close in the suite. On a first-name basis even. Of course, it was sort of his job to schmooze the bigwigs if he wanted to keep his sponsorship. But just how badly did he want to keep Sicianni happy?

What had he said? *You're playing with fire.* At the time I'd assumed he meant where Sicianni's carnal appetites were concerned. But now I wondered. In his suite Sicianni had all but confirmed that his investors were less than upstanding citizens. And Rafe hadn't seemed surprised to hear they were planning a big meeting at the dinner. The dinner that had been Rafe's idea in the first place. I bit my lip. Could Rafe be the connection between the Mafia and my casino that Ryder had been looking for all along?

I snapped my gaze to the floor, avoiding Rafe's stare as I heard an announcer come over the loudspeaker. "Taping will begin in five minutes. We ask that everyone please take your seats, turn off your cell phones, and enjoy the show!"

The announcement was met with thunderous applause from the assembled crowd. I dutifully set my phone to vibrate as I took a seat to watch the beginning of the show. Two of the six original contestants had been eliminated already, their kitchen sets lit with ominous red X's in contrast to the brightly staged other four. I noticed the tattooed woman was still in, contrary to Dubois's assessment of her mature skills. She was joined by a tall man with a head of stark-white hair, a round grandmotherly-looking woman, and a dark-haired lady with mounds of hair in a huge ponytail. All four stood at attention in their stations as the lights went up, the cameras started rolling, and Chef Dubois made his grand entrance onto the stage.

The crowd went wild, and Dubois ate it up, bowing for a sold thirty seconds before even acknowledging that the contestants existed. When he finally turned to them, the audience went silent, listening intently to what today's challenge would be.

I felt my phone buzz in my pocket and looked down at the readout to see Ryder's name. My lips instantly tingled at the thought of The Kiss.

I quietly got up from my seat, moving toward the exit as I heard Dubious bark out his culinary demand to the contestants. "You will have thirty minutes to make an Asian-inspired appetizer using only freeze-dried fruit and canned fish. Your time starts...now!"

I shuddered at the thought of having to taste those as I pushed through the exit and swiped my phone on. "Tessie King."

"It's Ryder," he replied. "Are you with the *Battle Buffet* group?"

I nodded even though I knew he couldn't see me. "I am. It's crazy in here. Good crazy, though." I couldn't help a lift of pride in my voice. The revenue this whole hoopla was generating was something that would've made my father proud.

"Can you meet me in the east hall? I'm here," Ryder said.

"Sure. I'll be right there." I swiped my phone off and made my way toward the east side of the auditorium. As I rounded the corner, I spied Ryder waving from down the hall.

He met me halfway. He wasn't wearing his usual suit coat, and his shirtsleeves were rolled to the elbows. His tie was loosened and askew. His hands were shoved deeply in his pockets, and he wore a welcoming smile that instantly gave me butterflies.

As soon as we were close enough, he pulled me in and gave me a light kiss on the cheek.

I felt myself flush.

"We need to talk," he said, either not noticing the blush or being gentleman enough to ignore it. "Some new information came in last night that I think you should apprise your security about."

I cleared my throat. "Right. Uh, what kind of information?" I asked, not sure I could handle much more. In the last two days I'd already dealt with a dead vintner, foodie mobsters, and angry strippers—*oh my!*

"We have it on good authority that the Gambias may not be the only crime family coming into the area," he said, concern puckering his brow.

"Oh, that." I waved him off, feeling relieved. "Yeah, I know. For the big supersecret Mafia meeting that everyone seems to know about," I joked.

Ryder's poker face came out. Clearly he wasn't in a joking mood. "Mafia meeting?" he asked, playing dumb.

I couldn't help feeling a little irked that he always expected me to share info when he was Mr. Tight-Lipped Fed. I narrowed my eyes at him. "You know the dumb-blond thing isn't nearly as cute on you as it is on me."

Ryder let out a big sigh, dropped the poker face, and grabbed both of my hands in his. Tiny little tingles danced across my skin. "I'm sorry, Tessie, but you know there are certain things I am not at liberty to discuss."

"Uh-huh…" My mind was stuck in a loop of how much his touch affected me and where those tiny little tingles were congregating. I forced myself to concentrate.

"Tell me about the meeting," he prompted.

"I don't know much. Just that, like you said, more than one family is involved," I hedged, not quite sure how he'd feel about the fact that I'd apparently be hosting said meeting.

"Any names?" he asked. He rubbed his thumbs across my palms, and my mind went numb.

"Um...I dunno. I tried to find out, but Mr. Sicianni changed the subject."

"Mr. Sicianni?"

"Huh?" Man, those tingles were distracting.

Ryder let go of my hands to tilt my chin upward, making my eyes meet his. "You asked James *Sicianni* about an organized crime meeting?"

"Uh...sorta?" Only it came out more of a question.

"And he just blurted this information out to *you*, the owner of the casino?"

"Uh...kinda?" My voice was rising in octave increments.

His eyes narrowed. "Why do I get the feeling that you're not telling me everything?"

Because he was a very perceptive man.

Ryder released a huge sigh and dropped his hands to his sides. "Tessie, these are dangerous guys we're talking about here—"

Only he didn't get to finish, as the door to the auditorium flew open and Rafe stepped out. "Tess, there you are." He made quick strides toward us. "We need to talk." He paused, looking back and forth between Ryder and me. "Am I interrupting anything?"

"No!" I said. Maybe a little too loudly in hindsight. I took a quick step away from Ryder as if I was guilty of something.

"Good. Because I need to get my jacket back from you."

"Oh, uh, right. Sure. I have it in my room."

Ryder cleared his throat, his hands firmly shoved back into his pockets now. "Tessie has your jacket?" He shot me a look that I couldn't read. "In her bedroom."

Rafe nodded. "I'm sorry—does that concern the FBI?" I could have sworn I heard a note of condescension in his voice.

Ryder stood up a bit straighter. "At the moment, everything that goes on in this casino concerns the FBI."

"Look, I just borrowed it last night," I said, trying to diffuse what was quickly becoming a tense situation.

Ryder's gaze whipped to mine. "Last night."

Uh-oh. "Uh...yeah?"

"Would that be before or after I visited your suite?" The words *and kissed you* hung unspoken in the air.

I bit my lip. "After?"

Ryder nodded, the set of his chin going granite hard.

"*You* were in her suite last night?" Rafe asked, his eyes narrowing suspiciously at Ryder.

"Official business," Ryder said. "I had some questions to ask a witness. That's *all*."

Ouch. Way to downplay the kiss.

"Hmph," Rafe grunted, crossing his arms over his chest as he glared at Ryder.

"Huh," Ryder shot back, lifting his chin to glare at Rafe.

Oh boy. If this went on much longer, I expected one of them to lift a leg and mark his territory.

"Oh, wow, look at the time. I'm supposed to be...somewhere..." I trailed off, leaving the standoff before things got ugly.

I skittered through the lobby toward the elevator. If LeAnna had a magical effect on men, I apparently had the opposite—the ability to turn them sour in one conversation. Not that either of those guys were *my* guys. I mean, Rafe was seeing Tiffany Weston *and* LeAnna at the same time. It's not like he had any time or interest in me, no matter how flirty his green eyes and warm hands had been. And Ryder had just made it abundantly clear that the kiss between us had meant nothing. And why should it? I was no glamorous LeAnna or bombshell Britton. I was just Tornado Tessie after all, the spastic little girl who awkwardly sat by the pool every summer with her father's girlfriend of the week while the other kids snickered and stared.

Yes, I was totally feeling sorry for myself. In my defense, I'd had a heck of a week. My eyes fought back tears of anger mixed with self-pity mixed with the oddest sense that I'd just experienced some sort of breakup. Though with whom, I wasn't sure. I needed a strong morning mimosa, a bubble bath, and a cuddly cat, in that order. I quickly pushed through the penthouse doors, slamming them behind me.

"Tess? That you?" Britton called, dropping a magazine on the coffee table before bouncing to a standing position.

"What's the matter?" She pounced at me in a skintight, animal-spotted microdress that showed more cleavage than I could ever hope to own. She'd topped it off with a furry, black three-quarter-sleeved shrug. Instead of looking like a fashion statement, she was leaning more toward an unkempt black panther wrestling a full-grown leopard. She brushed back a loose curl from her face.

I resisted the urge to pet her arm. "Nothing. I'm fine."

"I've lived with you for about a year now. You've never slammed the door. This isn't you being fine." She waved a hand around my general direction for emphasis, a dozen or so bangle bracelets clinking together at her wrist.

"Where's LeAnna?" I sniffed. The last thing I wanted to do was break down in front of the she-devil.

Britton shrugged. "I haven't seen her since last night. I figured she went back to her suite."

I shook my head. "No, I just signed off on it this morning." I fought back a sickening image of LeAnna lounging in Rafe's suite, enjoying a breakfast in bed after a night of playing tonsil hockey.

Britton bit her lip. "You know, I've tried calling her a couple of times. Her phone's off. We were going to do some shopping together this morning."

"I'm sure she's just sleeping in and enjoying her morning-after somewhere."

Britton slapped me on the shoulder. "Tess! She may not be a saint, but LeAnna wouldn't do that. She's pregnant and a grieving widow to boot."

Widow—yes. The grieving thing I'd yet to see.

"Maybe she went to the *Battle Buffet* shoot?" Britton mused.

"Actually, no," I reluctantly told her. "I was just there. I didn't see her in the VIP area." Which, now that I was thinking about it, struck me as odd. LeAnna had been glued to that set since taping had started. LeAnna and TV cameras went together like a sparkly cocktail and a bubble bath. Two things that were looking like less and less of a possibility as I watched Britton's features grow more and more distraught.

"Tess, I'm starting to worry about her. Her bed hasn't been slept in," she admitted. "And you've seen her around here. That phone goes wherever she goes. Why isn't she answering it?" Tears welled in her eyes.

"Maybe it's just out of charge," I offered, though the excuse seemed weak even to my ears. Britton was right—I'd never seen LeAnna without her phone on. "Tell you what—let's ask around. Maybe some of the staff have seen her. Maybe she just…needed a little alone time, you know?"

Britton sniffed back the tears and nodded. "Right. Yeah. Okay. I'm sure we'll find her and bring her right back home."

I paused. "I'll help you look for her, but the police are done with her room. Home is no longer here. Deal?"

"Deal." She picked up her leopard-print clutch and trotted toward the door.

"Aren't you going to change?"

She blinked at me a few times before scanning her outfit and then looking back at me. "Why?"

"Okay, then."

CHAPTER THIRTEEN

———

After I grabbed Rafe's errant jacket and left it at the concierge desk for him, our next stop was the local rumor mill at the front desk. Had Tate been manning the front desk, we would have undoubtedly found LeAnna within seconds. Unfortunately, he was nowhere to be found and not answering my texts. I suspected he was in hiding, somehow aware of how closely I'd come to being Sicianni's plaything and afraid of my wrath. I hadn't quite yet decided how afraid he really should be.

Britton leaned across the front counter, chatting with the tiny brunette wearing a blazer with the Royal Palace logo. "I have a photo of her on my phone," Britton offered, pulling it from her furry clutch, swiping across the screen repeatedly until she found one. "Here, this is LeAnna Taylor. Have you seen her this morning?"

The brunette shook her head. "Sorry, no."

Britton's shoulders drooped.

"Not since last night," the brunette amended.

"You saw her last night?" I pounced, watching Britton perk up again beside me.

"Yeah. I think I saw her head out the front doors, but..." The girl backed away from Britton, confusion etched on her face, her fingers nervously fidgeting with her jacket buttons.

"But what?" Britton pushed. "Was LeAnna..." She looked over both shoulders before continuing in a whisper, "Abducted?"

The brunette shook her head so hard that her hair flipped in front of her face. Swiping it from her eyes, she leaned back toward Britton. "It's just that I'd heard she was pregnant, and Mrs. Taylor was...staggering."

LeAnna Aiden-Taylor, mother of the year, folks.

Britton waved her away much like a queen dismissing her staff. "We'll check with the valets. I'm sure she was just tired."

As I followed her toward the front doors, I muttered, "Tired people generally go up to their rooms to get some sleep, not stumble out the front door to God only knows where."

Britton flashed me as much of a dirty look as her face would allow. "She hasn't really had a place of her own to go back to, *and* her husband was just totally murdered."

I nearly bit a hole through my lip to keep back the retort about her being under investigation for said murder. Instead I tried to put myself in LeAnna's spoiled-rotten shoes for a few seconds. She really was under a lot of pressure, and as much as I hated to admit it, I couldn't actually see her killing anyone, much less her husband.

Cheat on them, lie to them, spend their money like it was going out of style, annoy them to death, and push *them* to kill *her*? Yes.

The smell of car exhaust and gasoline combined with copious amounts of Axe Body Spray. Britton sauntered up to the head valet, who was responsible for the more overpowering of the mixture.

He yanked his vest straight and smoothed his long, dark hair behind his ears, snapping to stick-straight attention.

"Mrs. King." He nodded at Britton. Peeking over her shoulder at me, he nodded again. "Ms. King."

"Ken, you know you can call me Britton," she gushed.

"What can I do for you," he asked in a shaky voice, swallowing hard before squeaking out, "Britton?"

"Who was working last night?"

He slowly raised his hand over his head.

"You know our guest LeAnna Taylor, right?" she asked.

He nodded, his long hair falling loose.

"Awesome!" she yelped, causing Ken to flinch into a slightly crouched defensive stance for a moment. He quickly bounced back to attention as she continued, "Did you see her last night?"

"Sure did. She told me you said she could have the Palace limo last night."

I raised a brow at Britton, and her head shook enthusiastically. It wasn't like it surprised me that LeAnna had lied, but I was losing the tiny ember of compassion for her I'd fanned just a few minutes earlier.

Britton grabbed Ken by the shoulders, his face instantly flushing pink and sweat beading on his forehead.

"When did she come back?" she grilled.

"I never saw her after that. The limo came back around two this morning. But it was empty." He paused. "I mean, someone was driving it, but there were no guests."

"Who was driving it? We need to know where she went." Britton's concerned voice raised several octaves, making Ken squint.

He bobbed his head toward the circular drive. "Lucas. He's out there now. Just brought a high roller in from the airport."

Britton released him and grabbed my hand, dragging me behind her as we darted outside. "Thanks, Ken!" she called as the doors closed behind us.

The bright morning sun was chipping away again at the snow banks, leaving us to dodge puddles as we scurried up the drive toward the limo.

"Lucas!" Britton waved her arms erratically as he stepped a foot into the vehicle, obviously ready to leave. He paused, looking over his shoulder, breaking into a big smile as we neared him.

"Hello, ladies." He pulled himself up, standing at attention next to the perfectly polished vehicle. "Are you in need of my services again today?"

Britton's eyes widened with a matching smile. "Can you take us to where you took LeAnna Taylor last night?"

He nodded and opened the door for us. I shrugged and followed her into the backseat.

Before shutting the door, the driver said, "She went to that new club next to Harrah's, Midnight Tahoe."

"Hashtag oh-em-gee," Britton grumbled as the driver shut the door. "*I* haven't even been there yet."

Technically we probably could have walked the block to the club, but considering the temperature was hovering in the forties, and we were both wearing skirts, we let the limo do the transporting. A few moments later, we were pulling up in front of the trendy two-story club. A large television-type billboard sign flashed clips of smiling, perfect people dancing in perfect designer outfits on a perfectly packed dance floor bathed in colorful lights and enjoying a stream of never-ending drinks brought by perfect waitstaff.

However when we entered the front door, we were struck with a much different scene. It was dead quiet, and the sticky floor was scattered with glitter, partially deflated balloons, and torn streamers. The scents of soured booze, stale cigarettes, and day-after regret hung in the air. Half-empty glasses and bottles dotted the multilevel dancing and seating areas, along with overflowing ashtrays and various articles of clothing. I felt a hangover coming on from just standing there.

A man in a tight T-shirt that stretched the words *Midnight Tahoe* across his impressive chest popped up from behind the chrome bar against the far wall. He braced his forearms on the bar top, affording us a view of his bulging biceps. "Sorry, ladies. We're closed."

"God, I hope so," I whispered to Britton as we made our way to him.

Britton tiptoed through the messes on the floor, gliding like Ginger Rogers in spike heels. As she neared the bartender, she announced, "I'm Britton King. Of the Royal Palace Casino?"

He nodded. Everyone in town had heard of the Kings and the Royal Palace. While Tahoe was a fully modern resort destination, it was actually a small town with very few permanent residents. And my father had been one of the most well known of those.

"I was wondering if you could help us track down one of our guests."

He frowned. "Why? He stiff you on the room bill?"

Britton smiled and shook her head. "No, *she* just hasn't come home yet."

His frowned smoothed out. "Oh. Gotcha. Pulling a wild overnighter somewhere, huh?"

Britton's smile faltered, though I found myself having to stifle an unladylike snort. I had a feeling the bartender had nailed it.

Britton pulled her phone from her cleavage (which explained some of the excess) and swiped through her pictures, finally settling on the same one she'd offered the girl at the front desk. "Do you remember seeing her last night?"

The guy shook his head. "Lady, I see a lot of people in a night."

"Take a second look," I told him.

His eyes left Britton and swung my way as if noticing I was there for the first time. Story of my life lately.

"And you are?"

"Ms. Tessie King, owner of the Royal Palace," I said, totally playing the name-drop game in an effort to impress him.

Which seemed to work. He stood up a bit straighter. "Really? You know, I applied for a job there last month. Haven't heard back yet."

I gave him a tight smile. "I'll be sure your application gets moved to the top of the pile. Mr..."

"Brad. Brad Duncan."

"Great. So, Brad, think you could have a second look at Mrs. King's phone?"

This time Brad nodded, more than happy to help. "You know what," he said, nodding his head as he squinted at the picture. "I do remember her!"

"Really?" Britton asked. "So you saw her here last night?"

His head bobbed up and down. "I sure did. She was hard to miss. She's very..." He paused and grinned. "Friendly."

"Yes, she is," Britton agreed, completely missing the man's point. "Do you know when she left?"

"Sorry, we were slammed last night. I can't tell you when she left. I didn't know the guy she was with, either."

"Guy she was with?" I jumped on the words. Though I shouldn't have been surprised.

He nodded. "Wish I could help more, but I haven't lived here very long, and this *is* a new club. We don't exactly have regulars just yet."

Britton's shoulders sagged, and she turned her pouty face toward me. "What now, Tessie?"

As much as I hated to do it...

I pulled out my phone, reluctantly scrolling through my own pictures until I found one of Rafe at a publicity event we'd recently done. I felt physically ill, clutching my phone to my chest as I replayed his and LeAnna's cozy bathroom moment. The last thing I wanted was actual confirmation that LeAnna had been barhopping with Rafe.

Turning the phone slowly toward the hunky guy, I muttered, "This is the guy, right?"

To my surprised, he shook his head. "Nope, the guy she was with was much older. And, dude, even I know Rafe Lorenzo. The man is a snowboarding legend."

I let out a huge breath, unable to contain my smile.

"How old are we talking?" Britton asked.

Brad shrugged. "I dunno. I mean, not ancient. The guy could party, that's for sure. But he had kinda graying hair. Like a George Clooney type."

Britton and I locked eyes, the lightbulb moment hitting us both at the description. Her hands flew over her phone until she had Jerry Taylor's LifeBling profile on the screen. She turned it triumphantly toward the man again.

He tossed his hands in the air. "Boom!" His voice echoed through the cavernous room. "That's the guy she was partying with. He was wearing a shirt last night, but yeah, it's him. They seemed fairly fond of one another, if you know what I mean." He waggled his brow and winked.

I raised an eyebrow. Looked like someone might not mind "parking in Daddy's garage" after all.

Britton turned toward me, shock making her false lashes blink faster than a hummingbird's wings. "LeAnna and Jerry? LeAnna and her stepson?!"

I grabbed her hand and tugged her toward the door. Waving a hand in the air as we left, I called, "Thanks for your help!"

"Hey, call me about that position!" he shot back. "I'm free nights and weekends!"

I nodded as we made our way back out into the biting cold and into our waiting limo.

As soon as we were inside, I pointed toward her phone and said, "Do that thingy where you find out where he's been most recently."

Obviously not completely over the blow of LeAnna being friendly with her stepson, her blinking had downgraded to an erratic strobe light. "What?"

"You know, check his account glittering and stuff. I saw Tate do it."

"Oh, right." Finally, she forced her attention to her phone. After a few taps and swipes, she wrinkled her nose in disgust. "He just posted that he's *getting all gooey and wet* at the Deep Blue indoor beach." She shoved her phone in my face so I could see an anorexic redhead smearing suntan lotion on him while he was sprawled on a beach towel by the pool.

I offered her my best *what the heck* look. "Is he afraid of a florescent light burn?"

"Weston has tanning tiki huts, so you can get the whole 'beach experience.'" She made air quotes over her last few words.

I pushed the intercom button. "Lucas, can you please take us to the Deep Blue."

"You got it, Boss," our driver said cheerfully, knowing better than to ask why.

Again, a walk might have been the faster way to get one block down on Lake Tahoe Boulevard during ski season, but a few warm minutes later we pulled to a stop in the circular drive of the Deep Blue. The driver scrambled to the door, opening it and standing at attention, hand extended in case we needed help.

Britton patted his arm. "Thanks for your help, Lucas."

"It's no problem at all, Mrs. King." He nodded my way. "Ms. King. Will you need me to stay until you're finished?"

I glanced across the road at the Palace. "I think we can make it."

With a nod, he headed back to the driver's seat and was gone.

I cast a glance at Britton. She hadn't said much on the way over. She hadn't even looked at me, just stared blankly at the empty seat across from her. She was obviously a bit disillusioned with her friend. I felt bad for her. While I'd expected LeAnna to sleep with anything that had a pulse, I was watching Britton's faith in her friend crumble before my eyes. I slipped an arm through hers. "Don't worry," I told her. "I'm sure LeAnna will have a good explanation for all of this when we find her." Okay, it was a total lie, but it served to bring a small smile back to Britton's lips.

We made our way past the enormous fish tank and down the sandy, etched path where I practically heard the bubbling pedicure tubs call my name from the spa. We paused at the entrance to the pool area. I could hear giggles, splashing, and squeals from the other side.

I paused with my hand over the doorknob. "You sure you wanna see this? LeAnna could be in there with him."

Britton's posture straightened bravely, the panther on her shoulders dancing to attention. "Let's do this."

We opened the door and were immediately assaulted by the pungent smells of chlorine with a dab of sickeningly sweet coconut. The air was way too hot and humid. Sweat instantly beaded on my forehead and upper lip.

I scanned the enormous indoor beach for any sign of Jerry and his emaciated date. To the left was a large, curling water slide emptying into one end of the Olympic-sized pool. It was filled with squealing, screeching children. To the right was a separate wave pool. Adults seemed to congregate there, most with a drink in tow. Several cabanas dotted the sand-covered area around the pools, with lounge chairs filling the empty spaces between. Some were open, their occupants enjoying the view, while others had theirs closed off for privacy. I grabbed Britton's hand and tugged her along behind me. The clip-clop of her shoes on the cement walkway echoed off the high ceilings, mingling with the ear-piercing kid noises.

I passed several open cabanas before pausing outside one where the curtains were shut tightly. A female giggle mixed with male whispers.

I cleared my throat loudly. "Jerry Taylor?" I asked from outside the hut.

"Who's asking?" came the reply. Definitely in Jerry's voice.

"Tessie King," I stated definitively. I contemplated barging in but was worried about just what I might see.

Britton pushed me aside and barked, "And Britton King."

After some shuffling noises, the curtains opened. Jerry was wearing just a towel around his waist, his tanned, chiseled chest glistening with oil. His eyes shifted between me and Britton, narrowing as he saw that neither of us was dressed for a day at the beach.

"Where's LeAnna?" Britton demanded.

"How should I know?"

The tiny redhead from the photo appeared behind him, dressed in nothing but a matching towel. She jabbed a pair of hands against her nonexistent hips. "Uh, who is LeAnna?" she spat.

He turned. "It's my father's wife. My..." He paused, seemingly swallowing back some choice words before continuing. "Stepmother." He pivoted back around to us. "And I haven't seen her." He moved to flip the curtain back into place and return to his redhead.

But Britton grabbed the cloth from his hands before he could. "Like hell you haven't. You were clubbing with Stepmommy all night."

"Hey!" the redhead protested. "You told me you were going out with the guys last night."

If looks could kill, Britton would be dead. Jerry's eyes narrowed on hers. His jaw clenched. A vein at his temple bulged. He pulled in a deep breath through flared nostrils, reminding me of a bull about to charge. Talk about a Dr. Jekyll and Mr. Hyde. Where was the flirty playboy we'd met on his yacht?

"Cassie," he said, addressing the now pouting redhead. "Why don't you go chase us down a couple more mai tais while I get rid of these ladies?"

"Fine," she huffed, clearly not all that happy about his whereabouts but not yet willing to give up her arm-candy status yet either. She flounced off to do his bidding, still dressed in nothing more than a towel.

Then Jerry turned to us. "You've got two minutes," he ground out.

"Where is LeAnna?" Britton asked again.

"Not here," he shot back.

Britton scoffed, her glossy lips scrunched in an angry pucker. "You were the last person to see her last night. At Midnight Tahoe. The bartender saw you two together. Hashtag busted."

He shrugged. "So I saw her last night. I don't know where she is now. It's not like I'm her keeper."

"Where did you guys go after your date at the club?" I interjected.

"Whoa!" He waved his hands between us. "That was not a date in any sense of the word. She said she needed to blow off some steam, and I told her I was going to the club. We hung out."

I so wanted to tell him what the bartender had said about them seeming *fond* of one another. "Fine. Where did you two go after *hanging out*?" I asked.

"Nowhere. I left her about midnight. She wouldn't put that damned phone away and kept getting texts." He waved a dismissive hand. "I was done with her."

"Do you know who the texts were from?" I asked, again envisioning Rafe's face.

He shook his head. "I didn't care, and I didn't ask."

"Did she say where she was going next? How she was getting back to the hotel?" Britton asked. I could hear the desperation creeping into her voice again.

"No and yes. I have no idea where she was headed after the club, but she said she was texting a friend for a ride. Why?" he asked, clearly picking up on Britton's worry.

"She hasn't come home yet," Britton answered.

Jerry shrugged. "I doubt it's the first all-nighter she's ever pulled."

The redhead took that moment to sashay back with a brightly colored drink in each hand. Jerry gave her a smile as he took one, the charming Dr. Jekyll back again. Then he turned to us, the smile faltering a bit. "Quite frankly, I honestly couldn't care less where LeAnna is. Now, if you don't mind, I have some very important business to attend to." He enveloped the girl in his arms and disappeared behind the curtain into the hut. When laughs and giggles mutated to groans and moans, I grabbed Britton's hand, pulling her through the exit and into the cool hall outside.

"So," Britton said, a lost look in her eyes. "What do we do now? I mean, LeAnna could be anywhere."

Had the Mafia not chosen this particular week to stay in my casino, I might have shrugged this off as LeAnna shacking up with one of her boy toys. But as it was, I figured it was better to err on the side of caution where the safety of my guests—even if they were she-devils—was concerned.

I pulled my phone out as I swiped the damp hair from my face. "It's time to call in the big guns."

CHAPTER FOURTEEN

Half an hour later we were sitting in my office at the Royal Palace—Britton pacing next to my bookshelf, mindlessly rearranging knickknacks, and me trying not to fidget behind my desk as I waited for Agent Ryder to meet us. As much as I wasn't looking forward to facing him after our three-way standoff outside the *Battle Buffet* set that morning, the truth was he had resources that we didn't.

I felt my knee start to jiggle up and down as a knock sounded at the door, followed by Agent Ryder's broad frame.

"Oh, thank God," Britton said, pouncing at him like the leopard she resembled. "You have to help us. LeAnna is missing."

Ryder cleared his throat, nodding stiffly in my direction. "So you said on the phone."

"Can you find her?" she implored.

"Uh, well, that all depends," he answered, sitting opposite me in one of the leather chairs.

"On what?" I jumped in.

"On whether or not she *wants* to be found."

"What does that mean?" Britton asked, her eyelashes doing their hummingbird imitation again.

He did another throat-clearing thing. "It's not uncommon for suspects to flee if they feel law enforcement is closing in on them."

"No, no, no, no!" Britton shouted, resuming her pacing with a vengeance. "You have got this all wrong."

Ryder raised an eyebrow her direction. "Okay, let's start at the beginning. Why do you think she's missing and not simply just window shopping at Heavenly Village?"

"Because her phone is off. It's *never* off."

He shot me a questioning look.

"It's true. It's like an appendage to her," I agreed.

"And her bed hasn't been slept in," Britton added.

"Isn't it possible," Ryder started slowly, "that LeAnna may have slept elsewhere?"

Britton scoffed. "She's a grieving widow!"

Ryder and I shared a look that told me he had the same thoughts on that subject as I did.

"Okay, tell me this: When was the last time you saw her?"

"Last night," Britton responded. "We had dinner together, and then she said she wanted to go out, so we split up."

"When was that?" Ryder asked, pulling out his trusty little notebook.

"I don't know. Maybe nine or so?"

"And that was the last time you saw her?"

Britton nodded.

"You didn't call or text her after that?"

"Not last night. I, uh, had plans. I was busy."

I narrowed my eyes, again wondering at these plans she wasn't elaborating on.

"But I know she wouldn't just leave," Britton added. Tears started to puddle in her eyes, threatening a mascara spill. "Look, I've learned some things about her today that I'm sure she's not proud of." She pushed her shoulders back, her spine straightening. "But, I still know she didn't kill Gerald."

"So where do you think she is now?" he asked.

She threw her hands up in the air. "I don't know. That's why we called you!" She shot him a *well, duh* look.

Ryder sighed deeply and turned to me. "Have you tried calling her today?"

"Of course we've tried calling," Britton shot back, not waiting for me to answer. "She won't answer my texts, and calls go right to voice mail." The tears spilled over her cheeks. "And it's totes full now!"

I stood and ran a comforting hand down Britton's fuzz-covered arm as I addressed Ryder. "LeAnna was seen at that new club next to Harrah's with Mr. Taylor's son last night. It sounds like he's the last one to have seen her."

"He totally abandoned her," Britton spat, clutching my hand in hers.

Ryder nodded and stood. "Okay. I'll get a statement from him."

I meekly raised a finger, clearing my throat. "We, uh, already did. That's why I called you."

His jaw clenched, and he released another sigh. "And why didn't you call me *before* talking to him?"

"Isn't a missing person more of a local police department thing?" I asked, doing my best to evade the question.

He glared. "In a normal case? Yes. But in this case LeAnna is being investigated in her husband's murder..."

"She didn't do it!" Britton cried, punctuating her statement with a productive sniffle.

Ryder ran an exasperated hand through his hair. "Whether or not she did it isn't a relative point in this particular conversation."

She shook her head. "It totally is."

His hand shot out between them. "She's already in our database, so the local guys aren't supposed to..." He craned his head to the side, his neck popping several times before he straightened it. "Bottom line, this is my job. Okay?"

Britton sniffed again. "But can't you check her phone records or something and see where she's been?"

"I'm not sure that LeAnna not coming home this morning is enough to warrant that invasion of privacy," Ryder argued.

Britton rolled her eyes. "Oh please. I watch prime-time TV. I know that the first thing you cops do when someone is a suspect is pull their phone records. So if you already have them, it's not an invasion, right?"

Ryder let out a long breath, like this conversation was taking years off his life. He took a step toward her, his expression an emotionless mask. "Look, I know you want to think the best of your friend. But you want the most likely scenario? She's taken off, possibly ditched her phone, and doesn't want to be found. I've seen this more times than I can count."

Britton's shoulders sagged farther and farther down with each of his words.

I placed a protective arm around her, suddenly feeling a mama-bear vibe on her behalf. While Britton might have some misplaced loyalty toward LeAnna, she wasn't stupid. She knew LeAnna, and I had to admit, I put more credence in Britton's version of events than Ryder's.

"Well, I don't think the best of LeAnna," I said defiantly.

He turned his expressionless fed face toward me. "You don't?"

"Tess!" Britton flashed me a hurt look.

Glancing between the two, I explained, "LeAnna has always been a mean, spoiled, childish, irresponsible, vindictive..."

Ryder made a circular motion with his hand in a gesture to move me forward. I'd obviously used enough unpleasant adjectives to get my point across.

Popping one more in just for funsies, I continued, "And a tacky-dressing woman-child. I'm still sticking with that. However, I know her phone is practically attached to her hand. She would answer her texts and check her messages even if she was sprawled on her death bed, let alone out on the lam. LeAnna would even glitter about it." My posture straightened with pride in my newfound social media lingo prowess. "So I agree with Britton."

Britton smiled, linking her arm through mine in solidarity. "See?" she told Ryder.

Ryder muttered something under his breath that sounded a lot like a curse word and pulled out his phone. "You win." He sighed, typing something in.

"I do?" I couldn't help the lift of surprise in my voice. I'd outfought the big bad federal agent? Go me.

Ryder nodded. "I'm having someone at the main office send over her phone records." He glanced up at the two of us. "Happy?"

"Ecstatic," Britton answered for us both.

"Good." He glanced my way just long enough for me to see the hint of a smile curling his lip before he bent his head over his phone again. "They'll need to send it as a secure email attachment that I'd rather see on a bigger screen." He scanned the office, finally settling on my rather barren desk. "Is there a computer I can use to view the report?"

I scurried around to the other side of the desk, unlocked the side drawer, and pulled out my laptop. Rolling back the cushy executive chair, I waved my hand across the seat. "It's all yours."

He sat at the desk, filling out the large leather chair very well, where I always felt like my feet never quite touched the floor. He slid open the laptop then crooked a finger at me, motioning me to his side. I resisted the urge to perch myself on the edge of the desk, cross my legs, and play sexy secretary with him.

Pointing to the screen, he said, "I need your password."

"Oh." I bobbed my head and leaned over his arm. The intoxicating scent of his cologne made me do a mental girly sigh and nearly melt into his lap. My fingers punched clumsily at the keys. On my third try, I got the password correct. As I backed away, he looked at me through his lashes, his blue eyes dark with something I couldn't read.

"What?" I asked.

He cleared his throat and shifted in his seat. "Uh, nothing." Was it my imagination or did his eyes stray to the region of my not-quite-Britton-quality cleavage?

"How long will this take?" Britton asked, nervously chewing on the tip of a manicured nail.

"Not long," Ryder promised, directing his attention back to the screen.

I took a seat in the other chair across the desk from Ryder and straightened my blouse as I watched Britton pace again. She had to be burning a thousand calories going back and forth in those heels.

We waited for what felt like forever, but in reality it was just a few minutes before Ryder finally said, "Got it."

Britton jumped behind him to stare at the screen, and I leaned forward in my seat.

"Well?" I couldn't help asking.

"Well," he responded, "she was at the club last night. That was the last ping on her phone. She either shut it off or it died."

Britton sucked in a breath and put a hand over her mouth.

"It's just her phone," I tried to comfort her. "This isn't confirmation of anything other than that."

She nodded, but her hand stayed firmly placed over her mouth.

"Huh," Ryder mumbled, pulling our attention back to him.

"What?" I asked.

"Well, there hasn't been any activity since last night, but I'm going back over her recent history."

"And?"

"There's definitely a pattern."

"Which is..." I prompted. He was killing me here.

"Well, I'm seeing a lot of calls and texts to one number." He paused. "Which can sometimes be easily explained," he added in Britton's direction. "But when the Bureau runs background checks, this is one of the things that causes a red flag to indicate possible infidelity."

"Shocker." I couldn't help the sarcasm.

Britton shook her head. "Or maybe it's her *husband's* number?" she said, ever the optimist.

Ryder leaned back in the chair, his hands lacing behind his head, impressive biceps straining against his shirt. "Not unless he's continued to call from the great unknown. The last one was just a few minutes before her phone shut off last night."

That sickening feeling hit my stomach again. Rafe? Just because it wasn't him at the club didn't mean he was completely innocent. I had seen the bathroom footage, after all. This was how it was all going to come to light. I'm not sure why I even cared, but for some reason, I did. I bit my lower lip.

Ryder closed the laptop and leaned forward, elbows propped on the desk. "What aren't you telling me, Tess?"

"Me? What? Nothing."

He shook his head, eyes narrowing. "That's not a nothing look. You nibble your bottom lip when something's wrong."

Obviously I'd done an awful job of pulling a poker face. I quickly let my lip go.

Britton nodded her head while inspecting her manicure. "He's right. You so do that."

"Look, if you want my help, you've got to honest with me," Ryder said.

Without showing my cards, I evaded with, "It's a local number. Right?"

His expression remained the same fed face he'd had on since walking into the room. "What makes you think that?"

"I, well, just think..."

"It's not," Britton said, still staring at the screen from her spot behind Ryder.

Whew. Saved by the blonde.

Ryder shot her a look over his shoulder like he didn't share in my relief.

"You sure?" I asked Britton.

She nodded. "Yep. It's a 707 area code. That's Napa."

My mental hamster suddenly went into overdrive. Napa? So she was seeing someone local at home. But if she'd been texting him for a ride from the Midnight Tahoe club just before her phone went off, that had to mean her mystery man was here, too. So, who had a Napa number and was in Tahoe right now? Jerry's angry face at the faux beach immediately popped into my mind. Just because he *said* he'd left her at the club didn't mean he really did. We only had his word for it. No one actually saw who LeAnna left with. Then again, if he'd taken her somewhere last night, where was she now? Clearly not at the beach with him and the redhead.

Of course, Jerry wasn't the only one with a Napa number. Hadn't LeAnna said that Dubois had a restaurant in Napa where the show sometimes filmed? And she *had* been a regular on the *Battle Buffet* set. With her teeny-tiny frame, I took her more for a survive-on-Tic-Tacs-and-water kind of girl than a genuine foodie. Had her interest in the cooking show been more about its star than the dishes? It was possible. Though, it was equally as possible that LeAnna hadn't so much as been *charming* a celebu-chef as much as being *charmed* by a handsome, rich, and just a little bit sleazy producer like Sicianni.

He seemed to flirt with anything in a skirt, and LeAnna was a prime target for a guy with more cash than moral compass. Considering hers seemed to point just shy of north as well.

"Earth to Tessie."

"What?" I shook myself out of my thoughts to find Ryder staring at me.

Ryder's hooded gaze studied me as he stood deliberately and walked around to my chair, offering his hand. "You really need to work on your poker face, sweetheart."

"Oh. I was just... Okay." I let him pull me up to stand right in front of him. I found myself trapped between his broad form and the chair, not that I minded. The closeness sent flutters of anticipation through my body.

"Okay," he repeated, a slow smile snaking across his face, which had danger written all over it.

I shuddered. In a really good way.

He turned to Britton, abruptly breaking the moment. "I'll run down this number and see what we come up with. It could be nothing, but it's worth checking." Then he offered a lopsided smile in my direction. "You'll let me know if you hear from LeAnna?"

I nodded dumbly, still trying to shake off the effects of his sexy grin.

Britton flounced toward him, throwing herself into his arms. "Thank you, Agent Ryder."

That hug so should have been mine. I needed to work on my flouncing.

* * *

Britton went back to the penthouse to look through LeAnna's things for any clue to where she might have gone, and I headed back down to the *Battle Buffet* stage to make sure taping was going smoothly.

Tate was just leaving and met me in the hall. The second he saw me he made a beeline toward me, wrapping me in a fierce hug.

"Ohmigod, Tessie, I'm so sorry about last night!"

"Which part?" I managed to mumble as he squeezed my lungs.

He pulled back, taking both of my hands in his. "I had no idea that Sicianni would expect a *happy ending* out of you! Who knew he had prostitutes up there? I thought they were just strippers."

I shook my head in amazement that gay or straight, all men saw a huge distinction there.

"Thank God Rafe was there to rescue you!" He hugged me again like a boa constrictor.

"Hre hidnt hescue he," I mumbled.

"What?" Tate thankfully took a step back, allowing me to breathe.

"I said he didn't *rescue* me," I told him, sucking in deep breaths of air. "I was fine on my own. Sicianni was talking." I paused. "How do you know all this anyway?"

Tate waved me off. "Honey, nothing goes on in this hotel that I don't know about."

Clearly.

"So, what did Sicianni say?" he prompted.

I quickly filled him in on the fact that there definitely *were* some shady guys backing Sicianni, who definitely didn't want the cops anywhere near them, and there definitely *was* a meeting of some sort going on between more than one crime family. Unfortunately, I had a sneaking suspicion it was going on at our VIP dinner tonight.

"I knew it," Tate said, shaking his head when I finished. "There are wiseguys everywhere."

"I don't know about everywhere—"

"That's why you need to protect yourself, Tessie," he cut me off.

I narrowed my eyes at him. "What do you mean?"

"I got you something." Tate beamed with pride.

I got a bad feeling in the pit of my stomach. "What sort of something?"

"Follow me," he said instead of answering. I reluctantly followed as he trotted toward the front lobby, stopping at the check-in desk. He disappeared behind it and into the back room for just a minute before emerging again with a neon-pink case in his hands. He did a quick glance over each shoulder then motioned me over to the desk with an exaggerated wave.

"What is this?" I asked. The last time he'd had "something" for me, I'd ended up in Sicianni's lap without my panties. "Wary" didn't even begin to describe my attitude now.

"Go on. Open it."

I shook the package, but nothing rattled. I popped the latch, and the box creaked open to reveal a small pistol the same exact color as the case. I slammed it closed. "You have got to be kidding."

I shoved it back at Tate, but he raised his arms in an effort not to take it. "You need to be able to protect yourself. I got this for *you*. It's a gift."

"Where did you get this?" I hissed.

"I have a friend who works in the hunting and fishing industry."

I shot him a *get real* look. "You have friends who hunt and fish?"

"Well, they sell things that people use to hunt and fish."

I looked down at the neon pink. I had a hard time picturing this taking down a bear. "I do not need a gun." I pushed it at him again, but he kept his arms in the air. If passersby knew what was in the box, it'd look like a robbery.

"I think you do!" he countered. "You said yourself that Sicianni all but confirmed we have *made men* meeting in the casino."

"Keep your voice down," I warned, watching a mother at the check-in desk pull her adorable little redheaded son a little closer to her skirt as she eyed us. "And he only confirmed that his VIPs were meeting here. For all we know, it could be a meeting of the Food TV workers' union."

Tate's turn to give *me* the *get real* look. "Tess, I will not be able to sleep a wink if I don't know you're safe," he whined.

"Is this even legal?" I asked, again glancing over my shoulder as if the feds were just waiting to swoop in and slap us with a carrying-concealed fine.

"Perfectly." Tate paused. "I think."

I rolled my eyes so far I could almost make out my hairline. "I know nothing about guns," I whispered. "And they kind of scare me. A lot."

He put his hands on his thighs, bending slightly at the waist. "They're a lot like babies—you just have to learn how to take care of them and understand how they work."

I tried again to make him take the pink case. He just backed away.

"Babies aren't loaded."

Tate scrunched his nose. "You've obviously never changed a poopy diaper."

"Ha! And you have?" The thought of Tate even contemplating a diaper change was comical.

"I have..." He looked down at his shoes, mumbling, "Seen it done."

"That's what I thought." I grabbed one of his hands and formed his fingers around the handle of the gun case. "When you've worked up the nerve to change a poopy diaper, I'll learn how to shoot a gun."

"Who is shooting a gun?" a voice behind me said.

I spun around, instinctively hiding the neon case behind my back, and found myself face to face with Rafe.

"No one!" I blurted out.

He frowned, craning to see behind me. "What's that?"

"Nothing!"

Tate let out a long-suffering sigh from behind me. "It's a handgun. A very nice pink handgun."

Rafe shot me a concerned look. "You have a gun?"

"No, I do *not*," I emphasized, shoving the case back toward Tate. "It's his."

"Good," Rafe said, the concern melting away. "Because you really shouldn't own a gun unless you know how to handle one."

I crossed my arms over my chest. "What makes you think I can't handle a little pink gun?"

He raised an eyebrow. "Can you?"

"No," I reluctantly admitted.

"Well, I, for one, think she should know how to handle one to protect herself," Tate cut in, pushing the case back along the counter toward me. "I mean, think about what might have happened..." Tate looked up and down the hall then whispered, "with Sicianni, if you hadn't been there last night?"

Rafe frowned. "How do you know about that?"

"Tate knows everything that happens in this hotel," I informed him.

"Huh." Rafe seemed to take that in for a moment. "Well, I have to say that I agree with him."

"What?!" I spat out. Tate beamed and shot me an *I told you so* look.

Rafe nodded. "I think it's a good idea for anyone to know how to protect themselves. Especially someone in your position."

"What? A poor defenseless woman?" I asked, giving him a challenging look.

Rafe grinned, popping a dimple in his cheek. "No, the well-known head of a casino. You're a public figure."

"Oh," I said, the flattery completely deflating my argument.

"Tell you what," Rafe said, the smile widening to show off a second dimple. "I've got a break from babysitting Sicianni for a couple of hours while the show tapes. Why don't you and I take your little pink gun to the range, and I'll show you how to use it."

I opened my mouth to protest that Alfie was all the security I needed, but Tate didn't give me a chance. "She'd love to! Wouldn't you, Tess?" he answered.

I looked from Tate to Rafe to those two amazingly sexy dimples flashing just below those emerald eyes. I was sorely outnumbered.

CHAPTER FIFTEEN

———

I stood with my feet plated wide in my heels, staring down at the paper human-shaped cutout at the end of our shooting lane. Each time another person's gun went off, I flinched. Granted, that flinch was much better than the jump-shake-scream thing I'd started with when we'd first arrived.

Rafe set a box of .22 shells on the ledge next to me and opened the hot-pink case. "Always assume that your gun is loaded, even if you were the last one who used it, and you're positive you removed the ammo." He grabbed the weapon from the case. It looked ridiculously tiny in his large palm.

I took a deep breath and nodded as he continued his lesson.

"Wrap your hand around the grip, with your finger resting on the outside of the trigger guard. Make sure the safety is on." He pointed to an orange button on the side. "Push the magazine release switch and pull out the clip." It fell loose into his other hand, and he laid it next to the ammunition on the shelf. He slid his hand along the top of the gun. "Rack the slide and lock it back, looking into the chamber to ensure it's empty. Then, and only then, you can load the magazine." He picked up the clip, pressing bullets into the open end until it was filled. "After it's full, you press it firmly back into the grip." He shoved it into place with the butt of his hand. "With the gun in your hand like this—" He held the gun out for my inspection. "—use your thumb to push the slide release."

The slide cracked back into place. The sound and thought of a loaded gun reverted me back to my jump-shake-scream thing. "I'm not sure this is such a good idea."

He placed a comforting hand on my shoulder. "Relax. It's a good thing you're afraid of it. Guns should never, ever be taken lightly."

Well, at least I had the right attitude.

"This is the last step, and the gun is ready to fire." He pushed the red safety lever. "Put on those *stylish* protective glasses and earmuffs. I'll fire the first few shots to give you an idea of how to hold it."

I followed orders and watched him, enjoying my surroundings much better with the gunshots being muffled. He shot four times, hitting the target twice in the torso. I vaguely wondered how Rafe knew so much about guns and hoped it had nothing to do with any Italian businessmen back at the casino. I watched him reset the safety, lay the gun on the ledge, and turn back to me. He pushed one side of his earmuffs off then leaned over and did the same to mine.

"Well, what do you think? Want to give it a go?"

While I felt a little better being around the gun after seeing him handle it, I was still majorly anxious.

"If I say no, can I leave?" I asked.

He grinned. "Give it a try. Hey, you may even like it."

I doubted that, but since I was already in earmuff and goggles, I humored him.

I took a deep breath and stepped up to the ledge. Rafe stood directly behind me. I could feel his hot breath on my neck and smell the mint of his gum as he reached both arms around me to help. Warmth filled every inch of my body as he molded himself to me. Teen-me melted into a puddle, but it was probably for the best. She had no business in the shooting range.

He settled the gun in my hands correctly, pushed the earmuff back into place, and removed the safety.

"Just slide your finger over the trigger and pull," he commanded.

I steadied my hands the best I could and tried to match his stance. I slid my finger over the trigger, squinted my eyes closed, and pulled. The shot rang out, and I heard Rafe whistle beside me.

I opened my eyes. "How did I do?"

"Hit him right between the eyes."

I blinked, looking at the neat little hole in the center of the paper man's head. While I should have celebrated my beginner's luck, suddenly all I could think about was how easy it would be to put a neat little hole in a person's head. A wave of dizziness hit me.

Rafe pulled the gun from my grip and laid it on the ledge. "You okay?" he asked.

"No worries," I lied, trying to get my heart to stop pounding like a jackhammer. I made a mental note to give the little pink terror back to Tate and never touch a gun again. I'd had enough dead bodies for one lifetime.

"You wanna sit down for a minute?" he asked, concern creasing his brow. "You look a little shaky."

Was it that obvious? As much as I wanted to play tough chick, I was pretty sure I was five seconds away from my knees buckling like a pair of Mary Janes. I let Rafe lead me through a pair of doors to our right, away from the noise and onto a bench set against the wall in the empty hallway. Though when he sat close to me, I'm not sure it helped my racing heart any. I inhaled the woodsy scent of his cologne as I took in shaky breaths.

"You doing okay?"

I nodded, touched at the genuine concern in his voice. I glanced at him out of the corner of my eye. I had to admit feeling majorly conflicted where Rafe was concerned lately. One minute he was driving my hormones into a frenzy, and the next he was topping my suspect list. It wasn't a roller-coaster ride of emotions that I was really enjoying.

He turned his sparking emerald gaze squarely on mine. "What?" he asked.

I bit my lip. "Can I ask you something?"

He shrugged. "Sure."

"How well do you know Sicianni?"

Rafe frowned. "I told you that Sicianni and your father go way back."

I tried to fight back any uncomfortable feelings about my father going way back with a Mafioso. "You seemed very friendly with him last night."

The frown deepened. "Of course I did. That's part of the job, isn't it? Catering to the guys like Sicianni, making nice with the whales and high rollers."

I nodded. "Sure. The high rollers." I paused. "Like Mr. Taylor?"

"What about him?"

"How well did you know *him*?" I pushed.

"Tessie, what is this all about?" he asked. I could see a million questions in his eyes. I'd admit I had a few more of my own too.

I took a deep breath and decided to lay it all on the line. "I saw you with LeAnna," I blurted out.

"With LeAnna? When?"

"The night Mr. Taylor died. She..." I trailed off, momentarily losing my nerve. I cleared my throat. I could do this. I was a tough chick at a gun range, after all. "I saw you two practically making out."

Rafe blinked at me, his green eyes a total blank. "Making out? Tess, what are you talking about?"

"Don't deny it!" I warned. "I have video footage."

He studied my face, his expression stoic. "Look, I don't know what you think you have, but there is nothing going on between LeAnna Taylor and me."

"Then why were you hugging her in the bathroom?"

"In the..." His voice trailed off, something flickering behind his eyes. Then he shook his head and ran a frustrated hand through his hair. "What are you doing, spying on me now?"

"No!" I scoffed, huffing at a deep breath and crossing my arms over my chest. "I was spying on LeAnna."

Rafe raised an eyebrow my direction.

"For her own good!" Sorta. "I was trying to help Britton prove that LeAnna didn't kill her husband by having Maverick follow her via the security footage on the night her husband died. Only I didn't count on seeing her throw herself at you in the ladies' room."

"Then I guess you didn't see the footage from us together on the set that night, did you?"

I wrinkled my nose. "You were making out on the *Battle Buffet* set too?"

"No! We weren't making out anywhere." Rafe shook his head again. "She showed up at the set asking for a behind-the-scenes tour from Dubois. He was explaining some of the weird food combos that the contestants had to cook with, you know like oysters and candy corn, when she started to look sick and bolted. I followed her to make sure she was okay, and she told me it was just morning sickness."

I bit my lip again, replaying the footage I'd seen in my head. Honestly, Rafe hadn't *actually* made out with LeAnna. He'd put an arm around her shoulders, and she'd grabbed his butt. But for his part, I guess that's the sort of thing one might do if he was comforting a woman who looked like she was going to puke her guts out.

"So you're not seeing LeAnna?"

Rafe's expression softened. "No, I am not seeing LeAnna Aiden-Taylor. And," he said, moving closer to me on the bench until his thigh rubbed against mine. "For the record, I'm not seeing Tiffany Weston either."

"You're not?" I somehow squeaked out through the rush of warmth running through my veins at the physical contact.

He shook his head. "No. She's just visiting her uncle for spring break, and she doesn't know anyone in town, so I was showing her around."

"Oh. That's...really nice of you," I said honestly.

"I'm a nice guy when you give me half a chance." His voice was low and deep, his eyes suddenly taking on a dark, dangerous look that had both teen-me *and* adult-me melting like a Hershey's Kiss right there on the bench. He reached one hand out and brushed the tips of his fingers along my cheek. I shuddered at the contact, my breath hitching in my throat as he leaned in and ever so softly brushed his lips against mine.

I'm not sure how long our lips were locked together, as I think I might've blacked out for a moment. Not that I minded. But from somewhere in the deep recesses of my ecstasy-filled brain, I heard my phone ringing from my pocket.

Reluctantly I broke contact and fished it out, happy to see that Rafe looked almost as disoriented as I felt. "Hello?" I breathed into the phone.

In hindsight, maybe I should have taken a moment to compose myself before answering.

"Whoa, sex kitten!" came Buddy Weston's voice on the other end. "You always answer the phone that way, darling?"

I cleared my throat. "No," I told him, this time putting on my no-nonsense businesswoman voice.

"Well maybe you should. You could start charging $3.99 a minute." I heard him cackling at his own joke.

"What do you want, Weston?" I sighed.

"Hey, this is a friendly courtesy call, King. I'm just doing a fellow casino owner a solid."

I rolled my eyes. "I highly doubt that."

"Come on—you don't think I can be friendly? I'll scratch your back this time, and maybe next time you can scratch mine..." He trailed off, and I tried really hard not to get a mental image of his hairy back.

"I think I'll pass."

"Oh yeah? Well maybe you want to check your guest register before you blow me off, doll."

"And why would I want to do that?" I asked, quickly losing what little patience I had left.

"Because I just watched half of the Gambia family pull up in front of your lovely establishment."

* * *

"Damn it, Buddy was right," I muttered to Tate twenty minutes later.

I stood behind the front desk, looking at about fifteen suites listed in the computer under the Gambia name.

I glanced out at the gaming floor. It looked like a cross between a scene from *The Godfather* and *Jersey Shore*. A big guy in a dark suit with a neck the size of my thighs stood at the roulette wheel, a towering pile of chips beside him. A guy with dark hair and about a million gold chains hanging around his neck chewed on a toothpick and adjusted his cufflinks as he bet at the blackjack table. A rotund, balding man in a designer suit and the shiniest pointy black shoes I ever saw sat at the video poker machines, playing virtual hands at lightning speed. Beside him sat a woman playing a keno machine and wearing leopard-printed leggings stretched way past their normal limits atop a pair of gold stiletto heels. At the end of the aisle was a tall, lanky guy with one hand tucked inside his suit jacket, his watchful gaze shifting from one patron to the next.

I wasn't sure whether to laugh, cry, or duck and cover.

"Didn't anyone notice all of these reservations under the same last name?" I asked Tate, scrolling through the register again.

Tate shrugged. "We get a lot of family reunions here."

I shot him a look. This was not the type of family I wanted reuniting in my casino. "Any idea how long they are staying?"

Tate clicked a couple of keys on the keyboard. "It looks like just the weekend." He looked up from the screen, giving me a pointed look. "Just until after the *Battle Buffet* finale."

I closed my eyes and said a silent curse word, mentally going over my options. I could turn them away, but with the board meeting coming up in just a few short days, was turning away revenue really the best thing for the casino? The whole point of the *Battle Buffet* show was to bring in guests. We had guests in spades. The only problem was there was the teeny tiniest possibility that one of these "foodies" might have killed Mr. Taylor. And then there was the whole Mafia meeting thing. *Battle Buffet* was supposed to bring in good press. If anyone got hold of the information that the entire VIP section of the show's theater now was filled with organized criminals, we'd be sunk.

I took a deep breath. I counted to ten. Okay, this would be fine. They were just guests. A big family of Italian, food-loving guests. They would enjoy their show, gamble a little, and be on their way. Hopefully, no one would be the wiser.

My phone rang from my pocket, and I pulled it out to see Alfie's name on the readout. "Yeah?" I answered.

"Are you seeing what I'm seeing?" Alfie's deep voice boomed at me from the other end. Clearly he had his "eye in the sky" on the proceedings in the lobby as well.

"A full gaming floor and lots of new guests?" I said, doing my best to pull out the positive spin I'd just talked myself into.

Alfie grunted. "I'm gonna need you to approve some overtime for security."

"Done!" I promised and hung up. Then I quickly shot a text off to Maverick.

Update on Hammerhead?

I nervously watched Alicia check in a portly man and woman at the next counter over as I waited for his reply. Giada and Giovanni Gambia. Both of whom also had tickets to this evening's VIP dinner, or so Alicia informed them as she handed over their room keys. I took a deep breath, hoping this dinner wouldn't be my last supper.

Three minutes later my phone buzzed with Maverick's response.

Slept off a hangover this morning, hit the lunch buffet, and been steadily losing money at the slots ever since.

I let out a small sigh of relief. I wasn't sure exactly what I was expecting Hammerhead to do, but at least the report hadn't listed any nefarious activities.

"Aren't you glad you have protection now?" Tate asked beside me, nodding toward a guy checking in who had a distinct bulge at his right hip. Either he was packing or he was *very* happy to be in Tahoe.

I shook my head. "Trust me...both I and the world at large are better off if I don't have a gun in my hand."

"Come on. Are you telling me the shooting range wasn't fun?" Tate said.

"Sure, putting little holes in guys is a riot."

Tate shot me a look like I was the world's biggest lightweight. "Honey, it's a baby gun."

"Well, consider it *your* baby. I put it back in your locker."

Tate pouted. "But it was a gift!"

"Yeah, well, get me a pair of shoes next time instead," I muttered as I glanced across the lobby to find a familiar face making her way toward me.

Britton was dressed in a white faux fur coat that went clear down to her ankles, looking like a chic abominable snow monster as she wove her way through the "foodies" to the front desk.

"Hey," she said, stopping in front of us. "You ready to go, Tess?"

I blinked at her, trying to remember if I'd agreed to go somewhere with her. "Um...where?"

A pucker of confusion pulled her eyebrows closer. "It is five, right? Alfie said we were supposed to go to Dickie's grave together at five."

I ground my teeth together and stared up at the nearest black, round security camera in the ceiling. "He did, did he?" I asked.

Britton nodded, her blonde hair bobbing up and down. "Are you ready?"

I sighed. "Look, Britt, there are about a million guests checking in right now." *Most of them mobsters.* "I really don't have time..." I trailed off, watching the pucker of confusion fade and her eyes turn down at the corners, quickly filling with tears.

She sniffed loudly. "It's okay, Tess. I can go...alone." The last word came out on a stifled sob.

I sighed, shot a few more daggers at that security camera, hoping Alfie was watching, and finally gave in. "Okay, let's go visit Dad."

* * *

The strong, bone-chilling breeze whipped my dress coat against my legs and tousled my hair, flinging stray tendrils across my face. Ominous clouds rolled in, covering the setting sun, matching the emptiness I felt inside as I stared across the countless rows of graves. I sniffed to hold back tears. I crouched, pushing slushy snow away from my dad's headstone before laying the yellow Gerbera daisies at the base. The vivid color fought desperately to brighten such a grim setting. I had struggled with what to bring when Britton had insisted we stop at a florist along the way, but I'd eventually went with what I loved—the same type of flowers he always got for me. I traced the letters of his name with my fingers, stopping when I got to the date. One year today. Alfie was right. As hard as it was to be here, I would have regretted not coming.

"I'm sorry, Daddy. I promise I'm still doing my best to preserve your legacy."

Britton's hand on my shoulder startled me back into a standing position. I swiped at my cheeks, realizing they were wet. "He'd be so proud of you," she said, doing nothing to stop my brewing tears.

All I could do was nod, feeling too choked up to answer.

She pointed toward my dad's grave. "He talked about you all the time. In fact, there were times when I almost felt like I'd been there while you were growing up, you know? I kind of felt like you were my daughter, in a way. Well, sort of. I heard *all* of the stories from your childhood." She made a huge circle outline with her hands, undoubtedly in an attempt to make sure I knew just how many stories there'd been.

"You're exaggerating."

She splayed a hand, ticking off each digit with a finger on the other as she listed things. "I knew you lost your first tooth in kindergarten, scared the hell out of everyone the summer between third and fourth grade with viral meningitis, that you started your period when you were twelve..." She paused, raising an eyebrow as far as her frozen forehead would allow.

If I'd had a white flag, I would've waved it. Instead, I used my hands, flailing them between us. "All right, okay, I believe you. Please spare anyone within earshot the horror stories from my teens."

Her face softened into a smile. "I'm glad we're friends at least. Dickie would have liked that."

"Me too," I muttered. Then on impulse I grabbed her in a bear hug so tight that I surprised myself. As her arms went around me, hugging me back, a sense of peace drifted through me. Maybe this was what my dad really wanted all along. It was as though he were there, smiling over us. The sun even peeked through the clouds for a moment.

I pulled away, letting Britton up for air. "But you're family too. Actually, more like a sister than a mother though," I added, trying to lighten the mood a bit. "Except when you pull out that *mother knows best* look."

She backed away, the exact look attempting to furrow her brow, one glossy lip ticked up near the corner.

"Yep, that's it," I said, stifling a laugh.

Her mom face morphed into a smile. "I just wanted to make sure we were talking about the same one." She ran a hand across the smooth top of my father's headstone, the smile tumbling from her lips and tears quickly brimming in her eyes. "I miss him so much."

Grief and regret twisted my gut. "Me too." I slid a hand over her shoulder, hoping to return some of the comfort she'd just given me. My phone buzzed in my pocket. I briefly contemplated not answering it.

Thunder rolled in the distance.

"Yes, Daddy," I muttered, pulling it from my pocket.

It was a text from Maverick.

Hammerhead just went down to the VIP cocktail party.

CHAPTER SIXTEEN

———

I checked my reflection again in the full-length mirror mounted on my bedroom door, giving my black satin evening gown one last look. I adjusted the crystal choker at my neck so the ribbons that cinched it dangled at my shoulder. The chunky matching bracelet slid back into place when I dropped my hand to smooth my skirt. Jack gave my legs the figure eight brush of approval, winding between my ankles several times. I sat on the edge of my bed, careful not to wrinkle anything as I mentally prepped myself for the *Battle Buffet* VIP party. Originally I'd been excited by the idea of a gourmet meal prepared by Chef Dubois and hobnobbing with our big spenders and the producers of the show. Only now, I wasn't so sure that the party would have as much hobnobbing as it would consorting with the criminal element.

I glanced at the clock. I was as fashionably late as social etiquette would allow without being rude. It was now or never. Jack stared at me. He let out a little purr-slash-meow of encouragement, kneading biscuits on my comforter. I stood up, scratched his ears, grabbed my crystal-beaded clutch, and put on my most professional hostess face as I made my way down to the party.

We had opened up three of our ballrooms to accommodate the impressive guest list. The first held the pre-dinner cocktail party, which was in full swing by the time I arrived. I scanned the packed room for a familiar face. I spied Dubois, circulating among the crowd in a suit and tie, though he still wore the white sneakers in some attempt to look too cool to be too formal. He was soaking up the many congratulations that were offered, clearly loving being in the celebrity spotlight.

Guys in dark suits circled the room, weaving through people, their gazes quickly shifting from person to person. I noticed quite a few had hands strategically placed in either their jackets or pockets. I suddenly felt underdressed, the only person in the room not packing.

I entered the crowd, making my way through groups of plump, middle-aged women with gaudy makeup caked on their faces, stuffed into evening gowns at least two sizes too small. They gulped wine, hoarded hors d'oeuvres, and complimented each other on their fabulous attire. I suddenly felt like a beauty queen, my ego inflating more and more with each new cluster I passed. Finally I spotted Britton, dressed in a gorgeous white, floor-length beaded gown, in a far corner with Alfie, chatting up a thin man in an ill-fitting tuxedo. He had an impressive scar that slashed across his face, putting Alfie's to shame.

As soon as Britton saw me, she waved my direction and threaded her way through the crowd to my side. "Great turnout, huh?" she asked, eyes scanning the room.

I nodded, trying to think of the revenue the extra guests were bringing in and not about how many of them might be on the FBI's Most Wanted list.

Britton grabbed my arm, turning me away from the crowd. "Hey, any word from Ryder about the owner of that phone number in Napa?"

I shook my head. "Nothing yet. Sorry."

"Tess, I'm really worried about LeAnna," she said, her lips pinching together in a way that would have produced wrinkles on a normal face. "I was looking through her stuff this evening and... Well, let's just say I know for sure she didn't leave on her own."

"What did you find?"

"Her wrinkle cream."

I gave her blank look.

"Tessie, there is absolutely no way LeAnna would have gone somewhere overnight without that, let alone gone on the run!"

From what I knew of LeAnna, I kind of agreed with Britton. However, it was hardly conclusive proof. "Are you sure she wouldn't just buy more?"

Britton shook her head. "No way. She also left behind her pore cleansing mask, charcoal scrub, eye cream, and lip plumper," she said.

"Okay, you're totally right," I agreed. "Look, I'm sure Ryder is running down every lead he possibly can to find LeAnna." Which was completely true. Whether Ryder believed in her innocence or not, I knew he wasn't the type to let a suspect slip through his fingers.

Britton nodded, though the pinched look didn't leave her face. "Tessie, I'm really worried about her. If she didn't leave on her own, that means somebody took her. Or worse," she added, her voice cracking on the last word.

I bit my lip. I had to admit that the more time that went on without an appearance from LeAnna, the more I kind of agreed with Britton's theory.

"I'm sure she's fine," I lied. "The best thing you can do is mingle and keep your phone on in case she tries to contact you, okay?"

Britton blinked back the unshed tears and nodded bravely. "Right."

I gave her a tight hug before she turned and made her way back toward Alfie and Scarface.

No sooner had she left my side than I heard a familiar voice call my name.

"Tessie, you look amazing!"

I turned to find Rafe at my elbow. "That dress..." He trailed off, grinning. "I love it when you wear your hair up like that." He reached out and wound a finger through one of the loose curls at my neck, sending wonderful shivers skittering through me.

"Thanks," I mumbled, patting the back of my hair.

I brushed away nonexistent lint from his black satin lapel, noting that our outfits matched in a happy accident. It was almost like the perfect prom, only with aging mobsters and casino patrons, but I'd take it. All that was missing was a gaudy wrist corsage and a bad cover band.

"You look pretty sharp too," I told him.

He offered me an arm. "Are you ready to mingle?"

I gulped back a lump in my throat and swiped on my happy face. "Sure, lead on."

We trailed through seemingly endless groups of people. I shook hands, gave air kisses, and navigated several jovial comments about how our slots weren't nearly as loose as the ones in Atlantic City.

"Ms. King," I heard someone call my name. I turned to find James Sicianni chatting with a man I recognized as the *Battle Buffet* director.

Sicianni abandoned the director and quickly strode toward me. His face was all charming smiles and shining teeth as he pulled both of my hands into his. "Ms. King, you look absolutely ravishing," he gushed, kissing the back of my hand, his unsettling hooded gaze never leaving mine.

Instinctively I glanced around for Rafe, but he was busy greeting a large guy in an Armani suit and at least half a dozen carats in diamonds on his chubby fingers.

Sicianni finished fondling my hands, and he released them, but he quickly draped a firm arm around my shoulder instead. It was like he could sense I was ready to bolt. "I believe I still owe you a drink."

Spying a woman with a drink tray, I raised my hand, getting her attention. I grabbed two flutes of champagne, handing him one. "Please, allow me."

A knowing smile twisted across his face. "This doesn't count, you minx." He punctuated his statement with a wink.

I laughed nervously and took a generous gulp from my champagne. I quickly glanced around for a polite out.

And locked gazes with an impeccably dressed Agent Ryder.

Crap.

I forced a smile as he made his way toward us.

"Mr. Sicianni." Ryder nodded toward the man attached to my side. "Would you mind terribly if I borrowed Ms. King for a few moments?"

If I wasn't afraid he was about to arrest me for aiding and abetting the entire criminal organization, I could have kissed agent Ryder.

Sicianni sent a wary eye toward Ryder, slowly lifting his arm from my shoulder. "Of course. I'm always cooperative with the FBI."

I gulped, hoping I wasn't reading deeper meaning into that statement.

If Ryder read any meaning into it, he didn't let it show. Instead, he offered me his arm. "Can we find a quiet corner to chat?"

I pointed to the one farthest from the open bar, and we wove our way through the tightly packed mob. Literally.

Finally able to talk without yelling, he asked, "When were you planning to tell me that you were playing hostess to the entirety of the West Coast *family men*?"

"Whatever do you mean?" I forced a surprised look to my face, clutching the neckline of my dress.

He crossed his arms over his broad chest, giving me a hard stare. "Tess…" he warned.

"They happen to be foodies," I protested. Hey, if that was the story they were going with, I was going with it too.

"Foodies?" Agent Ryder repeated.

I nodded, crossing my arms over my own chest. "That's right. Restaurateurs, food critics, bloggers," I said, repeating what Rafe had told me.

"Really?" Ryder said, the same challenging tone in his voice. He pointed to a guy in a dark suit near a potted palm, who was wearing a pair of leather gloves. "So, exactly what food blog does Eight Finger Eddie write for?"

I gulped. "Uh…"

"And, I'm assuming Ned the Knee-Capper," he said, gesturing toward the guy with the impressive scar, "reviews for *Better Homes & Gardens*?"

I closed my eyes and thought a really dirty word.

"But you know what, Tess? You're spot on about 'Judge and Jury' Jonathan. He and his *lovely* wife, Badass Becca, are restaurateurs. They own a chain of pasta shops." He paused. "They also own a racetrack, a betting parlor, and a construction company known to specialize in cement shoes."

I threw my hands up. "Okay, I get it. I'm hosting my big, fat, Italian Mafia dinner."

Ryder grinned, clearly reveling in his little victory.

"Look, I had no idea they were coming, okay?" I whispered, lest I garnered unwanted attention from Badass Becca. "They just sorta showed up. I swear I thought they were foodies."

He raised one eyebrow at me.

"Well, up until recently," I amended.

"And why didn't you call me when you realized they weren't?"

"What was I going to do?" I whispered. "Call the whole show off?"

Ryder's smile faltered. "Tessie, these are not the kind of guys you want in your casino." Or girls," he said, turning toward Becca. "Trust me—you don't want to piss that woman off. Even her own husband doesn't trust her. Rumor has it he sleeps with a gun in each hand." He pointed to another group of people and started again. "And don't get me started on Stubby the Snuffer, Max the Impaler, Vicious Vito…"

I grabbed his finger and pushed his hand down, stepping between him and, evidently, pretty much every known Mafia figurehead. "Fine. So what do we do now?"

"We? *We* don't do anything. *I* make sure we have FBI surveillance on the casino twenty-four seven until your friends leave, and you try to stay out of trouble."

Trust me. I had no problems with that. "Speaking of staying out of trouble…" I started, my eyes resting on Britton across the room. "Did you find out whose number LeAnna was calling?"

Ryder shook his head. "It was a burner phone."

I felt my shoulders slump in defeat.

"Not uncommon for a guy seeing a married woman. But don't worry," he reassured me. "We'll find her."

I hoped so. I only prayed she wasn't wearing cement shoes when they did. I looked around the room. Could one of these men—or women, I amended, my eyes resting on Becca—have killed Mr. Taylor and abducted LeAnna? I felt panic starting to set in as I put a hand to my throat, feeling my erratic pulse. I had real-life mobsters packed into what I *had* considered a large space, but it seemed to shrink right in front of me.

I fanned my face, feeling light headed all of a sudden.

"Let's go get some air. I think Mr. Lorenzo has this covered." He nodded in Rafe's direction, where I could see him chatting up another expensively dressed couple.

"I'm supposed to help host tonight." I inhaled a deep breath and let it out slowly, but it did little to help my panic.

"Come on," Ryder said, grabbing my hand and pulling me toward the door. "Just for a few minutes. I'll take you for a drive."

I glanced over my shoulder. Ryder was right. The staff did look like they had everything under control, and Rafe did look like he had the hosting duties down better than I could muster at the moment. "Okay," I conceded. "But just a short one."

Five minutes later we were standing in the circular drive as Ryder handed the valet his ticket and a twenty-dollar bill. The cold night air brushed gooseflesh along my bare arms. I rubbed my hands over them in an attempt to stave it off.

"Maybe we should wait inside," I said.

Without hesitation, Ryder slipped out of his suit coat and draped it over my shoulders. I pulled it tightly around me. The intoxicating smell of his cologne enveloped me as well, quelling my anxiety instantly.

The valet pulled up in a newer sleek, black Chevy Camaro. As Ryder opened the passenger door for me, I offered him a nod of approval as I got in. Within seconds he flew around to his side, and we were off.

As he pulled into traffic, he offered, "I figured we could drive out by the lake." He leaned forward, looking up at the vivid moon in the night sky. "There's a full moon tonight. Who knows—we may even have a Tahoe Tessie sighting."

I shot him a look. "Ha-ha. I've never heard that one before." Thanks to my father's wry sense of humor and never-ending quest for a great publicity stunt, he had named me after the legendary Tahoe Tessie monster that was rumored to live under Cave Rock on the Nevada side of the lake. Fashioned after her Scottish Loch Ness cousin, Tahoe Tessie had been sighted by many drunken fisherman over the years, though, shockingly, none had actually been able to snap conclusive photographic evidence of the monster.

Ryder's eyes whipped toward me, twinkling with amusement. "Sorry, I couldn't resist."

"Yeah, well, apparently my father couldn't resist a good publicity stunt."

"Wait, are you saying that he actually named you after the monster?"

I nodded.

"Wow. I thought it was just a cruel coincidence. I'm so sorry," he said, but I noticed his eyes were still twinkling and his mouth had snaked up into a grin almost the size of his face.

I turned in my seat to study his profile. "Okay, you can either stop laughing at the unfortunate accident of my parents' sense of humor, or you can even out the playing field by telling me something personal about yourself. Preferably incredibly embarrassing."

He smoothed his hands over the steering wheel several times, a smirk tugging at his mouth. "It's going to be difficult to top that."

I swatted at his arm playfully. "Try."

"Okay, but you have to promise not to laugh."

I traced an *X* over my heart. "Promise."

"So, this car…" He slid a hand over the dashboard. "The only cars I've ever owned were black Firebirds. When they stopped making them, I had to go with this Camaro since it was the closest thing out there."

"Why would I laugh at that? You know what you like and don't settle for less." I had to admit, it was a nice car. I'd been tempted to ask him to let me drive it when the valet had pulled it around.

"Well, yeah, there's that too."

He watched the road in deep thought, and I waited patiently for the rest of his story. "Come on—you owe me." Well, sort of patiently.

"Fine," he muttered within an overly dramatic sigh. "Do you remember the show *Knight Rider*?"

I nodded slightly. "Vaguely." I snapped my fingers. "KITT! That car was a Firebird."

He looked at me for a second with a sheepish grin. "I used to watch the show with my dad. He had me convinced that his first name was Knight."

I laughed. "You thought your dad was Knight Rider?"

"I was five, okay?" he protested, but he was laughing now, too. "Anyway, when I hit kindergarten, the other kids set me straight about him. Next came the truth about the Easter Bunny, Tooth Fairy, and Santa. I had a heyday at the mall that year. I climbed up on Santa's holly-jolly lap and called him a fat lying bastard. Totally worth getting grounded."

Laughter bubbled from me, infecting him to join along. I was still giggling when he pulled off the road.

"You promised not to laugh," he said with a wink as he put the car in park.

"It was the Santa comment, and you know it." I glanced away from him in a pretend pout, but the glittering lake took my breath away. The moon illuminated the mountains, accentuating the peaks and making the valleys look dark and foreboding. The reflection on the water looked like a huge, rippling diamond. "Wow, that's beautiful," I whispered as though I could scare it away.

"Yeah, beautiful," he repeated.

I turned to share a look of wonder with him, but he wasn't looking out the window. He was staring at me. His heavy-lidded gaze locked with mine, sending a shockwave of pleasure down my spine.

He reached out, drawing his thumbs across my chin, his fingers sliding along my jaw. He pulled me toward him. His lips met mine in a soft, sweet kiss, his hands framing my face. I clung to his elbows, leaning across the center console, melting against as much of him as I could. Need blended into the mix, deepening the bond. His hands skimmed down my neck, pushing the coat from my shoulders. His lips followed the same path, in a trail of soft caresses, culminating at the nape of my neck, sending a jolt of heat through my body. One of his hands threaded into my hair, and the other trailed lightly down my spine. My head fell back into his hand, and I heard myself moan. I was floating somewhere inside myself, caught up in the feel of his lips, his fingers, the sound of his breathing, the smell of his cologne...

...the feel of his phone vibrating in the pocket of his coat against my leg.

Talk about a mood killer.

I pulled back from him reluctantly, heaving a huge sigh of regret when I saw the look of confused disappointment on his handsome face. I wiped the secondhand gloss from his lips with one hand and extended the buzzing killjoy with my other.

He sighed and flopped back against his seat, swiping on his phone then huffing, "Ryder."

I tried to busy myself by looking out the window at the scenery again. The lake just didn't hold the same magic without his attention. I tried not to eavesdrop, but the space was a little confined for me not to hear at least his side.

"Where?" he asked, casting a glance my way. He paused. "Any ID?"

I felt the shift in him from lover boy to federal agent in seconds flat, and it was a bit unnerving. But his next words sliced clear to my bones.

"Do you know how long she's been dead?"

CHAPTER SEVENTEEN

I stood in the circular drive of the Royal Palace minutes later and watched Ryder's car disappear into traffic. The night air was just as cold as earlier, if not colder, but I felt nothing. I was numb. Even though the agent who'd phoned Ryder hadn't been able to give a positive ID on the body that had been found in a Dumpster just the other side of the Y where Highway 50 met 89, I had a sinking feeling I knew who it belonged to.

LeAnna.

Ryder hadn't given me any details. He told me not to jump to any conclusions, but his emotionless fed face had told me he already was. He promised to call me as soon as he knew something for sure. Though I had no idea how I was going to face Britton in the meantime.

I tried to regain my composure somewhat before I wound my way through the busy lobby and casino area, hoping to find Tate at the front desk. Instead, it was Marcy training with another woman. For a moment, the happiness on her face as she listened intently to her trainer made me forget about dead bodies and missing people.

But only for that short moment.

I chose not to disturb them. Instead, I knew I had to bite the bullet and tell Britton the news. I would've wanted her to do the same for me. I rationalized that it would be best to ease her into it this way and spare her the shock when they identified the body. I straightened my spine, powdered my nose, reapplied my lip gloss, and forced myself down the long hallway to the VIP dinner.

The crowd was now gathered in the second two ballrooms, seated around large tables. Plates of creamy pasta, steamed mussels, herbed chicken, and roasted duck filled the tables as loud conversation filled the room. The air was thick with enticing aromas that spoke to Dubois's culinary talents. But even though I'd yet to eat, my stomach roiled at the thought of food as I scanned the room for Britton's face. But it was Rafe I saw first.

He quickly excused himself from the table, where he'd been sitting between Sicianni and a leggy blonde who'd spent one too many hours in a tanning bed.

"Tess, where have you been? The dinner is a total success. I think we'll get some majorly good reviews from these people."

"Uh-huh." While I had heard his words, they didn't really register. I was still scanning the crowd for Britton, mulling over what I was going to say to her.

Rafe grabbed my arm. "Are you okay? Did you hear a word I said?"

I looked up at him, my brain still in too much of a shock-induced fog to force anything but what I felt to my face. I nodded. "That's great."

"Where did you disappear to?" He stepped back, assessing me.

"I needed air. I, uh, went for a drive." I paused. "Do you know where Britton is?"

He shook his head. "Why? What's going on?"

"Agent Ryder said they found a woman's body tonight. He's checking into it." I looked away from him, fidgeting with my handbag, fighting back unexpected tears.

"A body? Who?"

"They don't know for sure yet." I took deep breaths to keep back the tears. "But I'm afraid it might be LeAnna."

"Oh, no," he breathed. He closed the gap quickly, brushing a reassuring hand on my shoulder, tucking me against him.

"Oh, yes," I blubbered, the floodgates opening, pouring down my cheeks as I briefly rested my forehead against his chest. I took a moment to get myself under control before backing away. I didn't completely understand my breakdown. It was not like there'd been any love lost between LeAnna and me.

But I knew how Britton was going to feel. I swiped at my face, undoubtedly smearing my makeup more so than drying my eyes. "Have you seen Britton? I need to warn her. It needs to come from me."

He brushed my hair to the side then pressed his lips lightly on my forehead. "I don't know. I haven't seen her since the cocktail party. My guess is she went back up to the penthouse."

I nodded. "Can you finish up here so I can go talk to her?"

He pulled me in for a hug. "Sure thing."

"I'll let you know if I hear anything from Ryder," I said, watching him flinch just the slightest bit at the mention of Ryder's name. I hoped that he couldn't read the sudden moment of guilt on my face as I flashed back to kissing Ryder in a parked car like a teenager.

"Go. It's fine," he told me.

I offered him a halfhearted smile before I left. On my way through the lobby and up the elevator, I went over a hundred different ways to tell her the news. None of them softened any kind of blow. I briefly contemplated a text, but that just felt like the cowardly way. The elevator dinged, opening on the penthouse floor. I just stood there, staring at the double doors. It wasn't until the elevator dinged again and started closing that I got out. I swiped my key, doing some yoga breathing in an effort to calm myself.

Opening the door, I called out, "Britton?" Jack quickly greeted me with his usual ankle circles, but other than a random meow and his loud purr, the place was quiet. I walked down the hall toward the master bedroom.

"Britton?" I knocked, and the door creaked open from the force. The room was dark except for the alarm clock on the nightstand. It was the same one my father had used when I was growing up. The neon-blue numbers had a slightly calming effect, but the empty apartment did exactly the opposite.

I pulled out my phone and texted Britton as I wandered back toward my room. I turned on the lamp next to my bed and sat down to wait for a reply. Britton always got right back to me. There was even a middle-of-the-night instance recently when I'd needed toilet paper and texted her. She hadn't been happy, but she'd responded.

I was still staring down at my dark screen ten minutes later. Panic squeezed my heart, making it hard to breathe. Dialing her number, I paced the floor. It never rang, instead going straight to her bubbly voice to leave a message.

I felt physically sick. I swallowed back the bile that threatened to escape.

I sent a text to Tate, asking if he'd seen Britton, clinging desperately to a crazy notion that my phone was on the fritz. But true to form, he texted right back saying the last he'd seen her she was showing off the *Battle Buffet* set to a VIP about an hour ago.

I tore out of the penthouse, willed the elevator to move faster, and jogged across the lobby then down the hall to the soundstage. I wasn't sure why, but I had a sense of foreboding deep in the pit of my stomach. I burst through the door to find the huge set dark except for a few safety lights glowing in the far corners. I was about to turn and leave when I spotted something out of the corner of my eye.

Remnants of a shattered mixing bowl. Pieces of glass were speckled across the floor, leading to Chef Dubois's side of the kitchen.

I moved closer, and as my eyes adjusted to the dark, I realized that his normally pristine area was trashed. Utensils were strewn across the counters and filled the sink. A thin layer of flour coated the cookbooks he'd used as props, a lone handprint smacked across the cover of one.

My knees wobbled as I turned several complete circles, scanning for anything that might make sense out of the mess.

Then I heard someone else moving in the soundstage.

I froze, listening to steps coming from the dark area where the cameras were housed.

"Britton?" I blinked several times into the shadows, but I couldn't make out who it was for sure. But who else would be down here? "Britton, is that you?" I asked hopefully.

Only I didn't get to hear an answer. I felt something heavy smack into my head at the base of my neck. Fireworks exploded before my eyes, matching the pain that shot through my body.

Then everything went black.

CHAPTER EIGHTEEN

The sound of moaning woke me, but the queasy feeling in my gut and the thumping in my head kept my eyes clamped shut. I felt like anything I'd eaten in the past decade was ready to make a hasty exit.

Swallowing hard, I forced one of my eyes open a slit. I was only able to make out shapes and outlines in the dim lighting, most of which still didn't make much sense. Was I still on the *Battle Buffet* soundstage? I opened both eyes and squinted in an effort to pull anything into focus. Only a sliver of moonlight illuminated my surroundings. There was definitely a bed. I tried to raise my head, but the room seemed to sway rhythmically. I'd either been hit harder than I thought, or I wasn't on land.

Or possibly both.

The moaning continued. As I tried to clear the fog from my head, I realized it was coming from the direction of the bed. I tried to speak, but it came out as a moan on my part as well when I realized my mouth was taped shut. The other sounds elevated to urgent whimpers.

I pushed past the hammering in my brain, attempting to pull myself into a sitting position. I fought against tape binding my wrists behind my back and at my ankles. Panic filled my gut, exploding through my entire body, as claustrophobia and my fight-or-flight instincts reared their ugly heads. I forced myself into yoga breathing, concentrating on my inner peace rather than the outside situation I had no control over. In that frame of mind, I pushed my torso into the fish pose, arching my back high, and then rolling onto my side. From there I was able to work into a handless version of a downward-facing dog, using my head instead of my hands and pushing my tush into the air. My forehead burned as I dragged it across the carpet to pull my knees under me. I shook off my high heels then sprang to my feet, all the while being serenaded with grunts and whimpers of encouragement from the bedridden cheering section.

I hopped once in that direction, nearly toppling back to the floor with the swaying of the floor and my throbbing head. I angled my feet out for more of a stance and hopped again, getting me close enough to the bed to make out two distinctive forms. One in a long white dress.

Britton!

I'd never been so glad to see anyone in my life. That is until I realized that meant we'd both been abducted and tied up by the same person.

I squinted through the darkness at the second figure, making out a formfitting, sequined microdress.

"Mee-maamaa!" I mumbled against the tape. Which of course didn't come out right, but I realized I was looking at LeAnna! She wasn't dead after all. I could have hugged the hussy if my hands weren't taped behind my back.

As my eyes adjusted more to the poor lighting, I could see that each woman's hands were duct taped to opposite ends of a scrolling, wrought iron headboard. Britton was closest to me, wiggling her hands and casting her glance back and forth between my feet and the nightstand next to her.

It took me a minute to figure out what her nodding and bobbing meant, but I finally honed into her thinking. She wanted me to get up on the bed so her hands could reach mine. I nodded at her as I bunny-hopped next to the ridiculously high piece of furniture. It was raised on a large frame so that the top was above my waist. I was going to have to channel my inner Michael Jordan to jump that high.

I moved backward slowly, sizing up the height. I then bounced as hard as I could, higher and higher until I reached it, slamming my butt against the nightstand in the process. We all three watched in horror as the brass lamp atop it tottered from side to side, finally crashing to the floor. Silence fell over us, and we froze, listening for anyone who might have heard the ruckus and would come to investigate. I heard nothing but lapping water and the soft creaking of waves against the side of a boat.

A boat? Where were we?

I released a huge sigh through my nose, matching the other two relieved glances.

I made another go at the bed. Several other failed attempts left my calves burning and me mentally promising I'd spend more time at the gym with Britton. On the fifth try, I finally sailed through the air, my aching hindquarters landing squarely just on the edge of the bedspread. I flailed about, much like a stranded mermaid, to stay on the bed as much as a person could without the use of her arms and legs. I finally came to rest with one cheek hanging off the side.

But I was on.

I heard all three of us heave a collective nose-sigh this time.

I cheek-crawled across the surface until I was next to Britton. She wiggled her fingers, which were, of course, still about a foot away from my bound hands. I snorted in frustration, knowing what had to be done. I worked my way into another downward-facing dog with my forehead again. Once on my knees, I felt like I'd just climbed Mount Everest. I pulled my ego into check and scooted back against her hands. After an accidental butt fondle and a few nail gouges to my back, she found the edge of the tape. It took a few minutes of careful peeling and prodding, but she managed to free my hands.

I reveled in the ability to move them for a brief moment before tearing the tape from my lips. I almost cried out in pain but forced my lips shut. Instead I settled for a quite impressive string of curse words under my breath. After freeing my ankles, I turned my attention to Britton.

I locked gazes with her as I loosened a corner of the tape over her mouth. "Ready?" I whispered.

She nodded lightly, her rounded eyes pleading for either mercy or to get on with it already. I tore the tape from her lips, and she let out a high-pitched squeal. I clamped one hand over her mouth while using my other to free her wrists.

While I worked on her ankles, I whispered, "I just saved you twenty bucks on a lip wax. You're welcome." I hoped my lightheartedness came across in my words.

"Where are we?" Britton asked, her eyes blinking back tears of fear.

I blinked, my eyes adjusting to the darkness just enough to make out that we were in some sort of small bedroom. A cabin? "I think we're on a boat." I looked out of the small window, expecting to see a dock. But all I saw was dark, black water. I turned to Britton. "You don't know how you got here?"

She shook her head. "One of the VIPs said he wanted to see the soundstage, so I was going to take him on a tour. But as soon as we got there, someone attacked me." The tears spilled down her cheeks. "I tried to fight back—you know, I have been taking cardio kickboxing lately—but I only got in one good kick before he hit me over the head with a mixing bowl." Her hand went to the side of her head, where I could just make out a knot forming.

"Just a wild guess, but that VIP wouldn't happen to be a Hank Gambia, would it?"

She blinked at me. "Yes. How did you know?"

I knew the Hammerhead was behind all of this! When I got my hands on that guy...

LeAnna snorted and moaned loudly, garnering our attention.

Britton propped herself against the pillows right next to LeAnna. She crossed her arms over her chest, the frown on her face looking almost clown-like with the reddened area around her lips. "Before we remove your tape," she whispered to LeAnna, "I want you to know how hard we worked to figure out what happened to you. Tessie and I totally worried our asses off. I also want you to know that I'm like in absolutely no mood for any more lies. Whatever comes out of your mouth had better be the God's honest truth. Do you understand?"

I looked over at LeAnna as she nodded slowly, her downcast gaze filled with shame. With my own eyes adjusting to the lighting, I was able to see her more clearly. Her hair lay in greasy ringlets. What was left of her eye makeup was smeared across her eyes or trailed into long streaks, more resembling war paint than beauty enhancement. Her tiny excuse for a dress was torn, stained, and wrinkled beyond any reparation. This would make for the most epic walk of shame ever known to womankind. Where were the reporters when you really needed them?

I yanked the tape off of her mouth, trying not to enjoy the yelp of pain it provoked. At least not too much. Britton quickly freed LeAnna's hands while I worked on her ankles.

Tears spilled down LeAnna's face, bringing with them gasping sobs. "We have to get out of here. He's going to kill me!" she cried.

Britton slapped a hand over her mouth, shushing her. "Who?"

LeAnna pushed her hand away and continued in a more hushed tone. "This whole thing is about the baby." She rubbed a few fingers over her belly. "But there never was one," she bawled, emitting a few more gut-wrenching cries.

Britton gasped. "Are you saying you're not pregnant?"

LeAnna shook her head. "No. I just wanted Gerald to get rid of the effing prenup. I deserve a cut of his money, damn it!"

I shushed her, glancing over my shoulder at the door to the cabin. I wasn't sure how long we'd been there or how nearby whoever had tied us up was. Or, more importantly, when he'd come back.

"You lied to me!" Britton said, clearly hurt.

"I'm telling you I worked hard for that money!" LeAnna countered.

Ew. I so did not want to know how.

"So you lied to your husband too," I said.

She nodded. "But, you see, I had to! I needed the money to leave him. To be with the man I love."

"Who is?" I asked.

But LeAnna ignored me, gaining momentum on her way to hysteria. "But I never expected he'd react this way to the thought of a baby. I thought he'd be happy, you know? But as soon as *he* found out about it, he completely flipped. Like, freaked out!"

"Then he picked you up from the Midnight club and has had you tied up here," I finished for her.

She blinked at me. "How did you know about the club?"

"Never mind that." I glanced at the door again. "Look, we need to get out of here."

LeAnna nodded. "I thought I could talk some sense into him. But he is freaking out. If he'd just listen to me about the baby being fake, maybe we could work this whole thing out, and he'd whisk me away to Belize just like he promised he would."

As our surroundings became more and more clear, I could make out details of the room, and I realized we weren't just in a boat...we were on a yacht. A yacht where, if I wasn't mistaken, an authentic Gustav Klimt was hanging on the wall. I sucked in a breath as I made out the image of a dark-haired woman surrounded by a mosaic of orange and yellow designs painted in oil on canvas. It had to be Jerry's. Apparently there had been some serious parking in Daddy's garage after all.

Britton must have noticed too, as she said, "Wait, are we on Jerry's yacht? Ohmigod, you're telling me that you're in love with your stepson? Hashtag gross, LeAnna!"

LeAnna gave Britton a funny look. "What? No. God, I wouldn't give a loser like Jerry the time of day."

"Well then, who are we talking about?" I asked, totally confused now.

From the inky darkness of the staircase, a man replied, "She's talking about me."

CHAPTER NINETEEN

———

I squinted to make out the figure at the bottom of the stairs. His face was in shadows, but he was at least a head too short to be Jerry. And the voice was wrong. Too high.

He took a step toward us, and I felt my breath catch in my throat as I spied a distinct pair of stark white, *never actually seen a sports arena* sneakers. Chef Dubois!

LeAnna scrambled into a kneeling position on the bed, hand waving frantically in front of her. "Please, don't kill me, Bastien. I love you."

I kinda doubted that, but I could believe that LeAnna loved his money and the fame that would have gone along with being Mrs. Chef Dubois.

Dubois slowly stepped into the room, his eyes going from me to Britton to LeAnna, all of whom he clearly expected to be tied up when he arrived. From the frown on his face, I could tell he wasn't pleased. But my attention was riveted to the long, thin chef's knife he held in his hands. If he'd looked menacing on his kitchen set with a meat cleaver, he looked downright deadly now.

"Just listen to me, Bastien," LeAnna said. "The baby isn't real. Honestly, I made it all up to trick Gerald." She turned her pleading look on Britton and me. "Tell him!"

I nodded. "It's true. She's a total liar. No baby."

Britton nodded emphatically beside me.

Dubois scoffed. "I'm not going to kill you because of du bebe," he said through his heavy accent.

I breathed a sigh of relief.

LeAnna released one too. "I knew you loved me. I'll make you so happy." She crawled seductively toward the end of the bed, her mannerisms the only thing even remotely sexy in her bedraggled state.

But Dubois held the knife out in front of him menacingly to hold her back. "Non, I kill you because you ruin all of my plans!"

She flopped onto her belly. "What?"

Britton whimpered beside me, clutching my arm.

My eyes darted from the long blade to the small door behind him. It was possible that with his attention on LeAnna, I could make a run for the doorway before he could react. But there was no way I could get both Britton and myself out of there. And there was no way I was leaving her. Instead, I stalled for time.

"What plans?" I asked.

Dubois spun his attention toward me, and I think I did a whimper of my own at the crazed look in his eyes. "And *you!*"

I gulped. "Me?"

"So nosey. You and your bimbo friend here always sticking noses where they no belong. Why couldn't you mind your own business, eh?"

"Sorry?" I said, though it came out as a wavering question.

The corner of his mouth hitched upward. "Oh, you will be."

Britton sucked in a breath beside me.

I cleared my throat, trying to be brave for the both of us. "You don't have to do this," I reasoned. "You haven't harmed anyone yet. You can let us go, and everything will be fine."

"Ha!" he cackled. "You really are a dumb blonde, aren't you?"

I blinked at him, his meaning slowly sinking in. "Wait, you *have* harmed someone already, haven't you?"

Dubois didn't answer but instead smiled widely at me as he twisted his knife back and forth in his hand.

"You killed Gerald Taylor," I whispered.

LeAnna sucked in a breath. "What? No!"

"Oh, yes," he hissed, turning his attention back to her. "That stupid old man wasn't going to ruin everything."

"How?" I asked, stalling again as I scanned the room for anything that we could possibly use as a weapon against the deranged Frenchman. Pillows, a cushion on a window seat, a pile of blankets on the floor. I cursed the plush, cozy room.

"How?" he repeated. Then he scoffed again. "As if it was hard. Non." He shook his head. "The old man—so predictable. Always drink too much. So I put on a disguise I take from the local—how you say?—sporting good store, and I wait. Then..." He made a stabbing motion with the knife and shrugged his shoulders. "Simple, non?"

I felt my stomach clench. The man didn't just play a hotheaded chef on TV. He really was nuts. The way he talked about stabbing Gerald as if he were slicing a pork chop made me physically ill. I felt Britton shiver beside me as well.

"But why use LeAnna's cuticle scissors?" I asked.

That creepy grin broke out across his face again. "Why not? Kill two birds with the same stone, as you say."

"Bastien?" LeAnna cried, tears filling her eyes. "How could you?"

"How?" he asked. He laughed again then held his free hand up to the light, attempting to inspect his nails. "The camera, it films my hands." He waggled his fingers. "All de times, it zooms on these amazing creators." He fluttered them in our faces as if to demonstrate the greatness contained within them then continued, "I had just finished having the sexy with LeAnna in her boudoir back home in Napa."

I gagged a little at the thought.

"My cuticles were incontrollable, so I borrow the scissors from my *mon chérie*, LeAnna." He snapped his fingers. "Voila! The perfect murder weapon, complete with her prints."

LeAnna sobbed into her hands. "You told me you loved me," LeAnna drew out in an annoyingly long whine. "How can you throw months of mind-blowing sex out the window?"

I was willing to bet it was more along the lines of *mind-numbing*. I scooted a little closer to Britton as Dubois's attention focused on LeAnna.

"Ah, the fantasies I had..." The corners of his lips curled into a smile.

"Really?" LeAnna asked hopefully.

"Fantasies of shutting zat big mouth of yours for good!" He flapped his hand like a blabbing mouth, his lips mocking along. "Blah, blah, blah. You cannot even shush during *le sexe*."

If I didn't fear dying at his hand, I'd shake it. I stifled a derisive snort with a cough.

"What?" LeAnna gasped. She wilted into a sitting position. "Are…are you saying you never loved me?"

Dubois threw his head back and laughed maniacally enough to audition as a cartoon villain. "You are a stupid woman, no?"

Yes, I almost blurted.

He took a step forward and wound one of her greasy locks around his finger for a moment then wiped that hand on the comforter. "You were a means to the end. A way to keep everyone happy and keeping their noses out of my family's business."

"Your family…" I said, the puzzle pieces starting to fall into place. "You mean, the Gambia family?"

Dubois swung his attention—and the tip of his knife!— my direction. "See, you never learn. You asking the questions again!"

I swallowed hard. "Sorry," I squeaked out.

"I don't get it. All you did was buy wine," LeAnna said, a crease of confusion trying to push through her Botoxed forehead.

"*Oui*. Lots of wine. The *grande* amount of wine ordered *was blanchiment d'argent*." He cast a gaze between Britton, LeAnna, and me. "How you say 'washing of the monies'?"

"Money laundering," Britton breathed beside me.

"And Mr. Taylor was involved," I mused out.

He raised one perfectly waxed eyebrow at me. "Involved? It was his idea!"

"Liar!" LeAnna cried from the pillows, where she'd retreated again. "I know my Gerald had nothing to do with it. He would have told me. He told me everything!"

"Not everything," I couldn't help mumbling.

LeAnna turned on me. "What are you talking about?"

"Your scheme never would have worked, LeAnna," I told her, taking just an eensy-weensy bit of pleasure in it.

"Gerald had just found out from his doctor that he couldn't have any more children. He was sterile."

"What?" Anger and confusion twisted her already distorted appearance.

Dubois laughed out loud. "No wonder that when *this one* started talking about babies," he said, waving the knife blade in LeAnna's direction, "Monsieur Taylor started asking questions about me."

"Too many of them," I surmised. "So you killed him."

He slowly took a step toward me, his features becoming clearer in the filtered moonlight. I briefly contemplated retreating, but there was precious little space for moving in the small cabin. His eyes narrowed on me, his nose nearly touching mine. "*Oui*," he shouted, his breath reeking of stale cigarettes and booze. He raised the knife in the air then slashed downward, imbedding it in the mattress between Britton and me. "*Il meurt!*"

It didn't take a French scholar to figure out what he said with his animated motion. Panic ripped through me, much like the knife had the bed, with the realization of what his confession meant.

He wasn't planning to let any of us leave the boat alive.

I sucked in shallow breaths as I watched Dubois slowly pull the blade from the mattress and advance on me. I bit my lip, eyes frantically searching for anything I could use to fend off his attack.

His eyes were wide, pupils dilated as if on some sort of drug-induced high. His usually coiffed hair stood out in tufts on the side, his nostrils flaring as he breathed hard.

Then I heard it. The sound of a motor in the distance. I felt a small lift of hope in my chest. Maybe someone was coming to save us!

Dubois must have heard it too, as he paused, cocking his head to the side. Then a slow smile snaked across his features. "I hear a *moteur* boat approaching. *Bien.*"

I felt that hope die a quick death. Dubois was expecting someone.

"Sadly, this is the end of our conversation. *Mes amis* will be escorting you elsewhere to clean up this mess." He waved a dismissive hand toward us as though we were merely fat to be trimmed off his fine steak.

I slid toward the edge of the bed. God only knew how many men were on that boat. While the crazy guy with a knife was bad, more crazy mobsters with guns would be worse. I glanced toward the floor, and in my peripheral vision I spied the lamp I'd knocked over earlier. I wasn't sure it was exactly a match for a knife, but it was the best shot I had.

I steeled my spine, ready to dive for it if he even flinched.

"Are you too good to bloody your own hands?" I taunted, hoping to catch him off guard.

"You speak grand for a petit one." He shifted his weight, his fingers clenching around his weapon. He took one step toward me...

And I dove for the lamp.

I grabbed it in both hands, lifting the heavy brass thing above my head just in time to meet his blade with a resounding clang. When he drew back to attack again, I swung toward him, the lamp catching his shins with a resounding crack.

He grunted, doubling over.

Britton took the opportunity to spring into action, grabbing one of her heels and clubbing at his temple. Dubois crumpled to his knees.

LeAnna reached off the bed, rapidly girly-slapping at his shoulder repeatedly with both hands. But with one strong sweep, he backhanded her right off of the bed like a rag doll.

Britton screeched as he rose up from the floor. He grabbed her by the hair and tossed her across the room, where her head the edge of the bed with a loud thud

"Britt!" I yelled, taking a step toward her.

One that was cut short as the tip of the sharp blade poked at my throat.

"Watch as I bloody more than my hands," Dubois seethed.

I froze, feeling hot tears blur my vision. I vaguely saw Britton's unconscious form and heard LeAnna's sobbing, though it suddenly felt like they were very far away. Like everything was far away or under water—my sight blurring, my ears ringing. Almost like every sense I had was focused on the tip of the knife poking harder and harder into my throat, threatening to spill the blood pounding in my ears all over Jerry Taylor's beautiful yacht. My head swam with random images—my father's grave, my soon-to-be orphaned cat. Ryder. Rafe. Tate's voice telling me how fabulous I am. My own high-pitched cry as I felt the blade of the knife pierce my skin.

Then I heard a voice loud and clear from the doorway, breaking through the fog.

"Are you feeling lucky, punk?" it asked in a deep baritone. "Well, are ya?!"

I blinked, looking toward the sound, but I could only make out a shadowy figure.

"Who are you?" Dubois squinted toward the doorway.

LeAnna must have noticed, as I did, that Dubois's attention was firmly on the figure now...and not on her. She slowly rose to her feet, standing tall behind Dubois like an unkempt phoenix rising from the ashes. Anger consumed her face—jaw set, nostrils flaring, tight fists clenching over and over at her sides. If she'd been scary as a seductive woman, she was downright frightening as a woman scorned. She scanned the room, her eyes landing on the Gustav Klimt painting, an evil smile curling her lips. She quickly grabbed it from the wall and reared it back. I waffled between my own safety and the painting's. The art curator in me wanted to scream out for her to put it back. Common sense made sure I kept my mouth shut. Thankfully, for the Klimt anyway, she kept the painting flat as she flung it at Dubois, catching the side of his head with the frame.

Unfortunately, with her spindly arms, the blow wasn't enough to stun him for long. It was just enough to piss him off. He dropped the knife from my throat and turned all of his aggression on her, raising his knife and lunging.

LeAnna screamed, I screamed, and I could have sworn that even the deep baritone in the doorway screamed as a shot rang out, ripping through Dubois's shoulder, slumping him to the floor as though he'd lost all bone structure.

For a moment, the only sound I heard was my own breathing coming out in short, hard gasps. Then I looked up as footsteps made their way from the doorway into the room.

Tate's bleached-blond hair glistened in the pale moonlight as he held a tiny pink smoking gun straight-armed in front of him.

CHAPTER TWENTY

A second later Maverick came in behind Tate, his own gun drawn—which was distinctly bigger than Tate's and decidedly not pink. His eyes bounced between Tate's gun, Britton on the floor, and Dubois's motionless body gushing blood. He quickly flipped Dubois over, checking for a pulse. "He's alive!" he shouted, a look of relief on his face, before he ran to Britt's side.

I was on the fence on how I felt about that, but mostly I felt numb. Though, it was a pretty safe bet prison food was going to be quite a shock to Dubois's delicate palate and a form of torture in and of itself.

The adrenaline had saturated every cell of my body, and my head was pounding with my erratic pulse. I felt tears streaming into my hair as I sat heavily on the floor, the lamp still clenched in my hands. I heard myself crying, as though I was observing. I heard LeAnna wail about the blood, and Britton moaning as she came to.

Trembling, I tried to stand, but gravity kept pulling me down. I didn't have the strength left to fight. The flurry of movement around me turned into a humming white noise as I pondered our fate if Tate and his tiny pink pistol hadn't come to our rescue. I changed my mind. I loved that thing.

The tears turned into sobs. I clamped my eyes closed, concentrating on my breathing, attempting to calm myself. I felt someone peel one of my hands from the lamp, grasping it firmly within his own, trying to wrench it away. I just wasn't ready to face whoever it was.

Tate's soothing voice pulled me from my hysteria. "You're safe now, sweets."

Opening my eyes, I glanced up into his handsome face. I tossed the lamp to the side and threw myself into his open embrace.

"Your Clint Eastwood impression was pretty badass," I blubbered.

"I was actually going for Jim Carrey in *The Mask*, but thanks." Tate wrapped me tighter in a bear hug. "Girl, I was so scared for you."

"Thanks for being my Prince Charming," I bawled.

He kissed my head. "As long as I draw breath," he whispered into my hair. "Though one of these days you're going to have to let me be Cinderella for a change."

A laugh escaped through my sobs. "Deal."

Gazing over Tate's shoulder, I smiled through the waterworks at Maverick. "How did you guys know where we were?" I asked.

Maverick pointed to Tate. "It was all his doing."

I could have sworn I saw Tate blush. "Well, when you texted about Britton, I started to worry. So I came down to the *Battle Buffet* set myself. Only neither of you was there, and it was a wreck. Like something bad had happened there."

"That's when he came to see me," Maverick jumped in. "And I pinged your cell."

"Wait—what do you mean ping?" I asked.

Maverick's cheeks went red. "Er, there's an app that Mr. Malone installed on your phone. It allows us in security to track you at all times."

I narrowed my eyes, mentally preparing the speech on privacy I'd be giving to Alfie when I got back.

"And it's a good thing they can," Tate jumped in. "Because when it came back with coordinates *in* the lake, we freaked, jumped in a boat, and came after you!"

"Well, *one* of us freaked. One of us was professional," Maverick corrected. "Not that it was too hard to find you. This yacht is the biggest thing on the lake."

"Well, I for one am glad you did," I said, giving Tate another fierce hug. I looked over his shoulder at Maverick. "Thanks for coming to the rescue. I owe you one."

He waved me off. "I'd do the same for anyone I loved." His cheeks went pink, and his gaze dropped to his feet. "Er, for any of my loved ones." His hands waved wildly. "I mean, for my family and friends." He slapped a palm over his eyes and turned away. "I'm gonna go call the authorities..." he mumbled, trailing off as he walked up the stairs.

Tate and I moved to Britton's side, each holding one of her hands. I wasn't sure just how long we sat there, but it felt like only moments later that uniformed police officers and EMTs started swarming the small room. They descended on Dubois first, clasping a plastic mask over his face and carrying him up the stairs on a stretcher way more carefully than he deserved.

One of the police officers told us that they were waiting to take our statements back at the marina, as the yacht was now a crime scene.

Tate scooped me up in his arms, and Maverick helped Britton up the stairs as LeAnna trailed behind on wobbly legs. I honestly didn't know Tate had the upper-body strength to carry me. I'd seen him struggle with a shopping bag full of clothes on several occasions. He was huffing and puffing by the time we reached the top of the stairs.

I slid from his arms. "I'd rather walk," I lied, releasing him from his unspoken duty.

"Are you sure?" he wheezed.

I nodded, wrapping my arms around myself and following him out onto the exterior deck, where a speedboat was tethered to the side of the yacht. A flimsy chain ladder with aluminum stairs had been secured to the railing, clanking against the yacht and stretching as the waves rolled past.

I shuddered as much from thoughts of the knife-wielding lunatic chef as the brisk night air billowing the skirt of my dress. My bare feet throbbed, feeling frozen solid as I padded across the deck to the ladder.

Tate kissed my forehead then waved a hand toward the speedboat to get Maverick's attention. LeAnna and Britton were already aboard, huddled together under a silver emergency blanket, directly behind the driver's area. Maverick smiled up at me from beside the ladder, his hand extended to help me steady myself on the steps. Between him holding the flimsy metal and

Tate following me down, my trembling legs didn't collapse, and I made it safely into the speedboat. Tate wrapped me in his arms, keeping the wind off of my face by arching his shoulders in front of me, taking the brunt of the frigid air. He proved yet again what true friendship was. It was a short drive from the cove where they'd anchored the yacht to Lakeside Marina. Just a few blocks from most of the casinos, it catered to the summer crowd, with small boat rentals and wave runners, but stayed pretty much closed in the winter and spring.

Maverick skillfully maneuvered his boat through the water to the end of the pier, and an awaiting officer wove the vessel's rope through the dock cleats. When he was done, he extended a hand to me and pulled me onto the dock. I made my way through the other officers, hoping to find a particular FBI agent milling about. Instead, one of the older policemen escorted me into a water-sports rental building they'd turned into a makeshift precinct. He pulled out a hard plastic chair, seating me at a desk with an attached placard touting the upcoming summer rental schedule and fees.

Sitting across from me in the high-backed rental agent's chair, he opened up a notebook and set a small tape recorder between us. "Are you comfortable enough to give me your statement, Ms. King?" He offered me a forced smile and an awkward pat on the hand.

I slid my feet together in an effort to warm them, but they were so numb I couldn't even feel my toes. I spied a lost and found basket against the far wall. Flipping my hand in that direction, I asked, "Mind if I dig through that for socks or something?"

"Not at all."

I sorted through the hodgepodge of items quickly, more than ready to get the statement over with and return to the penthouse. I could almost hear my jetted tub calling my name. I found a beach towel and wrapped it around my shoulders in a makeshift shawl. Luckily, I also found an old pair of slip-on deck shoes about two sizes too big and smelling of aged cheese, but I was in no place to haggle. I slid them on to my feet and slopped back to the desk.

I recounted every detail to the officer, reliving parts of it as I spoke, feeling the knife grazing my neck as though it were happening. I didn't even realize I was crying again until the tears hit my hands. I heard Britton talking and LeAnna wailing in an adjoining room, pulling me from my inner turmoil and back to the here and now.

Then I heard another familiar voice.

"Thank God you're okay." I looked up to find Ryder standing in the doorway.

I swiped a hand across my eyes before turning toward him. Only I didn't get a chance to answer as LeAnna sprinted from the other room, throwing her hot mess of a self into his arms. "Oh, thank heavens that you're here, Agent Ryder."

LeAnna hung from Ryder's forearms, his hands splayed out rigidly behind her. One finally gave way to lightly pat her back. "Um," he muttered. "I've got to get back to the office. There's a black and white ready to take you to the hotel, though, as soon as your statements are finished."

LeAnna dropped back from his arms, smiling up at his face. She leaned in as if to kiss him, but he expertly bobbed and weaved to avoid her lips. After wearing him down, she finally landed one on his cheek with just a tiny bit of lip.

"Mmmm," she purred when she was done assaulting his face. "I don't want to make a scene here in front of your fellow officers." Patting his chest, she made a kissy face as she returned to Britton in the other room.

As soon as she looked away, he emphatically shook his head while making his way to my side. He dropped to his knees, taking my hand in his. He cast a wary look at the officer. "Can you give us a minute?"

"Sure. We're pretty much done anyway." He slid the report over to me. "I just need your signature. You can leave this with Agent Ryder."

I nodded my head in response as he left, scribbling my name at the bottom of the paper.

Ryder let out a sigh. "I'm so glad you're alive. I have to admit I was worried as hell." His hands framed my face. He leaned in closer and closer, our lips almost touching.

Then another officer slammed through the door, bellowing to the guys in the other room.

Timing.

Abandoning the almost-kiss, Ryder rested his forehead on mine. "Are you okay?"

"Yes." I nodded, feeling my bottom lip quiver, contradicting my response. With a couple of deep breaths, I wasn't lying nearly as much. "So, Gerald really was dirty?"

"No. Where did you get that?"

"Dubois said that it was Mr. Taylor's idea to launder the Gambias' money through the winery. Why would he lie?" It felt good to talk, to get some questions answered and try to make sense of what had happened.

Ryder grinned at me, pulling back just a little. "It was. Just not *that* Mr. Taylor."

"Shut the front door." I swatted Ryder on the chest. "You mean Jerry?"

He nodded.

"And you knew this all along?" I narrowed my eyes at him.

Ryder cleared his throat, but for once the fed face didn't cover his expression. "We knew that there was some connection between the Taylors' winery and the Gambia family. Exactly what that was? No. But there were things that pointed our suspicions in Jerry's direction far more than his father's. At least until Mr. Taylor Sr.'s death."

"So, when Gerald suspected that Dubois was the father of LeAnna's baby, and he started asking questions about Dubois..."

"Dubois needed to shut him up before he exposed all of them," Ryder finished for me. "We've already picked up Jerry, and he's singing like a bad lounge act. The truth is, Gerald found out about Dubois's connection to the Gambias and told Jerry that he had to stop doing business with him immediately. Only when Jerry told Dubois, he found out that the chef didn't take no for an answer. He claimed he had no idea what Dubois was going to do until after his father turned up dead."

"But how did LeAnna fit into all of this?"

Ryder shrugged. "She was an innocent bystander."

I raised an eyebrow at him. "Bystander? Yes. Innocent? That's a word that would never apply to LeAnna."

He chuckled. "Point taken. But from what we've gathered from Jerry, when LeAnna took an interest in Dubois, the chef encouraged her as a way to keep close to the Taylors. He never realized that decision would blow up in his face when she decided to fake the pregnancy."

"That's Hurricane LeAnna for you," I mumbled, kinda liking my new nickname for her. "So how did Dubois get involved with the Gambias in the first place?"

"Well, that's where this story gets fun. Bastien Dubois is an alias. When we ran his prints, we found out his real name is Bernard Roche. He's got quite a rap sheet, often being arrested alongside various Gambia family members. He used those connections to finance his show and his restaurants, which in turn have all provided various covers and tax shells for the Gambias' less than legal dealings. I'd imagine he ditched the name because of his past."

I did a little giggle-snort combo without thinking. "And who would want to watch a cooking show when the star's last name sounds like roach?" I shuddered at the thought of little roaches crawling across his elaborate meals. Chances where that Dubois would be seeing a few of those where he was going.

"What about Hammerhead Hank?" I asked. "Did you arrest him yet? He's the one who lured Britton onto the set!"

Ryder's expression turned dark. "You know that woman's body that was found earlier tonight?"

I nodded, not liking where this was going. "The one we thought was LeAnna."

His nodding cadence matched mine. "Turns out that the victim was Jerry's personal assistant. She'd provided Gerald with the final clue to what his son was really doing with the family's winery business. When we were able to trace the murder weapon, in this case a 9-millimeter Beretta, back to Jerry, he admitted that he gave it to Hank to 'take care' of the problem."

I shivered, feeling sorry for the poor woman. "So he's in custody?"

Ryder nodded. "We caught him at the marina. Turns out he was supposed to meet Dubois on the yacht to take care of you girls too."

I shivered even deeper.

An officer appeared in the doorway. "Sir? We're ready to take the ladies back to the hotel."

I turned in my chair and saw Britton beam at me from beside the officer, waving me toward her.

Ryder slid a finger under my chin, pivoting my face back toward his. "I'll be by to check on you in the morning. Please call me if you need anything."

I nodded, fighting back those damned tears again.

He stood, holding out a hand for me, which I gladly accepted. I wasn't entirely sure my trembling legs would support my weight. He glanced down and then back up at me with a single brow arched high. "Nice shoes."

"Thanks." I wiggled my toes. "I saw them in the box and just had to have them."

* * *

During the short drive back to the hotel, I shared the information Ryder had given me with the girls. LeAnna just stared out the window. I couldn't tell if she was upset or melancholy. I'm sure it was a lot to process, since it all hit close to home for her.

Britton reached over and tucked a strand of hair behind my ear. "I'm just glad we all made it out okay." She bit her bottom lip, concern morphing her weary features. "There's...well, there's something I have to tell you."

"What is it?" I asked, turning to face her.

"Well...it's sort of hard. I totally thought I was going to die without coming clean back there. I've been keeping a secret, Tess, and it's totes eating me alive."

I patted her arm. "I'm sure it's not that bad."

"No." She shook her head wildly, hair flipping across her face. "It is. It's really, really bad."

Now I was worried. "What is it?"

Her big blue eyes looked at me, brimming with tears. "I've been cheating on your father," she whispered.

"What?" I felt as if someone had punched me. "You cheated on Dad?"

She blinked rapidly. "No! I mean...not like that. I mean...I've been seeing someone. For a couple of weeks. Secretly."

My turn to blink at her. "Dad's been dead for a year."

"I know! Only a year," she wailed. "I feel so guilty."

I patted her arm. "Britt, it's okay. My dad would have wanted you to move on." I paused. "Was this guy the 'plans' you had the night LeAnna went missing?"

She nodded. Then Britton looked up at me through her lashes, guilt still marring her perfect features. "That's not all though. It gets worse."

"Worse?" I wasn't sure I could take much more after all we'd been through that night.

She nodded. "It's not just that I'm moving on...it's who I'm moving on with." Her teeth bit into her lower lip.

"It doesn't matter," I said, shaking my head. "I'm happy for you." I slid a finger under her chin, forcing her to look at me again.

But her eyes welled with tears. "It does matter."

"Seriously, it's okay."

"It's Alfie."

I froze at the mention of my father's good friend and right-hand man. Alfie?! Seriously? *This* was the blonde that someone had spotted Alfie making out with in the back of a cab?

"I can see it on your face. You're upset!"

I shook my head, tying my best not to picture her and Alfie lip-locking on their way up to the tower suites. "I'm...surprised. But I'm not upset."

"Really?" The hope in her teary eyes was actually kinda adorable. And I'd meant what I'd said. She did deserve to be happy. I guess if she had to move on with anyone, my Dad couldn't have complained about her choosing his most trusted ally. Though I still had my doubts about Alfie having a single romantic bone in his body.

"Are you one hundred percent sure?" she asked.

I dropped my head on her shoulder. "One hundred and fifty percent, as long as you're happy."

The police car pulled to the back parking garage entrance. Alfonso Malone himself greeted us, stone faced, menacing, and surrounded by backup. I turned a knowing smile to Britton.

"Thank you," she muttered. Turning toward the doors, she practically pushed LeAnna from the car in her haste to exit. The moment she hit the pavement, Alfie pulled her into a hug that would have signaled to anyone just how they felt about each other. I felt myself smiling, hoping Alfie enjoyed his *personal* time off.

I looked away, pulling myself out of the car as I spotted Rafe pushing through the security team.

"Tessie," he breathed, pulling me into his arms. I finally felt warm and safe for the first time since the nightmare had begun. I sighed, melting against him, my head resting on his firm chest, listening to his strong heartbeat.

I watched from the safe cocoon of his arms as Alfie escorted LeAnna and Britton through the back entrance, followed by most of the security staff.

One of Rafe's hands came around, his fingers sliding against my cheek, tilting my face upward. "When Alfie told me what happened..." He trailed off, his face going a shade paler under his warm tan. "This whole thing is my fault."

I shook my head. "No, it was a deranged chef and the mob's fault," I said, trying to bring a little levity to the situation.

But Rafe just shook his head, the same concerned frown between his dark brows. "Yes, and I'm the one who brought them here, to your casino. I'm so sorry, Tess." His gaze dropped to my mouth, his lips soon following suit, brushing mine in a sweet, chaste kiss. Backing away slightly, he whispered, "I don't know what I'd have done..."

I placed a finger to his lips. "I'm fine." I forced a smile to my face.

"Liar. I know when you're faking it. What do you need? Anything. Just name it." He studied my face intently.

"Fine," I conceded, holding up both hands between us. "Honestly, I just want a hot bath and to curl up in bed with Jack for about two days."

The worried expression melted from his face, and he offered me a lopsided smile. "Have it your way." Then he paused and sent me a wink. "Lucky Jack."

CHAPTER TWENTY-ONE

———

LeAnna stood before me in the lobby, all primped and styled, dressed in a skintight black dress and matching glossy designer heels, not even a split end to hint at the hot mess from the night before. Her head was tilted to the side, with a thoughtful look on her face, for a change. "We should probably forgo all of the weepy thanks and just skip to the hugs of appreciation."

I grinned. As I welcomed her into my embrace, I couldn't help but think about how I would've never even considered hugging her before all that had transpired the night before. Maybe people can change after traumatic experiences. Maybe LeAnna was finally maturing. I was impressed.

She pushed me back to arm's length, hands gripping my shoulders. Her eyes brimmed with tears. "We all know I saved your lives with my quick thinking, using the painting and all. I don't need all of the hoopla."

And maybe not.

I briefly considered recapping for her all of the lengths to which Britton and I had gone, trying to find out who had killed Gerald and then to find her when she'd gone missing. The haughty, self-serving look was back on LeAnna's flawless face, her nose once again lofted so high she had to peer down it to look at me. I'd probably have better luck teaching a fish to climb a tree than helping her see the light. I just plastered my professional smile to my face and waved as she turned away from me and made her way toward the door, followed by a concierge with her mound of luggage. That was definitely the way I liked seeing her best—leaving.

I breathed a heavy sigh of relief, shaking my head as she crossed the lobby to bark orders at the bellhop. I really had to learn to lower my expectations where she was concerned.

Tate slid up next to me, handing me a folded copy of the *Tahoe Daily Tribune*. "This should turn that frown upside down."

I flashed him a confused look. "Is there a good hotel review that's come out of this huge mess?"

"Nope. Even better. Just look."

I flipped open the paper to see LeAnna's haggard, smudged face, complete with greasy locks and disheveled dress, plastered on the front page. The headline even read "LeAnna Aiden-Taylor Cleared in Husband's Murder." There was no way she could deny that it was her. I'm sure she'd try, but I didn't much care. I enjoyed the picture entirely too much.

I threaded my arm through Tate's. "And it's not even my birthday. Do you think framing it and putting it in my office is a bit too much?"

Tate's head tilted back, his hearty laugh filling the air. "Yeah," he sputtered between giggles. "Maybe just a little. We can scrapbook it together later though."

I stared out over the casino floor and sighed, watching what seemed like a mass exodus from the hotel. Unfortunately, the photo of LeAnna looked like it was going to be the high point of my day. According to the computers, at least half of our guests had decided to check out that morning. Not that I blamed them. With the *Battle Buffet* set now being cordoned off as a crime scene, we'd had to refund all of their tickets for the finale taping. I wasn't sure I could count high enough to calculate how much revenue we were losing now.

"Giovanni Gambia, checking out," I heard from the front desk.

I turned to find the portly Italian man and his wife with a pair of rolling suitcases at their sides.

"I hope you had a pleasant stay?" Alicia asked them, ever the professional as she pulled up their bill on the computer.

"You gotta be kiddin' me," the woman said. "There's cops crawling all over this place. Gives me the creeps."

"I'm so sorry," Alicia said, her smile faltering for only a moment. I had to remember to give that girl a raise. "Is there anything I can do to compensate you for the inconvenience?"

"Nothing doing," Giovanni answered. "We don't feel comfortable staying here any longer. We're finding other accommodations for the rest of our vacation."

"At the Deep Blue!" his wife jumped in. "Now that's our kind of hotel!"

I stifled a laugh. I had to agree with her. The Gambias and Buddy Weston were like two peas in a sleazy pod.

I hope that Buddy realized this made us even—as happy as I knew Buddy would be to have the business, I was more than happy to go back to my regular clientele of retirees and skiers.

As the Gambia coupled dragged their luggage behind them and exited through the glass front doors, I spied a familiar face entering just beside them.

Agent Ryder.

Tate must have spied him too, taking that as his own exit signal. "Well, I've got about a hundred mobsters to check out, so I better get back to work. Meet me for lunch later?"

I pulled him in for a hug, hoping he was feeling my thanks and gratitude all over again as I squeezed the air from his lungs. "Absolutely, and I'll buy. Anything for my hero."

Tate sighed then whispered, "Can you keep a secret?"

"Always," I promised.

"I was trying to fire a warning shot. The shoulder thing was an accident."

I tried to keep from giggling, but I couldn't contain it. Thoughts of how close I'd come to the end of Dubois's knife tried to flood back, and laughter was my way of shaking it.

"Guess I need a few more lessons on the range myself," he admitted.

"I'm sorry, Tate. It still stands that you saved us. We would have been goners if you hadn't."

"She's right," Agent Ryder's voice announced, coming up behind us. He clapped a hand against Tate's shoulder. "You did good, man."

Tate's dark lashes fluttered at light-speed, a smile consuming his face. "Thanks, but I think I'll leave the gun stuff to the professionals like you from now on, Agent Ryder."

"Please, my friends just call me Devin." He offered a hand to Tate, who quickly shook it.

"Well, *Devin*, duty calls." Tate turned to me. "Noon-ish, Tess?"

I nodded and waved as he backed down the hall then turned my attention to the hot federal agent at my side. He wasn't dressed in his usual suit and tie. Instead he wore jeans and a simple gray sweater. The casual look softened him a bit. I had to admit it looked good on him. Even so, I couldn't help teasing the usually perfectly put-together agent a little. "Laundry day?" I asked.

He grinned. "What, I'm not allowed to be comfortable on my day off?"

"Day off, huh?" I asked, turning toward the front doors so he didn't see the goofy smile on my face. "Does that mean you're here in a *personal* capacity and not professional?"

"Could be," he hedged, his casual tone matching his attire. "I see the family reunion is over?" he added, glancing around to the couples in suits and spandex, rolling luggage toward the circular drive.

I shrugged. "I heard a rumor it's moving across the street."

Ryder raised an eyebrow at me.

I put my hands up in a surrender gesture. "That's all I know, I swear! I'm so over the whole 'foodie' thing."

Ryder chuckled. "I wish I could say the same, but it looks like as long as the Gambias are in town, I will be too."

"Oh really?" I asked, not altogether hating the idea of seeing a little more of him.

"Yep." He nodded and leaned his elbows on the counter, glancing over the gaming floor. "So, any chance you're free sometime this weekend?"

That goofy grin took over my face again. "Maybe," I said, playing at coy. "Depends on what you have in mind."

He turned toward me, a smile curling one side of his mouth. "I'd like to take you out. You know, on a real date, for a change."

I bit the inside of my lip to keep from squealing out a resounding *yes*. "So, the stuff at the lake in your car wasn't a real date? Felt pretty real to me."

He stood up straight, towering in front of me, his blue eyes twinkling with mischief. "Oh, I'm hoping for more 'stuff' like that, but maybe dinner and drinks too."

"Sure." I tried my best to match his nonchalant tone. But I couldn't help adding a small jibe. "Only this time, you better actually show up."

His smile faded for a fraction of a second. "New Year's again? You're still on that?"

I shot him a look. "Don't press your luck. Maybe *I'll* be the one who suddenly has somewhere else to be this time."

He did an exaggerated sigh. "Okay, okay. I'm sorry. The truth? I was called away at the last minute for work."

"And, what, your dog ate your phone for the next three months?" I challenged.

He cleared his throat. "No. I was undercover."

"I...oh." I paused. Wow, that was actually a great excuse. And one I hadn't seen coming.

"Look, I'm really sorry. I would have called if I could have, but it was a situation that was very time sensitive. And happened to take longer than I'd anticipated. By the time the job was over, well, a lot of time had passed. I wasn't sure if you even wanted to hear from me again."

I bit my lip. He was right. I almost hadn't.

Almost.

"So now that it's over, tell me, what sort of job was it?" I asked.

He looked over both shoulders in an exaggerated move. Then he leaned in. "Can you keep a secret?"

"Yes?"

"So can I." He winked at me.

I shoved him playfully in the arm. "Come on. That is so not fair. I waited for two hours in that restaurant. Two!" I held up two fingers to emphasize my point.

"Okay, okay," he relented, though his mouth was hitched upward in a smile now. "One of the organized crime groups we'd been tracking was set to receive a large delivery of illegal merchandise from overseas. They needed me to pose as a potential buyer in order to track where the goods were being dispersed in the US."

"Drugs?" I whispered.

He shook his head. "Handbags."

I blinked, not sure I'd hear him right. "Come again?"

He grinned. "Knock-off designer handbags from China. Hey, those babies are big business. I hear women pay crazy amounts for a bag with a logo on it."

"Crazy is subjective," I said defensively.

"Anyway, I'm sorry. About the whole thing," he said, taking a step toward me. "Forgive me now?"

"Hmph," I huffed, though it was getting harder and harder to hang on to any sort of grudge.

"Pretty please?" he asked, taking another step closer.

I bit my lip. "Fine. On one condition."

"Anything" he said, his voice low, warm, and dangerously sexy.

"Next time we go out, I get to drive KITT."

* * *

I sat outside the boardroom, nervously jiggling my knee up and down in my black skinny slacks. The board of directors had been behind closed doors deciding the fate of the Royal Palace for the last...I checked my phone readout again...15 minutes and 32 seconds. Not that I was counting.

I thought I'd made a fairly convincing case to them that while the casino had not seen the *significant* change in revenue that the board of directors had wanted, we had seen a small upward trend. Of course they had then countered with the entire *Battle Buffet* fiasco.

With its star behind bars, this is one show that did *not* go on. The finale had been canceled, and even then reruns of the show had been pulled from the network the moment the news hit the entertainment airwaves that Chef Dubois was a cold-blooded killer. Sicianni had been furious at first. However, being the enterprising producer he was, he'd quickly turned around and pitched a brand new show to the network. It starred the final two contestants from *Battle Buffet*, the man with the shock of white hair and the woman with the tattoo of the whisk on her arm, as they went undercover and behind the scenes to expose America's most violent chefs. They were pitching a pilot that was rumored to focus on the terrifying reign of Dubois over his kitchen staff before he finally snapped. Personally, I thought they had a fighting chance. That sounded like good TV to me!

With the show a bust, and the ensuing swarm of press scrutiny and law enforcement officers who descended on South Lake, the Gambia family quickly left town. Whatever they had or hadn't been meeting with other families to discuss remained a mystery to me. Which was fine. I vowed to leave the organized crime to the FBI from now on. And with the way Jerry Taylor was wheeling and dealing to keep himself in a white-collar prison, Agent Ryder was hopeful that he would get enough dirt on the family men to make more arrests soon.

LeAnna had gone back to Napa to settle her husband's estate, which, according to Britton, turned out to be much more sizable that LeAnna had ever hoped. Since Jerry was unable to profit from his crime, the entire estate now went to LeAnna. While the idea of her in endless designer dresses didn't fill me with any warm fuzzies, at least she would no longer be trying to get her hooks into wealthy older men. In fact, from what Britton told me, LeAnna was now having to fight off gold diggers of her own.

"Tess?"

I bounced to my feet at the sound of Alfie's voice hailing me from the doorway to the boardroom.

"They're ready for you, kid," he informed me.

I sucked in a deep breath and let it out slowly, hoping to release some of my nerves as well. I knew our profits hadn't lived up to the board's expectations. I had a sinking feeling I knew what they were going to say. I steeled myself against the words as I straightened the lapels on my cropped blazer, held my head up high, and marched into the boardroom ready to meet my fate.

A long wooden table held several well-dressed men and women, all with piles of spreadsheets and pie charts in front of them. I gulped back fear, knowing exactly what those charts showed. Less than stellar profits over the last four quarters.

"Ms. King," the white-haired man at the head of the table began. "The board realizes that we put you in a difficult position when we voted you in as a temporary chairman of the Royal Palace Casino and Resort. We realize you had precious little experience in the hospitality industry and a very sharp learning curve ahead of you."

I nodded politely, silently waiting for him to go on. So far this wasn't sounding like a glowing performance review.

"The board is grateful for all of the work that you have done over this past year as a temporary director. We are, however, concerned about the lack of a significant change in our profit margins."

I opened my mouth to protest, but Alfie's hand on my arm stopped me. He gave me the slightest shake of his head. I shut my mouth with a click.

"We have an obligation," the white-haired man went on, "to our shareholders that we feel has not yet been fulfilled. There have been some good ideas for special revenue-generating events, but they have not *quite* worked out exactly as planned, have they?"

If he was referring to *Battle Buffet*, that was the understatement of the year.

"As such," he said with a quick glance at the others around the table, "we are removing you as temporary chairman."

There it was. I felt as if I'd been punched in the gut. I'd known this was coming, but actually hearing the words out loud had tears pricking at the back of my throat. I blinked, trying to keep a calm professional facade even as my sentence was being handed down. I only prayed that while they might be letting me go, they hadn't given up hope on the casino yet.

"And the Royal Palace?" I asked, amazed that my voice wasn't as shaky as my knees suddenly felt. "Are you closing the doors?"

The white-haired man blinked at me as if he didn't understand the question then turned to a man in a three-piece suit sitting next to him.

"I am afraid you may have misunderstood our meaning," Three-Piece Suit said. "The board has decided that running the day-to-day aspects of the casino and the public relations and event planning that go with that are just too much burden for one person to take on. We are removing you as the temporary chairman and reinstating you as the permanent cochairman."

"Wh-what?" I asked, my gaze whipping from the man at the table to Alfie standing beside me. I could tell from the small smirk on his face that he'd been in on this.

"You have the deepest respect of the staff and patrons of the hotel," White-Haired Man picked up again. "We think your father would be very proud of the way that you run the day-to-day business of the Royal Palace."

I did some more blinking, unable to keep those tears from hitting the back of my eyes now. "Thank you," I managed to whisper without completely breaking down.

"In fact," Three-piece Suit said, shuffling some papers, "we were rather impressed with the numbers that you brought in this weekend."

I scrunched up my nose. "*This* weekend?" I asked. As in the weekend we'd had to refund nearly a thousand *Battle Buffet* finale tickets?

He nodded. "Yes. Even with the swift vacancy of the rooms after the...unpleasantness," he evaded, "we had an unprecedented uptick in revenue on the gaming floor for the short time our, er, foodies were staying with us."

I shot a look at Alfie. He grinned back and mumbled, "Turns out the 'foodies' liked to gamble big. And they weren't very good at it."

I didn't know what to say. Apparently the event hadn't been a total bust after all. "You mentioned I'd be *co*chairman?" I asked.

White-Haired Man spoke up. "Yes, we have made the decision to appoint a cochairman who will take over the special events planning and media for the casino, to ensure that our next event goes off without incident."

While I could've argued that a homicidal chef had hardly been my fault, the special events and media planning had never been my strong suit anyway. The idea of leaving that to someone else wasn't altogether unpleasant. Then again, it all depended on who that someone else was. "May I ask who the cochairman will be?" I said.

"We have decided that the natural choice is someone who is familiar with the Royal Palace, has the social and traditional media contacts to properly promote our casino, and experience planning large-scale promotional events."

I nodded along with them, agreeing on all points. "And that person is?"

Alfie spoke up beside me. "Rafe Lorenzo." He grinned again, his eyes lighting up in a mischievous way that told me he might have had a hand in the selection.

I watched the board members nod their agreement to each other as the white-haired man went on to talk about all of Rafe's wonderful qualifications for the position. But in all honesty, I was kind of only halfway listening at that point, relief ringing in my ears that the Royal Palace really was going to be okay. I had to agree that Rafe would be perfect for the job. He'd practically handled all the planning for the *Battle Buffet* show anyway. And while he wasn't ready to retire from snowboarding anytime soon, using his celebrity in this capacity was a natural progression of his career.

My eyes had wandered to the large windows overlooking the sparkling crystal blue Lake Tahoe and the snowcapped mountains beyond. Now that I had an official partner in crime, I might even actually have some free time to paint. I could almost feel my fingers tingling with the itch now as I watched the bright March sunlight create sparkling diamonds across the surface of the lake. I swore I could almost see my father winking at me in the twinkling lights.

"Tess? You okay?" Alfie asked, coming up behind me and putting a hand on my shoulder.

I turned to him, not able to keep the smile off my face. "Never better, Alfie. Never better."

ABOUT THE AUTHORS

Gemma Halliday is the *New York Times* and *USA Today* bestselling author of the High Heels Mysteries, the Hollywood Headlines Mysteries, the Jamie Bond Mysteries, the Tahoe Tessie Mysteries, as well as several other works. Gemma's books have received numerous awards, including a Golden Heart, two National Reader's Choice awards, and three RITA nominations. She currently lives in the San Francisco Bay Area with her boyfriend, Jackson Stein, who writes vampire thrillers, and their three children, who are adorably distracting on a daily basis.

To learn more about Gemma, visit her online at
www.gemmahalliday.com

T. Sue VerSteeg was born and raised in the small town of Grinnell, Iowa. At the age of 21, she moved her family—parents and all—to the beautiful Ozarks region of Missouri where they have lived since. She is blessed with an adoring husband, two wonderful kids, the best sister in the world, and amazing parents. Writing has always been a passion in her life, to which family and friends can attest. From her first attempt at a spin-off of Dick and Jane, to her latest novel, her heart and soul has been poured into each word. Her most sincere wish is that you will find as much enjoyment in reading her stories as she did in their creation.

To learn more about T. Sue, visit her online at:
www.tsueversteeg.com

Want to get a free ebook?

Sign up for Gemma Halliday's newsletter and get a free ebook as a thank you!

www.gemmahalliday.com/contact

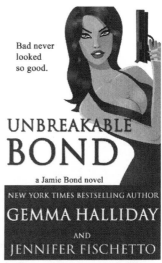

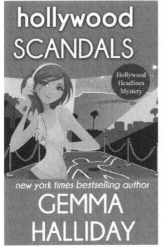

Made in the USA
San Bernardino, CA
23 November 2015